Escaping the Past

by

Tammy Falkner

Night Shift Publishing

Copyright © 2012 by Tammy Falkner

Escaping the Past
Second Edition, Paperback – published 2007
Night Shift Publishing
Cover design by Kim Killion, Hotdamndesigns.com
ISBN-13: 978-0615734880
ISBN-10: 061573488X

Prologue

Mary Lou Smith woke to the sound of humming. It was sweet, soulful humming; the kind that makes you wish you could carry a tune. Lou opened her eyes and there sat a heavy, dark skinned woman with a smile as big as all outdoors.

Not completely sure where she was, Lou lurched upright, desperately searching the room.

"Whatcha lookin' for child?" the woman quietly asked.

She laid back quickly, her hand pressed to her forehead, the pain still with her from the previous night.

"My…" Her tongue came out to wet her parched lips, but her mouth felt like it was lined with cotton.

"If you are looking for that sweet child, she's in the kitchen with my husband, Jebediah. He's the one who found you in the road last night. Him and John." The woman clucked as she leaned over the bed to survey the damage to Lou's head. "I'm Sadie. Jeb is my husband and we take care of this place for the owner. Her name is Margaret Wester. You'll be meeting her later. How does your head feel?"

"Hurts," she mumbled around the cotton filling her mouth. Sadie placed an arm beneath her shoulders, raised her to a reclined sitting position, and lifted a glass of water to her lips.

"Where 'bouts you from, child? Do you have a name? How old are you?" Sadie hit her with all the questions at once.

She wasn't from anywhere. Not anymore. Tears stung the backs of her eyelids as she said, " My name is M…Lou! My name is Lou. It's short for Louise. Louise Smith. I am almost nineteen years old, ma'am. The baby's name is Sarah. She's two months old." Unable to hold back the tears, they rolled like two swollen streams down her face. She sniffed and wiped her nose with the back of her hand. "I'll be out of your way today if you tell me where I am, ma'am."

"You're not going anywhere with that gash on your forehead. You and the baby will be just fine and safe right here. We'll figure out what to do with you when you're better." Her voice lowered to just above a whisper. "You had a black bag with you. We put it away for you. When you need it, you just let us know."

The man she called Jebediah walked through the door of the bedroom. He was a tall, skinny man with a warm look in his eyes. Beneath one arm, he held a bassinet. On the other arm lay a cooing Sarah.

"I sent John into town to get diapers and formula for the little one. She seems to go through both pretty quick," he mumbled as he bent and placed Sarah in Lou's arms. Sarah reached up with a clumsy fist and hit Lou in the cheek. She grabbed that tiny little fist and placed a quick kiss to it. They would be all right. Wouldn't they?

"That, she does, sir. Thank you. And thank you for last night." Lou's smile was genuine despite the worry that plagued her. "I am sorry for all the trouble I must have caused you."

"Don't you worry your pretty little head none. I have been through worse, although it has been many a year since then. So far, ain't nothing broke that can't be fixed." He winked at her. "One broken window on my truck." He shrugged and then slipped an arm around Sadie's thick waist. "The last time I got shot at, it was Sadie's father who held the gun." He scratched his forehead. "Man always was a poor shot." Sadie elbowed him playfully in the side.

The heavy tread of boots stomping down the hallway met their ears and then a young man with flaming red hair and bright green eyes appeared in the doorway. "Jeb, you ain't gonna believe how expensive it is to have a baby. The lady at the store told me I needed all this stuff even though I told her we only one." He held up a single finger for emphasis. "One." With a disgusted sigh, he dropped six bags filled with clothes, diapers, toys, formula and other necessities on the edge of the bed.

"Good Lord, boy, I'll never send you out with another hundred dollar bill again. I should have known you would bust it wide open." Jeb took his hat off his head and playfully swatted the young man with it. Sadie reached into the bags and grabbed bottles, formula, and other supplies before waddling toward the kitchen.

The man's red hair stood in loose curls atop his head. Six feet of skinny boy walked to the side of the bed with an awkwardness that bespoke of his youth. He extended a hand. "My name is John, ma'am. Who might you be?"

"My name is Lou and this is Sarah," she said, looking down into the baby's brown eyes. "Thank you for last night."

Sadie entered the room, shaking a bottle of formula and carrying a burp cloth in the other. She reached over and gently took the baby from Lou, placed her in John's arms, and put a bottle in his hand. She threw the burp cloth over his shoulder. Swatting him on the rear, she said, "Why don't you make yourself useful while Lou and I get cleaned up?"

Lou couldn't hold back a grin the look of shock on his face. Jeb clapped him on the shoulder and said, "Come on, boy, I'll give you some moral support."

Sadie closed the door. She crossed her arms over her chest and glared at Lou. "I don't particularly care where you came from as long as you have no secrets that will hurt those I love. Is there anything I should know?"

She couldn't hide from the searching, brown eyes. The sobs started low down in her belly. Sadie sat beside her on the bed and listened to her story, never once scowling or showing emotion. She gently patted her on the back and dried her tears when they were spent.

"Let's get you cleaned up." Lou had just bared her soul to Sadie and she barely blinked an eye? Let's get you cleaned up? No threats to toss her and her daughter into the street? No worries about the people who'd shot out her husband's windows the night before after he'd stopped to pick Lou up on the side of the road? Could anyone truly be this kind?

As Sadie helped Lou to the shower, they heard a disgusted yell from the kitchen. "Well, damn! She puked on me!" Jeb's low laughter could be heard as well. Lou felt like the weight of the world had been lifted from her shoulders. She didn't, and wouldn't, allow herself to think about her mother or the past. Not yet. Not today.

Chapter One

2010

Lou waited for Sarah to get off the bus at the end of the long drive, sweat rolling from her brow. At seven years of age, she was still too young to walk the long, gravel drive to the main house alone. Some days Sadie was there to greet her because Lou was busy in the house. Sometimes, John would come to meet her. Sarah enjoyed these days most of all, because she got a laughing pony ride back to the big house. Today, Lou was there waiting.

"Hi, Mommy!"

Lou said, "Hi, Baby. How was your day?"

Youthful exuberance met her as Sarah bubbled over with her tales of school. "Do you know Kerry's mom says butterflies are not the most beautiful creatures in the world? She says there are a lot of things more beautiful than butterflies. I decided today I want to be a singer when I grow up. Gina's mom is a singer and she gets to travel to the ocean and back…"

Sarah could never be accused of being quiet. Once she learned to talk, she had never stopped.

Lou used the long walk back to the main house to think about how lucky and how thankful she was for her good fortune. She was proud to have been offered a job and a home by Margaret Wester, the owner of the grand old home and breeding stable where they now resided as a part of the family. Mrs. Wester had no responsibility toward Lou and Sarah, despite the fact two of her employees had brought them home like lost kittens on that fateful night seven years before. Never in her wildest dreams could she have imagined Mrs. Wester would choose to hire her as a personal assistant, educate her at the local college and prepare her for life in the way she had.

Western Skies Breeding and Horse Stables had never been so prosperous. The barns were filled with quality quarter horses—broodmares and stallions of the greatest beauty and temperament. Horse owners drove for days to deliver a mare to the stable for breeding. The lush pastures were well tended and horses were thriving because of it. The stable hands were the best of the best, and they knew quality horseflesh when they saw it.

Lou walked down the long, gravel drive to the house, taking in the scenery as she enjoyed the shade thrown by the huge magnolia trees that hugged the lane. The scent of honeysuckle hung in the summer air. She inhaled deeply, smiling as she thought of her good fortune.

The main house was a beauty in and of itself. In true antebellum style, multiple Greek columns supported porches that graced all four exterior walls on both the lower and upper levels. A hipped roof sloped from a single point down on all four sides to the eaves of the home. Four dormers hinted of a large attic that stretched the length of the house. Each of the thirteen bedrooms had access doors leading to the porticos on each level. Wrought-iron railings with ornate details garnished each floor. A large ballroom remained unused since the early 1900s. Central entryways at the front and the back of the home were a welcome site after the long walk from the bus stop.

Sarah ran through the back door, thunked her book bag on the kitchen table, and skipped toward the bedroom of Margaret Wester. Mrs. Wester sat supported by a chaise lounge and had a book propped in her hand. Sadie stood by the bed, fluffing pillows before turning to straighten the room. Sarah crawled into Mrs. Wester's chair and deposited a loud kiss on her cheek. The old woman's eyes opened slowly.

"Whatcha doing?" Sarah asked.

"I was checking my eyes for cracks," Mrs. Wester said feebly.

"Did you find any?" Sarah asked, touching her eyelids in wonder.

"Nope. But I'll be sure to look again in a few minutes. How was your day?"

"My day was great. You're not going to believe what happened…" Sadie and Lou listened as Sarah told Mrs. Wester about the butterflies and the happenings at school. Pretty soon, Mrs. Wester was visibly fading, so both the adults worked to shoo Sarah from the room. Lou kissed her employer on the top of the head before they walked out the door. Mrs. Wester was already asleep.

Lou stopped to gaze back at her mentor and friend. Her heart broke as she looked at the once strong body, now weak. Mrs. Wester couldn't withstand the rigors of social interaction for more than a few minutes and could only get about thirty minutes of clarity before sleep would again reclaim her. She no longer accepted callers, but she insisted Sarah visit at least once a day.

Lou's eyes met Sadie's. "I think it's time to call Brody," Sadie said.

Brody was Mrs. Wester's son. In all her years at the farm, he had never once come home to visit, but he had sent Christmas and birthday gifts with nice notes like clockwork for Mrs. Wester, Jeb, Sadie, and
John. He never missed a birthday. Every year Lou opened the UPS boxes full of gaily wrapped packages at Christmas and placed them beneath the tree.

"Do you know how to reach him, Sadie? I agree and think we need to call him soon," Lou said as they walked into the library. Mrs. Wester had not stepped foot in the library in years but her desk remained. Lou used it to care for the finances of the farm.

Sadie turned a small, black Rolodex until she reached the card she wanted. She plucked it from the card holder and held it out to Lou. Lou sat down behind the desk and picked up the phone. Holding the card in one hand, she dialed with the other.

"County Hospital," the distracted voice said.

"May I speak with Mr. Brody Wester, please?" Lou asked patiently.

"You mean Dr. Broden Wester?"

"Um, yes. My name is Lou Smith. I work for his mother."

"Oh. He is in surgery right now. May I take a message?"

"Yes. Could you please tell him his mother is ill and she needs him?"

The voice paused. "I'll do that," she said.

"Thanks." Lou hung up the phone.

A few hours after her phone call, Lou read Sarah a story and tucked her into bed in the room adjoining her own. After making sure the child was settled for the night, she decided to go out to the barn and check on a new foal that had not looked very sturdy earlier in the day. She quietly closed the bedroom door.

The air outside was so thick you had to chew it before you could walk through it. Her long, brown hair stuck to her face like seaweed wraps around your legs at the beach, and her clothes were soaked before she ever reached the barn. She peered over the stall door, happy to see that the new baby was on her feet and looked much stronger than she had earlier in the day.

"She's a beaut, ain't she, Lou?" John said as he stepped beside her and peered over the stall door. He took off his hat and wiped his forehead with his forearm.

"She looks better than she did this afternoon."

"I know. I was worried there for a while." John, although he was Margaret Wester's nephew, was in charge of the stables and the foals, and it was his job to oversee the birth of the new arrivals. With some, like this one in particular, Lou sat up with him all night to wait for the new baby. This one came pretty quickly. As they waited patiently, they had discussed their worries about the old matriarch, Mrs. Wester, and they shared the same concerns.

"It's hotter than seven hells out here, Lou. What do you say we get cooled off?" John asked, a mischievous look twinkling in his green eyes. "I thought we might take a dip in the pond behind the house. What do you think?"

Lou thought about it for no more than a second, plucked the sweaty shirt from her skin one more time, and nodded her head. "Race you!" she called out as she streaked by him, heading for the huge farm pond. An excellent runner, she outdistanced him by three car lengths. She reached the dock long before he did. She turned her back to John and kicked off her worn jean shorts and sandals.

Before John could get his shirt off, she was slicing through the water wearing only a lacy, matching bra and panty set. John performed a perfect cannon-ball wearing only his boxers. He disappeared into the water. She waited for him to resurface. After a minute, she began to worry. Could he have hit his head? Where was he? He tugged her ankle and pulled her under. Her head went under water, and she came up sputtering.

She smacked the surface of the water before she struck out after him, grabbing his head and pushing him below the surface of the water. Their water play continued for about a half-hour before they both tired. They swam back to the dock, and he climbed the ladder first. He turned his back and started to pull his jeans on while she climbed out herself. She bent to pick up the faded jean shorts.

"Uh-hum!" The clearing of a throat grabbed their attention.

Lou gasped and crossed her arms over her wet t-shirt. She looked into the distance and could see the taillights of a cab as it pulled out of the gates. It had left the tall man who stood before them, one eyebrow cocked slightly and a bemused look upon his face.

"Brody!" John exclaimed as he walked forward to greet the newcomer.

****

The woman obviously knew no shame. She stood there, nearly naked, the moonlight shining on all of her assets. The wet cloth of her shirt and panties was nearly translucent and did little to hide the shadows and curves beneath. Her long legs and graceful, bare feet were exposed for his view. Long, dark waves of wet hair clung to her shoulders.

When she realized someone had interrupted their tryst, she had tried to hide herself behind her shirt but he had already seen her. Her curves were in all the right places. Her nipples pressed against the wet, transparent fabric, hard and dark. Her flat stomach led to dainty panties that stuck to her like glue.

"John! It's so good to see you," Brody said. They shook hands and clapped one another on the shoulder.

The girl turned her back and took a moment to pluck her shirt from her body. Pulling her shorts up and fastening them, she turned to face the men.

"Brody, this is Lou. We just took a swim. We were about to…"

"I can see what you were about to do, John. There's no need to explain. You're a chip off the old block." Brody punched John softly in the arm with a knowing smile.

John had the decency to flush before turning to Lou. "Lou, this is my cousin, Brody."

Lou extended her hand to shake his. "Nice to meet you, Brody."

He grasped her hand firmly, allowing his gaze to roam freely up and down her body. He wasn't completely sure if it was because he wanted to unnerve her, or because he enjoyed the view. He was taken aback by the spark of sensation he got when her dark eyes finally met his, yet he forced himself to hold firmly to her hand. He raised one brow at her and she tore her gaze from his.

Lou disentangled her hand from his with a gentle twist, pointing toward the house. "You guys go ahead. I'll meet you both back at the house. Do you mind?" Lou asked.

"If you asked my mother," he drawled with a slight southern accent. "She would tell you that I never did mind very well."

Broden James Wester, III was home.

Chapter Two

Brody clapped John on the back as they walked side-by-side to the big house. "Your girlfriend is something."

"Who? Lou? Oh, no, it's not like that, Brody." John stammered, shaking his head. "She's just—"

John's thought was cut off mid-sentence when an excited squeal arose from the porch. "As I live and breathe! It's Brody!" Sadie shrieked as a huge grin erupted on her face.

Brody dropped his bags and rushed forward, wrapping his arms around Sadie's waist to lift her ample body from the ground and spin her slowly. "Well, aren't you the prettiest thing I've seen in years, Sadie?" He placed her on her feet. "And light as a feather, too," he said, unable to keep her excitement from flooding him as well. He placed a kiss on her weathered cheek.

"Oh, you, stop. I ain't no such thing." She reached up to tousle his sandy hair. "Ain't you a sight for sore eyes, boy?"

"Sadie, I left the boy back on the farm twelve years ago."

"I can see that, Brody." She stepped back to look appraisingly at him. It was like he'd never left. Like he hadn't been gone for twelve years.

"What's all the racket out there on the porch? You would think you had seen a snake," Jeb said as he walked outside. His eyes lit up as he saw Brody, and he extended his hand. Brody bypassed the outstretched hand and embraced him.

"Your mama is going to be so happy to see you, boy," the man said low against Brody's ear.

"Where is she, Jeb?"

"She's in her room. You can run right along and go see her. She needs you right now," Sadie said with a gentle push toward the door.

****

Lou circled the house and went in through the front door, in hopes of avoiding Mrs. Wester's son, particularly in her wet and bedraggled state. She cringed at the knowledge that *that* man had seen her in her wet underwear. Even now, her wet hair clung to her face and her clothes stuck to her body. She went up the stairs to her room and stripped down to nothing. She turned on the shower and stepped beneath the spray. A few moments of solitude to redirect her thoughts were all she needed. She appraised herself in the mirror, and then walked from her room and down the grand staircase toward the kitchen. She walked by Mrs. Wester's room and stopped to listen at the sound of a male voice chuckling. She paused in the doorway and quickly stepped back, hoping no one would see her.

Mrs. Wester still sat in the chaise lounge, her book laid delicately on the arm of the chair. Brody sat at her feet, leaning toward his mother. His sandy-colored hair hung lightly over his forehead. Mrs. Wester raised her weakened hand to brush the lock of hair to the side. He grabbed her hand in his and lowered it to her lap but did not release it. His steely eyes were full of worry, his brow knit with concern. His six foot two inch frame dwarfed Mrs. Wester's smaller one.

Lou stood in the doorway for a moment longer and then coughed gently to announce her presence. Two sets of eyes met hers as she walked into the room. Mrs. Wester's were welcoming; her son's were not.

"Are you ready for bed, Mrs. Wester?" Lou had taken it upon herself to be sure Mrs. Wester was clean and placed in bed before she went to bed at night.

"I can take my mother to bed, thank you," Brody said, his jaw tight.

"Why don't you do it together?" Mrs. Wester asked, as she patted his hand gently.

Lou filled a basin of water in the bathroom sink and carried it to the chaise lounge where mother and son sat. She wet a cloth with a small amount of soapy water and passed it to Mrs. Wester. She had quickly learned Mrs. Wester valued her independence and wanted to take care of her own needs as much as she could. Mrs. Wester washed her own face, neck, and hands. She passed the cloth to Brody and he handed her a clean cloth to dry her face. He took the basin from Lou and went to pour it in the sink as Lou chose a nightgown from the wardrobe. Brody turned his back as she helped Mrs. Wester to disrobe and don the nightclothes.

"Ready to move to the bed?" Lou asked gently. Mrs. Wester was often so tired after washing her face that she needed help to get to the bed. Lou placed one arm beneath her legs to swing them gently to the floor. At that moment, Brody placed a hand on Lou's shoulder and moved her out of the way. He put an arm beneath his mother's shoulders and one beneath her knees, and gently lifted her from the chair.

Lou moved ahead of him to turn down the bed. He laid his mother gently between the sheets and Lou arranged the covers around her. She fluffed the pillows and made sure the matriarch was comfortable. She then took Mrs. Wester's hand in her own and bent to kiss her on the cheek. "Good night, Mrs. Wester."

She stepped back and tried not to listen when Brody whispered, "Good night, Mama," before he did the same.

Mrs. Wester fell asleep with a smile on her face before they ever left the room.

Lou turned with a smile to Brody to say thanks for all the help. She was met with cold, gray eyes that seethed with anger. He was obviously furious.

"How long has she been like this?" he demanded, stepping into the hall and pulling the bedroom door shut behind him.

"She started to go downhill about two weeks ago," Lou replied as they walked into the kitchen.

"Why didn't anyone call me before now?"

"She told us not to. As she became weaker and weaker, Sadie and I decided you needed to know," she added. "She seemed very happy to see you. How long has it been?"

He sighed and some of the anger left his eyes. "It's been twelve years." The silence hung like a cloak as she waited for him to elaborate. He didn't. "I talk to her on the phone every chance I get. I just didn't think that I would be coming home."

"We're glad you did." She grabbed a bottle of water from the fridge. "Good night." She turned and went back up the stairs.

****

The next morning, the alarm clock buzzed loudly beside Lou's ear at five a.m. She reached over and tapped it lightly. She rolled over in the big bed, slid from beneath the covers, and headed for the bathroom. She pulled her long, dark waves of hair into a high ponytail. Shedding the T-shirt in which she normally slept, she put on a pair of shorts and a cotton top, and then laced up her sneakers. She quickly checked herself in the mirror, brushed her teeth and headed down to the kitchen. The day started early on a ranch this size. When Lou had first arrived at the ranch, Sadie was still taking care of the breakfast and feeding all the hands who worked the stables. As the years passed, Sadie still made the plans, but Lou did most of the work. Sadie stood by to help, but Lou did the physical labor, lifting and serving.

Lou wiped the sleep from her eyes and entered the kitchen. Brody, Sadie, Jeb, and John were seated at the kitchen table drinking coffee and looking over the day's news.

"Good morning," she chimed.

Brody looked up with a surprised look on his face. "Morning," he mumbled as he crossed to the coffeepot. "Want some coffee?" he asked, extending the pot in her direction.

"No thanks. No time. I'll put on more for the hands, though," she said, taking the pot from his hand. She quickly filled the reservoir, added coffee, and started the perk. She then grabbed a basket and headed out to the hen house to get the fresh eggs for breakfast.

She returned to the house with a basket full of eggs and the beautiful day made her add a spring to her step. She started cracking eggs into a bowl. For the next thirty minutes, she scrambled eggs, fried piles of bacon, and boiled grits. She took out biscuits Sadie had cut by hand the day before and warmed them in the oven. When she was done, she rang the bell to beckon the hands to come in for breakfast.

****

In the kitchen, she washed her hands before heading back upstairs. Brody watched it all trying to keep his admiration for her from showing on his face. He turned to Jeb. "Does she do that every day?"

"Five days a week," Jeb replied.

"She certainly earns her keep." John went to join the hands at the buffet table.

"I thought she was your girlfriend, John?" Brody asked. Several of the hands snickered behind their hats.

"Who? Lou? Nope. She's works on the farm, just like the rest of us." John's face reddened.

Just then, Brody heard small feet scurrying down the stairs. Lou followed, and held out her hand for the brush and ponytail holders the child held.

Brody leaned closer to John. "Who's that?"

"That's Sarah."

"But, Mom, I want Sadie to fix my hair!" The little girl screeched with a flurry of activity.

She ran around the room and landed at the Sadie's feet, wrapping her arms around the old lady's thick calves.

"Do you mind, Sadie?" Lou exhaled.

"Nope," Sadie replied. "How do you want them, princess?"

"Two ponytails, please."

"You look like a pony's tail, squirt," John said, pulling Sarah's hair gently.

"I do not!" Sarah squeaked.

"Enough!" Lou said, just as Sadie finished working magic on the unruly mass that the child had for hair. "Go and get your breakfast."

The dining hall was filled with twelve hungry men, all of whom wanted their breakfast. However, the line parted swiftly as one of the hands offered Sarah a plate and helped her to fill it. She sat down among the men as though she belonged and started to eat her breakfast.

"Uh, hum." Sadie coughed gently.

Sarah laid her fork beside her plate. Every head in the room bowed as Sarah said, "Thank you, God, for this food, for the people who are here, and for our health. We pray You keep everyone safe while they do their chores today and that You will keep an eye on Mrs. Wester. Amen."

A chorus of twelve amen's joined hers and the commotion began anew.

Brody stepped in line behind Lou. "Which of the guys does that little nymph belong to? And where's her mother?"

"You're looking at her," Lou replied, her eyes meeting his, daring him to pass some judgment about her daughter.

"Does her father live here, too?" he asked casually.

"No," was her only reply.

Lou joked with one of the men about a date he had been on the night before, and another of the hands quizzed Sarah on her spelling homework. Then Lou rose, placed her plate and cup in the sink, and grabbed Sarah's backpack from a post by the door. She beckoned for her daughter. "Move your butt, little lady. You're going to miss the bus."

"I'll take her down, Lou," John said, grabbing the backpack and bending over so Sarah could climb on his back. They walked over close to Lou so she could get a peck on the cheek.

"How about me?" John asked with his bottom lip poked out.

Lou smacked him soundly on the rump before she said, "Giddy up."

The hands all laughed as John walked out the door with a false look of dejection on his face.

Through the screen door, all the hands could hear Sarah say, "I'll give you a kiss, John." Then she squealed with laughter.

Lou stood in the doorway and watched them walk to the end of the lane. Then she turned and started clearing the dishes from the table as Sadie loaded the industrial sized dishwasher. When the task was complete, Lou threw the towel down and looked at her watch. "Sadie, I'm going for my run. Be back in about an hour."

"Jogging?" Brody asked.

Lou just nodded, glancing at her watch with impatience.

"Care if I join you? I want to talk to you anyway."

She looked slightly annoyed. "Can you hurry? I have a lot of work to do today," Lou replied.

"I'll meet you outside in five minutes. I just need to change my shoes," Brody said.

****

True to his word, Brody stepped off the back porch steps no more than five minutes later. Lou could almost feel his gaze on her as she stretched against the board rail fence. Her right leg was extended in the air, her ankle resting on the top rail. She bent with her nose nearly touching her knee. She flexed and extended her arms toward her toes, taking full advantage of the stretching position.

She dropped her leg. Her eyes met his, not comprehending the reason for the sudden darkening of his slate gray eyes.

"Ready?" she asked, checking her watch.

"Always," replied Brody.

She started the jog down the trail slowly, regulating her breaths as her feet hit the path. The jogging trail took them down the dirt drive that led to the bus stop. Lou then turned and cut across a small path that led around the edge of the property. The path was well worn and wide enough for the two of them to run abreast.

"Do you run every day?" Brody asked between breaths.

"Five days a week," Lou replied shortly, still timing her breaths to her coincide with her footfalls. "You?"

"Every day, if I have an opportunity. I am on a tight schedule at the hospital."

"You're a doctor, right?"

"A surgeon."

"I thought so. When I called, they said you were in surgery. How did you get here so fast?"

"They interrupted me during a procedure. I caught the first plane out. Sorry about catching you in your undies with John. I didn't mean to ruin the moment."

"What moment?" she asked, nearly tripping over an exposed root.

He reached out to catch her fall and her eyes met his. What she wouldn't give to know what he was thinking.

"You were in your underwear and John was shirtless so I just assumed." He shrugged.

"You know what they say about people who assume, right?"

"They make an ass out of you and me?" he asked with a smirk on his face.

She did not reply but merely picked up the pace of their run, making it harder to talk. The path became too narrow to run side-by-side so he dropped in behind her. She was almost relieved, until she realized he was in a perfect position to watch her butt muscles flex with every step. She winced at the very thought. And wished she hadn't had ice cream two nights the week before.

The path widened and he moved back up to where he could run beside her. She tried not to look when he grabbed the tail of his T-shirt and pulled it over his head. He then pushed the tail of the shirt into his waistband. Lou turned her face to him and couldn't draw her gaze away. It moved as though of its own accord from his steely gray eyes to his neck. His strong jaw was clenched with concentration. Her gaze stopped when she met the hair on his belly that dipped into his waistband.

"You want me to remove those, too?" he asked with a smirk.

"Suit yourself," she said, as heat crept up her cheeks. Damn him for noticing her appraisal.

A small chuckle was his only response. "You can take yours off, too, you know."

"You couldn't pay me enough," she replied.

"So money is a motivator? Is that why you have attached yourself to John? You think he might be worth part of the farm some day?"

Her breath stopped in her throat as she realized his meaning. She stepped in front of him and stopped abruptly. He stopped short, nearly knocking into her as she blocked his path. Her back straightened as though her five foot eight inch frame could meet his six foot two. She poked a finger in his chest and forced herself to speak around heaving breaths.

"How dare you! You don't even know me! How dare you make an assumption about my motives?"

He placed two hands up in mock surrender. "I just know I saw you almost naked. You're living here with your child who has no father, freeloading off my mother. You have Sadie and Jeb wrapped around your pretty little finger." He held his little finger up in the air and swirled it like a lasso. "What else am I supposed to think?"

Tears pricked at the backs of her lashes. She turned from him quickly and resumed her run, the pace becoming faster and faster until she left him far behind. He was just out of her eyesight as she turned the corner at the pasture fence and slowed at the back steps. She did not stop to stretch again but blasted through the screen door, heading for her room and a shower. The door slammed behind her.

****

"What's wrong with Lou?" Sadie asked, rising from her chair when Brody walked into the kitchen

"Who knows, Sadie? I guess I offended her," Brody replied, shaking his head. "All I did was ask her some questions. About why she's here."

Jeb rose from his chair and crossed the room to stand before Brody. "What do you mean, boy?" he asked, his brow drawn together.

"I already told you, Jeb, I left the boy back on the farm twelve years ago." Brody couldn't help but bristle.

"Then I suggest you act like the man you claim to be and tell me why Lou just flew through here like a cat with her tail on fire, and about as mad, too. What did you do?"

"It's not about what I did, Jeb. It's about what she has done. She's not what she seems. I can tell it. There's something I don't trust about her."

Jeb took a deep breath and looked Brody in the eye. "Say again?"

"She must have y'all snowed, Jeb. Those calf eyes and the ponytail make her seem so innocent."

"Boy," Jeb began. Brody clenched his jaw at the comment, yet the man continued his speech. "You don't deserve to know but I'm going to tell you anyway just to set my own mind at ease. She came here when she was almost nineteen years old. She had a two-month-old baby and no home. I found her lying in the middle of the road and brought her here. We have all been happy with her being here ever since. She didn't know much about life and she knew even less about mothering. But she learned. Your mother saw some potential in her and made sure she had an education and a roof over her head. She had a built-in family with Sadie and me and John and your ma. She pays us back for it every single day, although we have never asked her to. We get the pleasure of her company and we get to see the benefits of her hard work.

Jeb took a deep breath as he continued. "That girl puts in more work on the ranch than any five hands we have out at the barn. She gets up with the chickens to save Sadie from having to haul food for the hands, and that's not even part of her job. She'll be here again at lunchtime, no doubt, for just the same reason. Her job here is to take care of the finances for the stables and the crew. She makes sure they all get paid well and on time but she's worth more than that. Both she and her daughter are a part of Western Skies. That's more than I can say for you." Jeb placed his hat on his head and walked out the backdoor. Brody winced as the screen door slammed.

He turned to Sadie. She shook her head in disappointment. "I thought better of you, son."

"Sadie, I didn't know," Brody said.

"Now you do," she said and walked out the door.

****

Lou stormed through the door of her room and flopped on the edge of the bed. Her shoes hit the floor with a bang and her socks followed.

"The nerve of some people," she hissed before she stepped into the bathroom. Her breath still rushed in anger as she flung clothes off with abandon. "I've lived and worked here for years, and he comes home for a day and judges me." She turned on the shower spray and placed her closed fist beneath the spray, testing for warmth. Her anger pulsed against the warm water until she stepped beneath it. The warmth hit her face and she placed both elbows against the wall, resting her weight against them. Only then did she start to relax.

She allowed the water to pour over her face and shoulders. The water served to wash away the sweat from the run as well as the tension in her body. She let his hateful words and antagonism wash down the drain. Taking deep breaths, she soaped her hair and washed her face, then applied scented shower gel to her legs and arms.

She stepped from the shower feeling much calmer and wrung her wet hair like a rope, removing most of the water. She then bent forward and wrapped a towel around the brown mass of hair. Lou wrapped her body in another towel and tucked it between her breasts. She then moved to the wardrobe to choose her clothing. She bent to open the bottom drawer and heard a rap on the door.

She heard her name called just as she saw the door handle jiggle. She turned, her bottom still in the air and was about to call out for whomever was on the other side to wait a moment when the door opened, and a blond head with a square jaw popped through. Flint-colored eyes met her own.

****

She gasped and reached to cover her breasts, even though they were well shielded from his gaze by the fluffy towel.

She shrieked. "Get out!"

"Oh, God." He closed his eyes but his head did not retreat. Her image was already burned on the inside of his eyelids. "I just came to apologize. I'm sorry. I'll come back later." He pulled his head back and something hit the door. Did she throw a shoe at him? On purpose?

Brody stood outside the door and could hear her curses from inside the room. His blood ran hot at the thought of her little bottom bent over in front of the wardrobe. He could see the curve of her rear in his mind's eye. When she stood up, he could see the cleft between her breasts, clenched tightly by the towel so they created small swells above the material. He shook his head to get rid of the image, but then his thoughts just jumped to her long, golden legs. In his head, he imagined them bare, and they seemed to be a mile long with no pants to mar the lines. He shook his head again.

Brody turned to walk down the hallway and couldn't suppress the grin that stole across his face. He also couldn't suppress the urge to adjust the fit of his pants.

****

Lou, freshly showered and dressed, applied a light bit of makeup and dried and brushed her hair until it shone. She left her room and took the stairs down to the library where her desk and files were located. Late mornings and early afternoons were reserved for office work. She often took a small break to help Sadie put lunch on the table but rarely stopped to eat more than a bite herself.

She turned to enter her office and was stunned to find her chair was turned backward and someone with broad shoulders was sitting at her desk. The figure in her chair turned and Lou groaned inwardly when she realized who it was. Broden Wester, III was reclining in her chair, talking on the phone. She crossed her arms in front of her chest and tapped her foot lightly as she waited for him to surrender her work area.

"I'll just be a minute," he said, covering the mouthpiece and stretching his long legs so he could put his feet on her desk. Of all the nerve!

Lou decided it wasn't worth the argument and walked beside the desk to retrieve a file so she could take it to the kitchen and work. She knocked his feet off the top of her desk with a gentle shove and opened the file drawer to the right of the chair in which he sat. The drawer bumped his knees so he turned slightly to the front to avoid a second blow. Her elbow brushed his thigh as he turned. He instantly reacted and flexed his thigh muscle in response.

She heard his indrawn breath and wondered if he was agitated because of her interruption, or if he had felt the same heat she did when their skin touched. She bet it was the former.

"Dr. Jones, can I call you back later today? Yes. I have some notes I need to review and then I'll get back with you. Thanks for understanding. Yes. This is a very trying time. I appreciate your help." He hung up the phone and his steely eyes met hers.

"Hi," he said.

"Hi," she clipped out.

"I think we got off on the wrong foot. Can we start over?"

"Does starting over include you berating me for being a freeloader again?" He at least had the good grace to flush.

"I'm sorry," he said, rising from the chair. "Let me introduce myself. My name is Dr. Brody Wester. And you are?"

"I am annoyed." He didn't deserve more from her than that, did he?

"I deserved that," he said beneath his breath. " Am I keeping you from work?"

"Actually, you are, so, if you don't mind…" She nodded toward the door. She could be civil if she had to, couldn't she?

"Well, it's nice to meet you, Lou." He extended his hand to shake hers. Her hand rose hesitantly but clasped his firmly. She wouldn't let him see any weakness in her. None at all.

"I'll let you get to work," he said, walking toward the door. "Will I see you at lunch?" he asked.

She mumbled, "Not if I see you first."

A mischievous grin lit his face as he met her eyes, and then he waved quickly and left the room.

After taking a few moments to collect her thoughts, Lou worked in the library, poring over figures and facts until her eyes crossed and she could no longer read the pages. She checked her watch and realized it was almost one in the afternoon. She went to the kitchen and helped Sadie carry two heaping trays of sandwiches and fruit, typical lunch fare, outside to the picnic tables under the shade trees. Jeb had already arrived and had iced down sodas, tea, and bottled water for the lunch crowd. Sadie also uncovered a plate of fresh-baked chocolate chip cookies.

After the hands were all settled for lunch, Lou grabbed a cookie, a bottle of water, two apples, and a sandwich for herself and headed for the barn. She stopped at the saddle rack and tucked her lunch into a clean saddle bag. Clucking softly to Sunny, a bay gelding of sixteen hands, she chose a leather bridle from a hook on the wall and approached a stall.

Sunny bumped his head against her shirt, demanding her attention.

"Oh, all right…here," she said, removing a peppermint from her pocket, unwrapping it and popping it into his mouth. He crunched heartily and snorted at her. She giggled and snorted back. Draping the bridle over his ears and fitting the snaffle bit between his teeth was the easy part. As was covering him with a blanket and saddle. She lowered the saddle to cover the blanket, tightened the cinch, and counted to sixty. She mumbled, "If you would just let out that last breath, we could get moving." She tightened the cinch again. Lou led Sunny from the stall and out into the bright sunshine beside the barn.

"Going for a ride?" a deep voice asked as she swung up into the saddle.

"Yeah. There's a wild horse out by the south pasture. John bought her at an auction, not realizing how wild she was. She's due to foal soon. I'm going to see if she's still hanging out in the same spot. She bred with Wester's Folly, one of our best sires, before she flew the coop."

"How far away is she?"

"About a half hour's ride north of here."

"Care if I join you?" Brody asked, his hands shoved deep in the pockets of his Levis as he scuffed up dirt with his heels.

"Not at all. I'll go and get you a horse." She started to dismount.

"There's no need. I can just ride with you." Before she could protest, he slid her foot out of the left stirrup and replaced it with his own. He swung up in the saddle behind her, his legs and calves touching her own as his lap pushed her to the front of the saddle. Her zipper nearly touched the saddle horn. His zipper touched her bottom. Her breath caught in her throat at the intimacy of the contact. She turned slightly so she could look him in the eye.

"This saddle is too small for both of us," she started.

He grinned at her and said, "If I'm not mistaken, this is the same old saddle Jeb used to ride double with all his nieces and nephews. So, it's made a little wider and just fine for both of us to share."

"Jeb's skinnier than you are." She tried one last complaint.

"You saying I'm fat?"

She sighed. "It would really be better if we got you your own horse, don't you think?"

"It's been twelve years since I've ridden, so I'm afraid I might be a little rusty. Do you mind?"

"I would rather…"

He cut her off with, "Aw, come on. Please..." His attempts to sound like a five-year-old failed miserably, especially since he was one hundred percent man sitting behind her in the saddle.

"Are you really scared to ride by yourself?"

"Yep. Terrified." He gave a mock shiver. "Let's go." Without waiting for her to agree, he wrapped his arms around her and took the reins from her hands. He clucked gently to Sunny and nudged the horse with his knees. "You don't mind if I drive, do you?"

"Actually, I do." She took the reins from his hands and sat straight up in the saddle, avoiding his length behind her as well as she could.

His breath bushed across her cheek when he spoke. "I want to apologize again for what I said earlier. I'm sorry. I had no reason to distrust you or to speak to you the way I did." His voice rumbled over her shoulder and across her neck. She fought a shiver.

"Apology accepted. If someone bothers my family, I am a little territorial, too."

"Where is your family? Nearby?" he asked casually.

"Sarah is my only family. I have adopted Jeb, Sadie, your mother, and John. Or they adopted me. I don't know which happened first." A grin tugged at her lips.

"They seem like they think the world of you."

"The feeling is mutual."

The silence was comfortable for a few moments as they were lulled by the gentle motion of the horse.

Lou shifted in the saddle, hoping for a more comfortable position.

"Would you be still?" he asked gruffly in her ear.

"Sorry." Her hand touched his thigh as she lifted her bottom and then settled back into the saddle. Her new position put her in closer contact with his maleness, and she could suddenly feel the hardness of him pressing against her bottom.

Lou looked over her shoulder in alarm and caught his steely gray eyes as they darkened slightly. His eyes met hers and he said, "Perfectly normal male reaction to being so close to a woman. Especially one that's acting like she has ants in her pants."

"Can't you…"

"Can't I what? Make it go away? Sure I can. I just need to put you about two feet away from me for the rest of the ride. How do you suggest we accomplish that?" he asked sarcastically, a small growl in his voice. "This wasn't my best idea ever," he admitted.

"But…"

"Just be still for a minute and it'll go away. I promise. Do you want me to explain the medical side of this kind of physical reaction? I could tell you why it happens from a non-emotional standpoint. Would that ease your mind?"

"Would it help to ease anything for you?" she asked.

"Probably not," he grunted.

"Then we can skip it. Thanks."

"Any time."

"Would it help to talk about something else?"

"Anything else, yes. You pick the subject," he urged.

She could barely think with him pressed against her. "Do you like your work?"

"I love my work. I get to be a hero and save lives every day. Those I can't save at least get a fair shot."

"Sounds like a noble profession."

"It is. It's what I wanted to be ever since I was a little boy playing doctor with the girl who lived on the next farm over."

"You never wanted to be a rancher?" she asked.

"Nope. Still don't. When I was eighteen years old, my father told me I could either be a rancher and continue to be his son, or I could be a doctor and do it on my own. I graduated from high school, left here, and never looked back. I left with $1000 in my pocket, a car that had been given to me for my sixteenth birthday, and a trash bag full of clothes. I don't know if I left because of the ultimatum or because I hated the ranch. It was probably the ultimatum that did it. I put myself through college using student loans and part-time jobs. I am in debt up to my eyeballs now, but it was all worth it." He finished his speech with bland smile in her direction.

She shifted in the saddle again and he groaned. "Here we go again..."

"Sorry. You're pressed against me like white on rice, Brody. My skin can't even breathe." She slowed the horse and tapped his knee with her palm, whispering, "There she is. See her standing by the rocks? She usually comes to me to get a treat, but I am not sure if she'll come with you here." She tapped his knee again. "Get off."

"Don't I wish," he mumbled under his breath.

"What?"

"Nothing," he said as he dismounted.

Brody threw one leg over the back of the horse and pivoted gracefully to the ground. He adjusted his jeans and reached to help her dismount as well. Her foot caught in the stirrup and she fell against him. Her blood warmed at the contact. He grabbed both her elbows and steadied her. One hand reached out and brushed the chestnut locks of hair from her face.

"You okay?" he asked.

"Yep. Just fine." She turned her back to him and reached into the saddlebag for her lunch. She carried it over to a large rock, climbed atop and sat down.

"Now what?" Brody asked.

"Now we wait," she replied.

"Wait for what?"

"For her to come over to see us. She's way too nosy to stay over there."

"Ah, I see." Brody hitched himself up on the rock where she was perched.

Lou found it hard to ignore him. "Pretty soon, we'll go ahead and move her up the foaling pens. She's going to be ready to have that baby within the next two months and we certainly don't want her to do it out here."

"That so?" Brody questioned, totally unconcerned with the topic as he eyed her sandwich.

"Got one of those for me?" he asked.

"I have a knuckle sandwich for you if you try to steal my lunch," she replied with as much cheek as she could muster.

"I guess I'll have to take my chances," he said, reaching for one triangle of the sandwich. She swatted at his hands, then gave up and offered him half with a loud groan.

"You'll have to fight me for Sadie's cookie," she said, her eyes narrowing.

"Point taken," he said.

She raised the water bottle to her lips and took a sip. "I guess you want some of this, too."

"You guessed right," he replied, taking the bottle from her outstretched hand. Her pulse sped up at the thought of his lips touching the rim of the bottle where hers had just been. He drank slowly as she watched his Adam's apple bob, and then he handed the bottle back to her.

Lou picked up one of the apples and bit into the flesh. A trickle of juice ran down her chin. Brody wiped the juice that ran from her lips with the pad of his thumb. He raised his thumb to his mouth. The jolt of electricity that sliced through Lou was surprising and fast.

"You want some?" she asked, her mouth full of chewed apple.

"Yeah. Got some extra?" he asked, his eyes never leaving hers.

"That one is for the little mama but you can share this one," she said, handing him the apple that already had a bite out of it.

He accepted it graciously and bit off a chunk.

Lou felt a snort on the back of her neck. Sunny stood grazing several feet from them so she knew he couldn't be the source. "Shhh...be very quiet," Lou whispered, her breath a mere few inches from his. She turned slowly and extended the apple to the mare. She didn't try to make eye contact or to touch the mare, but simply extended her shaking hand toward the huffing animal.

The mare took the apple from her and stomped away to enjoy the treat.

"Six months ago, I couldn't even get close to her," Lou said. "She was way too skittish. She would run about a hundred yards away and stand there, stomping, taunting me. She has gotten closer and closer each time I came out here and seems to be starting to trust me."

"Now you have her eating out of the palm of your hand. Literally," Brody replied. "That was amazing." He passed her own half-eaten apple back to her.

"If you hate ranching so much, why did you want to come out here with me?" Lou asked, her brows knit together as she took a healthy bite.

"I don't hate ranching. I hated having my choices taken away," was his reply. "And besides, I had a hunch."

"What kind of hunch?" Lou asked.

His hand gently cupped her neck and threaded into the air at the back of her neck as he pulled her forward. "A hunch you would taste like this." His head tilted and his lips gently touched hers. He tasted of warm apple. His firm lips closed over hers as he lingered at her mouth. He deepened the kiss by turning his head and taking firmer possession of her lips. "Open your mouth, Lou," he whispered gently.

She was so surprised by the command that her breath caught in her throat. Her mouth opened of its own free will, and his tongue slipped inside. He traced the line of her teeth and the inside of her lips with gentle circles. He gently and tenderly touched his tongue to hers. It rose in response. The kiss deepened and Lou's heart began to pound in her chest. His hands played in her long dark hair, holding her head still as he assaulted her senses. His strong fingers cradled her head, gentle but insistent.

Just then, she heard a snort behind them again. Lou stiffened and tried to move back. Brody's hand tightened in her hair, his tongue still probing her mouth. His eyes opened, and he took the half-eaten apple from her hand. He did not break the kiss but reached behind her and held out the apple to the mare. She ate it from the palm of his hand just like she did with Lou. Like before, she ran away after she stole her prize.

Brody broke the kiss and placed his forehead against hers, his breath coming in gasps. A small smile played across his lips.

"You had a hunch, huh?" she asked, her heartbeat returning to normal.

"Yep," was his only reply. "I was right. You're not as untouchable as all the hands seem to think."

It took a moment for his words to sink in and then her spine stiffened. Her hand met his cheek with a resounding thwack, leaving behind a red handprint that covered the side of his face.

A muscle jumped in his jaw. He stepped back and raised a hand to his cheek.

"Don't ever do that again," he ground out.

"Ditto," she ground back.

Chapter Three

The ride back home was completed in silence. Lou sat stiff as board in the saddle. She ate her cookie without a word and did not offer even the smallest crumb to Brody, who sullenly looked on. She figured his ardor was sufficiently dampened by the slap, so there were no issues with squirming and movement. Nonetheless, she was about as inviting as a cactus sitting in front of him.

As they rounded the corner and came out of the north pasture, Lou straightened in the saddle, realizing there was a vehicle with flashing lights parked in the driveway. She shielded her eyes with her hand to see what was going on.

"I think that's an ambulance, Brody," she said, concern evidenced by her tone.

Brody tore the reins from her hands and kicked the horse into a gallop. He held the reins in one hand and the other wrapped firmly around her waist with his arm beneath her breasts. He pulled her back against him so they fit as one in the saddle. They tore across the last half mile of open pasture and skidded to a halt before barn. Brody quickly dismounted and pulled Lou from the saddle. He handed the reins of the horse to a stable hand that stood nearby.

Both Lou and Brody ran toward the ambulance as Margaret Wester was being lifted into the back on a stretcher. She had an oxygen mask over her pale face and blue lips.

"Mom, are you alright?" Brody asked, his voice clouded with anxiety as he grabbed his mother's hand.

Mrs. Wester's eyes opened slightly but she did not speak.

Sadie placed her hand on Brody's arm, "She wouldn't wake up from her nap, son. I didn't know what to do."

"You did the right thing, Sadie. Thank you." He squeezed her hand and climbed into the back of the ambulance with his mother. He was taking a stethoscope off a technician's neck and listening to Mrs. Wester's chest as the doors closed and the ambulance came to life.

Lou turned to Sadie and was immediately enveloped by her welcoming embrace. Sadie wrapped her arms around Lou who buried her face in the old woman's neck. "I'm sure she's going to be all right, child. Just you wait and see. Why don't you get the car and meet them at the hospital? I'll stay here and John will get Sarah off the bus. She can keep Jeb and me company until you come back. Go on, now," she said, patting Lou on the arm.

Lou walked quickly to the backdoor and retrieved a set of keys from the peg on the wall. She grabbed her purse and ran to the Jeep that was normally for farm use, started it and left, rocks flying in the driveway behind her.

Mrs. Wester would pull through this, wouldn't she? Lou entered the emergency department via the sliding doors. She walked toward the reception desk to inquire as to the whereabouts of Mrs. Wester when she heard the shouting.

"Damn it! She's my mother! I'm a surgeon for Christ's sake!" said Brody.

"You very well may be, Dr. Wester, but you don't have privileges at this hospital so you cannot be present during the diagnosis and testing phases. Your mother is critically ill. We need to concentrate on her care." The doctor's voice lowered and he asked, "Do I need to have someone escort you to the waiting room?"

With an exasperated look and a roll of his eyes, Brody shook his head. "Hell, no. I don't need an escort to help me move to the waiting room." His voice was suddenly nasal as he mocked the doctor's tone. The doctor closed the curtain that separated mother and son and stepped behind it.

Lou approached Brody and laid a hand on his shoulder. "Do you know what's happening yet?" she asked.

"Not yet. The sons of bitches won't let me go in there," he ground out.

"That's ok. We'll just wait out here until they're ready for us." She patted his shoulder gently and encouraged him to move to the waiting area. "Sadie said your mother took a nap like she normally does in the afternoon but she didn't respond when Sadie tried to wake her up?"

"That's what she said. I didn't get a chance to examine her because the little bastard in the ambulance took the stethoscope back. I should have just clobbered him over the head with it."

Lou couldn't hold back a small smile at the idea of Brody knocking out the ambulance technicians and stealing their equipment. "I don't think that would have been a very good idea," she chuckled.

"Sure would have made me feel better," he flopped into a waiting room chair and lifted his feet onto the coffee table. His fingers drummed on the arm of the chair.

"I'm sure they'll come out and tell you something soon. Is it okay if I wait here with you and keep you company?" she asked.

"You're welcome to stay but I'm not sure how much company I'll be," he responded.

"I'll take my chances."

The minutes became hours as the day went on. The doctor came out once and explained to Brody that they were taking his mother down to x-ray and then get an ultrasound of her heart. He did assure Brody his mother was now stable yet they were very concerned. He had not returned since that time.

Brody was restless and couldn't sit still in his chair. He shifted and moved constantly, looking at his watch every five minutes. At 7:30 in the evening, he checked his watch again and was stopped by the rumbling of Lou's stomach.
"Why didn't you tell me you're hungry?" he asked as he lowered his feet to the floor.

"I'm not hungry," Lou replied, her face heating in embarrassment.

"Bullshit. Your stomach says otherwise. When was the last time you ate?" he asked.

Lou straightened in her seat, her back stiffening and she replied, "The same time you did." Her face warmed again as she remembered sharing the sandwich earlier that day.

"At least you had a cookie," he mumbled under his breath.

"What did you say?"

"Nothing," he sighed. He rose from his chair. "Come on. Let's go and get you something to eat." He waved his hand at her with an impatient gesture.

Brody stopped at the emergency desk and checked out a pager that would alert them if the doctor was ready to see them or if there was a problem. He put it in his back pocket and touched his hand to the back of her arm, urging her to precede him into the elevator. She leaned against the wall and closed her eyes, exhaustion taking over. She yawned loudly and long.

"Am I boring you?" Brody asked with a small smile on his face. "I must be keeping you from a date or something."

"I don't date and I'm not bored."

His eyes narrowed. It was almost imperceptible, but it was there. "Why don't you date?"

"I just don't go out much. I work a lot of the time and spend the rest of the time with my daughter." Lou shrugged her shoulders. "She's my number one priority."

"But surely someone who looks like you takes some time off for a date very now and then?" Brody cocked one eyebrow with disbelief.

Lou looked down at her jeans and t-shirt. "What do you mean, someone who looks like me?"

"You can't tell me that someone with your..." He stopped as though looking for the right word, "assets..." His eyes finally found their way back up to her face. "Has a hard time finding a date."

"Are you going to tell me next that I have great birthing hips?" she asked, a grin tugging at her lips.

Brody chuckled. Under his breath he said, "Those hips may be made for something but it sure ain't birthing."

"What?" He didn't really say that, did he?

"Nothing." He swiped a hand down his mouth.

The elevator doors opened and Brody landed at the small of Lou's back, nearly stealing her breath. She stepped away from him as they reached the counter.

"What's your pleasure?" Brody asked.

"It doesn't look like any of this will be pleasurable," Lou said under her breath and then turned to the attendant behind the counter. "Vegetable soup and a diet soda will do it for me."

"Same here but add a burger and fries to mine," Brody requested.

"You're going to eat all that?" Lou asked.

"Yep. I'm a grown man. You have to feed us every now and then." He patted his stomach playfully like he was playing a drum. "Keep in mind I work at a hospital. You eventually get used to the really bad food." Brody took the tray from Lou and guided her to a table where he clunked it down. He passed her soup and soda over and sat down across from her.

"So...let's get back to the conversation we were having." He dipped a French fry into a huge pile of ketchup and talked around it. "Why don't you date? My mother can't possibly keep you that busy."

"My life keeps me that busy. I have Sarah, my work, and your family. They all keep me busy. I don't leave the ranch unless Sarah has something going on at school or Sadie needs something from the store. I make it a rule not to date the hands, because it just causes bad feelings if it doesn't work out. I can honestly say I have never been on a real date." She tapped her fingers lightly on the tabletop and thought about it.

"Surely you dated Sarah's father?" he asked.

"That was different. Why are we discussing this?"

"I just wanted to find out a little about you. That's all." He shrugged his broad shoulders.

"You're hoping I'll spill the beans and tell you my life story. Okay. Here goes. My mother was a stripper. She worked in the shadiest places in the worst parts of town. She used her body to keep me clothed and fed. I had a different 'Uncle' every month or two. He moved in long enough to screw my mother. When he pissed her off, she would move on to the next one. And then another one after that. The last few years she was alive, she was almost never sober. Except for the night she died." She paused briefly. "I'll never, ever, let anyone use my body like she did to survive. Now you know the reason I don't date. Happy?"

Brody shoved a French fry in his mouth and chewed thoughtfully for a moment. Then said softly, "Tell me something good about her."

"What?"

"It can't have been all bad. Tell me about a good memory you have of her."

Tears suddenly pricked at the backs of her lashes. This was why she didn't talk about her mother.
"I don't have any."

Just as softly, "I don't believe that."

Lou shook her head. "She never made cookies like the other moms."

"What did she make?"

"What?" Why did this matter?

"She had to make something. She obviously fed you. What did she make?"

Lou shrugged. "Regular stuff. Pizza. Burgers. Hot dogs. But nothing was ever called by its name." Lou smiled. "Everything had a crazy name, like you would see on a menu at a restaurant. When we had burgers, we were having Ole Bessy over to dinner." The grin was now unmistakable on her face.

"See. I told you that you had some good memories," he said quietly.

A grin tugged at her lips. "Yeah. I guess I do," Lou smiled as she stole a French fry from his plate and dipped it in his ketchup. The ketchup smeared the corner of her mouth so he reached over to wipe it with his napkin. Her eyes met his, and electricity moved between them just as his pocket started to buzz. He retrieved the pager from his pocket.

"Looks like they're ready for us. Let's go." The rest of the food was left uneaten as they rose from their seats. Lou dumped the contents of their tray in the trash on the way out the door.

They entered the elevator and Lou looked over at Brody. He wasn't at all what she'd expected. "Thank you."

"For what?" he asked.

"For giving some of my mother back to me," Lou replied quietly. She hated the quiver in her voice.

But he just heaved a sigh and looked directly into her eyes. His slate grey gaze was slightly disconcerting in its intensity. "You did the same for me when you called and told me to come home."

Lou jerked her gaze from his and raised a fingernail to nibble on it. It would be nice to find out the prognosis for Mrs. Wester. The floors dinged by slowly on the display until the doors opened and they stepped out. The doctor was hunched over the nurses' station with a pen in hand. He looked up and scowled as they approached.

"Your mother, Dr. Wester, is suffering from congestive heart failure." Brody's indrawn breath and swear were all Lou needed to realize the seriousness of the situation. "I need to ask you some questions." The ER doc motioned to a chair and indicated they both should sit.

"How long has your mother had a cough?"

Brody looked toward Lou and she replied, "About two months. It has gotten worse in the past week. She coughs more when she is lying down."

"And her shortness of breath?"

"She hasn'tt been very active in the past few months. She just said she was extra tired."

"I can see why. Her x-ray showed there is fluid in the lungs and her heart is enlarged."

"Can I see it?" Brody asked.

"Sure." The ER doc moved over to the lighted x-ray viewer and switched it on. He hung the x-ray on the viewer and pointed with a pencil to the right side of the heart. "You can see here that blood has engorged the right side of the heart."

Brody nodded. "You can see the blood backed up in the veins. Damn it." He swore.

"Your mother's fingertips and toes were blue when she arrived…"

Brody cut him off mid-sentence. "Indicating a loss of blood flow to the extremities." Brody sighed again. "What's your recommendation?"

"I would suggest using a combination of diuretics like Lasix, vasodilators, ACE inhibitors, and calcium channel blockers," the doctor replied.

Brody nodded. His jaw tight enough that it was ticking.

"I know it's not easy for you, son, being a surgeon and not being able to help someone so close to you." The ER doctor squeezed Brody's shoulder gently.

"You have no idea," Brody responded as he extended a hand to shake.

"Let me know if you need anything. You can go in and see her briefly in the ICU, but she needs to rest."

Brody wiped his hand over his face as though he could wipe away the frown lines that now marred his features as the other doctor walked away. Lou reached out her hand to touch his shoulder.

"What did all that mean?" she asked gently.

"It means my mother is dying," he breathed in response.

Lou's hand fell from his shoulder as her world narrowed to black.

****

Lou felt a tickling breath on her cheek as her name was spoken softly.

"Lou…wake up, sleeping beauty."

Lou stretched her body only to find she was reclining in Brody's lap in a chair in the waiting room. One of his arms was behind her back, supporting her and his other hand was holding her wrist, checking her pulse as he counted the seconds.

"What happened?" Lou sat forward in his lap.

"You fainted." Brody mouth quirked like he was holding back a grin.

"I do not faint." Lou laid a hand on her chest. Of all the ideas!

"Then how else did you get in my lap? You didn't crawl there, as pleasant as that may sound."

"Oh, you!" Lou growled as she sat forward and quickly remembered the events that had just transpired. "Your mom…"

"Is waiting to see us, I'm sure. Feel up to it?" he asked gently. His voice was soft and his gaze wary.

"Absolutely. Can I go, too? Or do you want some time alone with her?" She lifted herself from his lap and stood in front of him. She brushed her hair from her face. His only response was to take her by the hand and go through the double doors leading to the elevator and then the ICU. The nurse pointed to a curtained area and they both poked their heads around the corner.

Brody walked to the right side of the bed while Lou walked to the left. Mrs. Wester was huddled amid the covers, her face as white as the sheets around her. Some of the blue tint had receded since the scare in the ambulance, so she looked more like herself. She woke briefly when Lou took one hand and Brody took the other. Her eyes opened slowly.

"Hey. My two favorite people," Mrs. Wester said softly.

"How are you feeling?" Lou asked quietly, still holding her hand.

"With my fingers. How about you?"

Brody chuckled softly. "I see you're feeling better."

"I'll be back up and about in no time, I'm sure." Her determined statement didn't quite reach her eyes. "You two should go home and get some rest."

"We will. We just wanted to say goodnight, Mom."

"Goodnight, son. 'Night, Lou," she muttered, her eyes closing as she spoke.

Brody released her hand and checked the IV bag that was pumping into his mother's frail arm. "What's that?" Lou asked.

"This one is a Lasix drip to help with fluid buildup and allow the heart to pump more normally. The other one is dextrose, saline, and potassium. The Lasix depletes potassium in the body so you have to add it back in." Lou looked at him with what must have been a blank look on her face. He groaned and said, "So, this one is sugar, water, and something like bananas. Make sense?"

"Clear as mud, Doc," she mumbled. "Will she improve with this?"

"She'll improve for a while." His voice was soft as he bent over the bed and brushed the hair from his mother's forehead and then kissed her gently. "But not forever."

Lou raised Mrs. Wester's hand to her lips and kissed it, then placed the hand back on the covers.

"Ready to go home?" Brody asked.

"Whenever you are," Lou replied.

Lou and Brody walked through the sliding doors and toward the parking lot. The pavement was blackened and damp with rain. Lou's shoes made slapping sounds as she walked toward the car.

"Mary? Mary Smith? Is that you, child?" Ssomeone called from across the parking lot and Lou heard quick footfalls approaching. A hand with skinny fingers clutched her arm. Lou turned and looked into a face that had been roughened by the hands of time. Her heartbeat quickened.

"I'm sorry. Do I know you?" Lou's tongue nearly refused to work.

"Mary Lou, it's me, Mrs. Downy. I lived next door to your family when you lived on Broad Street. That must have been about eight years ago."

Lou raised her nose a few inches and she assumed a rigid pose. "I'm sorry but you must be thinking of someone else." She removed the older woman's hand from her arm and turned to walk away.

Mrs. Downy said softly, "I'm sorry. I had you mistaken for someone I used to know." She said something more, but Lou didn't hear the words, because she was already in the Jeep with the door closed, sweat beading her forehead.

Brody walked over to the driver's side door and motioned for Lou to move over. She hesitated briefly and then slid across to the passenger's seat.

Brody slid into the driver's seat and held out his hand for the keys. "Are you okay? You're not going to faint on me again, are you?" he asked, backing out of the parking space.

"No! Of course not. Once in a lifetime is plenty." She'd never live it down if she did it more than once.

Brody raised a hand in mock surrender. "Hey, I'll take any excuse I can get to have a woman sprawled across my lap." His attempt at levity eased some of the tension that hung in the air like a wet blanket.

Lou bit back a grin. "You probably have women sprawled across your lap all the time." Why did she say that?

He grinned at her. "Actually, my lap is usually too busy to have anyone sprawled across it." His eyes cut in her direction as they narrowed. "I stay pretty busy at the hospital."

"When do you have to go back home to go to work? Soon?" she asked, realizing it would be better to change the subject.

"I'm going to take a short leave of absence. I have a month of vacation time to burn and I am not leaving until something happens with my mother. You do know it's just a matter of time, right?" He put on his best doctor's face despite the fear that must be gnawing at his gut.

"I understand." Tears filled her eyes, yet refused to spill. "Is there any chance she can come home?"

"Maybe. It's something we have to discuss with the doctors. We have to let her come out of the ICU before they'll even consider it."

"I can help take care of her when she does come home. We all will." Her innocent comment had him raising his eyebrows.

Brody's eyes met Lou's. "That's what you do, isn't it? You take care of people?" His voice softened. "Does anyone ever take care of you, Lou?"

"I don't need-"

Brody cut her off. "We all need to be taken care of, Lou... Even you." He reached across the seat and took her hand gently in his. Her next comment was as lost as the breeze coming through the open window. His strong hand enveloped hers and held it gently between them on the console. "Thanks for sitting with me today, Lou. You made the hours seem bearable."

"You're welcome. I wouldn't have had it any other way." The sentiment was cut short as her stomach betrayed her again with a loud growl. She removed her hand from his and pressed it to her belly. "Good grief," she mumbled.

He chuckled lightly. "Feel like some ice cream?" he asked as they passed the Dairy Barn.

"I always feel like ice cream," she responded, a grin stealing across her lips. "Sarah convinces Sadie and Jeb to hook up the hay wagon all the time, and we all pile in the back and come here for ice cream. She would be jealous if she knew where we are."

Brody circled the building and pulled into a parking space. "We'll bring her next time. Come on," he said, shutting off the car and opening his door.

They walked up to the counter together. Lou ordered a scoop of chocolate and a scoop of sherbet on the same cone. Brody ordered plain vanilla in a cup. "I thought you had an adventurous spirit," she commented playfully.

"I have an adventurous spirit. I just don't have a cast-iron stomach. How can you eat those flavors together?" He shivered dramatically.

"You don't eat them together. You eat them separately. If you are lucky, they mix a little as they melt." They took a seat outside the Dairy Barn at a picnic table. Rather than sit on the bench, she climbed on top of the table and sat down. He eyed her skeptically for a moment and then joined her. They sat in companionable silence for a short time. The lights flickered off at the Dairy Barn. It was obviously after the ten o'clock closing time. The area was devoid of other cars and people. "We had better go," she said, her half-eaten ice cream in one hand.

He waved impatiently at her. "We have plenty of time. I want to finish my boring old cup of vanilla," his voice dripping with heavy sarcasm.

She sank back down on the tabletop, her feet on the bench below. Her elbows rested on top of her knees. "Mine is much better than yours." Her attempt at a singsong voice and a teasing tone were muffled by her tongue swirling the cone.

"I don't know how it could be. Are you sure you didn't hit your head when you fainted?" He reached over and placed the back of his hand on her forehead as though checking for a fever.

"Positive. Here." She held her cone out to him. "Try it."

"Nuh-uh. It's much more fun watching you. I'll stick with vanilla."

"Sure?" she asked pleasantly, extending her cone toward him again.

"Oh, all right," he finally acquiesced with a big smile. He grabbed her hand to steady the cone and took a bite of the sherbet. "Not bad," he said, nodding his head.

She extended the cone again. "Now you have to try it with the chocolate."

"That's disgusting." He chuckled.

She extended the cone again and he once more took her hand. He bit a section of the chocolate scoop at the bottom of the cone. "You're not going to get me to try them combined no matter how cute you look doing that."

"You think I look cute?" she asked as her tongue swirled around the section where the two flavors met.

"You know you look cute," he mumbled under his breath as he watched her swirl the two flavors with her tongue again. "Would you stop that?" he asked more loudly.

"Stop what?" Her tongue stopped in mid-swirl.

"Never mind," he snapped, standing up quickly.

"Are you mad at me?" He rolled his eyes and groaned heavily. "I offered to share my cone."

"You can't be as innocent as you seem," he mumbled. He took a deep breath. "I want to try the two flavors mixed." His voice deepened as he moved to stand before her. Chocolate and sherbet glistened on her lips. She extended the cone again but he caught her wrist and deflected it. Instead, he moved closer to her knees and met her lips with his. His tongue gently and tenderly flicked against her closed lips, tasting the flavors of her cone. "Mmm..." he growled. "I think I like it."

Her breath caught in her throat at the simple assault on her senses. "What-" Her words were smothered by his lips as they closed more fully over hers.

"Can I have some more?" he asked playfully against her mouth. He stepped back slightly and she unwittingly raised her cone back to her mouth, her wrist clasped in his large hand as he guided the cone back to her lips. She swirled her tongue around the cone again. His mouth once again descended and met hers. He groaned again.

"Mmm...that is good." He dropped his own cup of ice cream on the sidewalk as his hand cupped her face, his fingers splayed toward her ear. His thumb touched her chin lightly, pressing insistently until her mouth opened under the pressure. She gasped softly, her indrawn breath bringing his tongue further into her mouth. He retreated slightly but did not remove his lips from hers. "You taste sweet," he said against her mouth.

Her only answer was a small whimper, as his tongue touched her lips again and traced a circle from lower to upper lips. His hands touched her calves and ran up behind her jean-clad knees. He very slowly spread her knees so he could stand between them. He reached around to the back of her jeans and pulled her bottom toward him so that she sat on the edge of the table.

His mouth continued the slow assault on her senses. His tongue probed gently and moved around her teeth. "Kiss me back," he whispered against her mouth. Her tongue rose to meet his and he made a rumbling little noise that skittered across her skin. He pulled her tighter against him. Her hand rose to touch his chest, the other still holding the ice cream cone.

Lou jumped when their kiss was cut short by the two-second peal of a siren. Brody broke the kiss, opened his eyes and noticed a police car parked ten feet from their perch on the table. Lou tucked her face against his neck in embarrassment.

"You kids want to move on out? It's getting late," the officer said through the open window. Lou smiled, trying to contain a giggle against his neck. A quick glance up showed her Brody was grinning too.

"Yes, sir. We'll be moving on out," he replied with a quick wave.

Brody lifted Lou's free hand from his chest and held it as she climbed off the table. She was a little unsteady on her feet. "You okay?" he asked gently, pressing the back of her hand against his lips.

"Yeah. I'm fine." Her legs felt like water but she would never admit it. He opened the passenger side door of the Jeep and she slid in, still clutching the melting ice cream cone. She started to lick the dripping streams of ice cream from the cone.

Brody crossed to the driver's side and slid into his seat. He started the Jeep and turned to look at Lou, her tongue once again swirling around the cone.

"Oh, Jesus," he groaned. He took the ice cream cone from her hand and tossed it out the window.

"What did you do that for?" She probably sounded like a whiny brat. But that was her ice cream for goodness sake.

"Never mind," he ground out as he again reached over and removed her sticky hand from her lap. He clasped it loosely in his own larger hand between them on the console.

The ride home was spent in companionable silence, the havoc of the day finally taking a toll on them both. Brody stopped the Jeep and turned off the ignition He squeezed her hand tightly. "Thanks again for sitting with me," he said gently, removing his hand from hers. Her only response was a slight nod.

They walked up the back porch steps together. He held the door for her. Sadie and Jeb were waiting up, sharing a pot of coffee at the kitchen table.

Jeb rose from his chair and turned to Brody. "How is she?" At the same time, Lou went to Sadie and walked into the old woman's arms. The stress of the day fell from Lou's body like the slow rain of her tears. Sadie patted her back and cooed to her like she was a child again. Jeb held out a handkerchief that was always in his back pocket. She took it and dried her eyes, thoroughly mortified to have been caught crying by Brody.

"Where's Sarah?" she asked softly.

"She's in our bed," Jeb said. "Do you want me to go and get her?"

"No. I can do it. You just stay here."

Lou walked from the kitchen to the long hallway that led to Jeb and Sadie's apartment on the lower level. She retrieved Sarah from atop the covers on their bed. The child did not wake as she lifted her but just wrapped her legs around Lou's waist. Lou placed her hands beneath her bottom and boosted her a little higher. Like most old homes, the stairway was centered around the kitchen so she had to walk back to where the family was seated.

Brody looked up from his coffee where he sat at the table with Jeb and Sadie and smiled softly at her as she walked by with the sleeping child tucked against her.

"'Night," she said softly as she turned to go up the stairs.

"'Night," he said in response.

Lou hauled the sleeping child up the stairs and entered her room. Once she was safely stowed beneath the covers, Lou kissed her forehead and walked through the bathroom that connected the two bedrooms. She typically slept with the adjoining door open so she could hear Sarah in the night.

Lou shed the worries of the day as she shed her clothes and stepped beneath the spray of the shower. The warm water washed away her worries. Her fears for Mrs. Wester began to diminish as she reminded herself that her mentor and friend was in good hands at the hospital. She lathered her hair with a lavender shampoo and washed her body with a soap that smelled vaguely the same. It was revitalizing and yet helped to relax her at the same time.

She stepped from the steaming shower onto a bath mat and rubbed the mirror clean with a towel. She dried her body with the same towel and then bent at the waist so her hair fell forward, allowing her to wrap it, turban style. She looked in the mirror and noted she looked reasonably good, even though she was still pale and tired.

She padded across the floor on bare feet and retrieved matching pajama shorts and a strappy pajama top. She unwound her hair from the towel and ran a brush through it. She looked at the hair dryer but then dismissed the idea. She decided, instead, to open the door to the portico and step out into the fresh air and let the wind blow-dry her hair.

In true antebellum style, the home had porches on both levels, and each bedroom had a separate entrance onto the porch. Outside each door sat double rocking chairs that faced the night. Lou quietly opened the door to her room and stepped out into the darkness. She chose not to turn on the porch light, preferring the glow of the moon over thousands of tiny bugs that would attack if she turned the light on. She sat down in one of the low-backed rocking chairs and hung her streaming mass of wet hair over the back so it swayed as she rocked gently. The small wind was a blessing after a hot day. The gentle motion of the rocking chair lulled her and eased some of the tension from her body. The creaking rockers on the chair sang a comforting tune. Lou closed her eyes and thought of the events of the day.

She felt like she had been rode hard and put up wet.

She had spent the day with a man who was at first accusing, then apologetic. He made her tremble, both with anger and with passion. She pressed her fingers to her lips, remembering the feel of his mouth against hers. *He must think I am such a child.* He had obviously had lovers before. Any idiot could tell he had experience. Unlike her, he had probably had more lovers than he had fingers and toes. She wondered if her lack of experience was obvious. It had to be. Not once, but twice, he had thrown out the bait and she took it like a starving mouse goes for rat poison. She was her mother's daughter after all.

That thought caused the acidic taste of bile to rise up in her throat. She swallowed it back as the ramifications of her actions hit her in full force. *I behaved like my mother.* She let her emotions and physical desires override her good sense and she was making a fool of herself in the process.

She ground her teeth in disgust. *How could I have been so stupid?* He was a man, and men only wanted one thing. They wanted to use you until they stole your soul, your pride and all your dreams. *How many times have I seen my mother discarded by a man over the years?* More times than she could count. She would never, ever be like that. She would let him know, in no uncertain terms, that she wasn't and would never be a whore, no matter how poor her decisions had been. She would tell him at the first opportunity.

Lou ran her fingers through her hair once more, feeling the silken threads fall between her fingers. Her hair was nearly as dry as her mouth. She rose quickly from the rocking chair and spun, opening the door to her room and letting it close not too gently behind her.

Lou crawled between the sheets with renewed determination, knowing she had to either put her foot down tomorrow or steer clear of one Dr. Broden James Wester, III.

****

Brody sat in the dark outside his own room, enjoying the peaceful evening as he tried to tidy the thoughts that ran through his mind. He tried to wade through the grief that accompanied the thoughts of his mother and her condition.

He sat in the shadows, chewing his fingernails, and was startled when he heard the sound of the door down from his opening. Lou stepped into the moonlight. She was wearing close fitting shorts and a small top that was so tight he could see her breasts jiggle slightly when she walked. They were obviously unbound but were still pert and full, her nipples pushing against the fabric in the gentle breeze.

He felt himself harden at the thought of her. Good God! He was acting like a kid with no self-control again. He could tell right off the bat Lou wasn't as experienced as he thought when he first met her, even though she had a daughter. Her inexperienced lips meeting his told him, plain as day, about her and her hesitation. If she had known how she looked eating that ice cream cone and interpreted his thoughts, she would have run for the hills.

If the cop hadn't shown up when he did, he would probably have stripped her right there on the table. He smiled at the thought of the cop calling them kids. He did feel like a kid again when he was with Lou, like the world was new and he wanted to explore all of it.

Her devotion to his family was unwavering. She would be at Western Skies long after he was gone. She didn't seem to be a one-night stand kind of girl, so the best thing he could do was keep his hands to himself and try to be friends with her—nothing more.

The scent of lavender tickled his nose as she lifted her hair over the back of the rocking chair. Her pose went from relaxed to rigid. He watched the expression change on her face as she rocked on the porch. He didn't understand the play of emotion that crossed her face but could tell she wasn't pleased just by the tension in her body. He was about to make his presence known and come out of the darkness to see what the problem was when she rose quickly from her rocker and stomped into the house.

The door slammed behind her.

What on earth had caused that?

Chapter Four

Chubby fingers clawed at the windowsill as banging hands slapped the front door. "We know you're in there, Lou! We know you have it. We want to talk to you." The banging stopped briefly and a new voice rang out—quiet, yet clear. The voice belonged to Mrs. Downy, the old lady who lived next door. "Lou, Honey, its Mrs. Downy. Why don't you just open the door for these nice gentlemen so they can get what you owe them, dear? They have been waiting for a long time…"

The voice faded away and was replaced by angry bursts and deep, guttural curses. The walls of the trailer shook as the hands beat against the rickety frame. A baby cried in a bassinet in the corner of the room. Lou grabbed the baby from the bassinet and crawled from the carpet of the living room to the cold linoleum floor of the kitchen. She climbed into the lowest set of kitchen cabinets and closed the door behind her. She placed a finger in the baby's mouth to keep her quiet. The baby suckled gently on her finger. She rocked her body back and forth. Was it more to comfort her or the baby? She wasn't sure.

The door splintered as the assailants finally found their way into the home. Heavy footfalls pounded through the rooms as they ran from one end of the mobile home to the other, opening doors as they walked through the house. They stopped and looked under beds and in closets. She heard them walk into the kitchen. Her heart started to race. She jumped as the first cabinet door opened. Her startled movement scared the baby clutched against her breast, and the baby let out a pitiful wail.

The door to the cabinet where she was hiding opened slowly. The kind, old face of Mrs. Downy peered into the darkness. Before Lou's very eyes, the kindly expression that was normally on the old woman's face changed to one of anger and hatred. The voice still belonged to Mrs. Downy but the face wasn't the same. "Just give them what they came for child," she chided as she reached out and grabbed the baby from Lou's arms with surprising agility. Lou held frantically to the child, trying to regain her grip but she was unable to hold on. A scream ripped from her throat as she realized she had failed to protect the baby.

"No! No! Nooooooooo!" she screamed.

Lou sat up straight in bed, sweat pouring from her body. Her hair was plastered to her face and sweat ran down her skin in rivulets. Her heart was pounding so fast she thought it would jump out of her chest. She scanned the room, looked through the open doorway into Sarah's room and verified the sleeping child was still tucked safely in bed. One day, the dreams would stop, wouldn't they?

****

The door to her room flew open with such force that it hit the wall with a thud. Brody stood in the threshold, wearing only a pair of boxer shorts. He held a baseball bat in his hand. Lou's eyes raised and met his.

"What's wrong? What happened?" asked Brody breathlessly, his eyes taking in the quiet state of the room where Lou had been sleeping. "Why did you scream?"

"I don't know," Lou stammered, clutching the comforter in front of her soaking wet body. "What did you hear?"

Brody sighed with relief and visibly relaxed. "I heard you screaming like someone was trying to kill you." Brody jumped when a hand touched his shoulder. He turned to find Sadie standing behind him, wearing a robe and slippers and her hair bound for sleeping. Jeb was directly behind her, dressed in lounge pants and a T-shirt. His feet were bare. "It's all right, Jeb. I think she had a bad dream." Sadie bustled by him, pushing him out of the doorway.

"You two can go on back to bed, now," she mumbled as she closed the door in their faces.

"But..." Brody stammered as the door was about to close.

She spoke through the crack in the door. "I'll take care of this, Brody. Take yourself off to bed, now."

"Come on, boy." Jeb placed a playful arm around Brody's shoulders. "Since we're both up, I'll treat you to a cup of coffee downstairs. You had better put some clothes on first, though." Jeb snickered and shook his head. A bat in his hand with him in his underwear. He'd blasted into the room like a naked avenger. He needed clothes. And coffee sounded good, too.

Jeb and Brody sat in companionable silence at the kitchen table until Sadie joined them thirty minutes later. "Is she okay, Sadie?" Brody asked, his eyebrows crunched together with concern.

"She's taking a shower, now. Poor thing was wringing wet with sweat." Sadie's eyes met Jeb's over the table. If Brody didn't know her so well, he wouldn't have seen the concern etched in her brows.

"Been a long time since she's woken up like that," Jeb said to Sadie with a sigh.

"Wait," Brody broke in. "She's done that before?" Surely it didn't happen often. It was terrifying.

"When she first came here, she woke up like that every night. Then the dreams started to get fewer and farther between until they stopped completely. She hasn't had one in years," Sadie clucked.

"What are they about?" Brody asked.

Sadie started to speak and Jeb cut her off. "That's her business, Brody. If she wants you to know, she'll tell you." Sadie nodded in agreement.

John walked into the room, rubbing his sleepy eyes as he tried to wake. "What's all the ruckus?" he asked around the yawn that filled his mouth.

"Lou had a nightmare," Brody announced. If no one else wanted to talk about it, perhaps John would.

John came instantly awake. "She hasn't had one of those in a long time. Did it wake Sarah up?"

"That child could sleep through a hurricane, John," Sadie replied with a slight chuckle.

"Was the dream as bad as they used to be?" John asked.

"Yeah. But she's fine now. You can go back to bed," said Jeb. He touched Sadie gently on the elbow to urge her back to bed as well.

Realizing no information would be forthcoming, Brody broke from the group surrounding the kitchen table and climbed the stairs back up to his bedroom. He passed by Lou's room and noticed the door was still slightly ajar. He tapped softly, calling out, "Lou?" He received no response.

He opened the door a few inches and peeked through the crack he had made. "Lou?" he called out again. Still no response.

Brody pushed the door wide open before he heard the creak of the rocking chair outside her room. Brody tiptoed through the room and opened the door to the porch slowly.

"Lou?" he called again, quietly.

Lou jumped as though someone had grabbed her. She was sitting in the dark in the rocking chair, much like before. Her long dark hair was hung over the back of the rocking chair, swaying in the breeze. She wore a fresh pair of pajamas, again a strappy pajama top and matching shorts. She sat forward quickly and was momentarily startled until she looked up and saw Brody standing in the doorway. Then she relaxed considerably, leaning back against the chair and wiping her wet hair from her eyes. "Hey," she said quietly.

"Hey, yourself. Are you okay?" Brody asked gently, sitting down in the rocking chair beside hers.

"Yeah, I'm fine." She dismissed his fear with a gentle wave in his direction. "Thanks for coming to my rescue with the baseball bat." She chuckled.

Her laughter lightened the mood considerably. He shrugged his shoulders. "It sounded like someone was trying to kill you. I had to do something."

"Next time, you might want to remember to put on some clothes before you go saving lives," said Lou, cutting her dark eyes in his direction. Brody could see the shine of her white teeth glowing in the dark, evidence of a smile.

Brody grunted. "You should be happy I wasn't sleeping naked."

Lou's grin got bigger. "If that's how you normally sleep, I'll consider myself warned and will try to keep my screams to myself." She put on a mock-offended look.

"Do you have nightmares like that a lot?" he asked gently.

"Is this Dr. Wester asking me or is this Brody?" she asked with a smirk on her face, one eyebrow raised.

"Both," was his only response.

Lou took a deep breath. "I used to have them all the time. I haven't had one in a really long time. I don't know if it was the stress of your mom being in the hospital or something else causing it. Let's both hope that was the last one for a while."

"I can give you something to help you sleep if you need it," Brody said. He didn't like to use medication to ease fears, and he had a sneaking suspicion that's what this was about.

"No!" Lou snapped, sitting forward in her chair. Then she sighed heavily and replied, "I don't drink. I don't smoke. I don't take drugs. I can get through this without any medication. But thanks for the offer."

"Is that because of your mother?" he asked gently.

Lou shook her head as she sat forward. "Boy, I've known you for all of twenty-four hours, and you're talking to me like you're my best friend. What gives?" Her eyebrows drew together, making a cute little check mark at the top of her nose.

"It's the doctor in me, I guess. I have to figure everything out before I can diagnose."

"Well, I'm not one of your patients, so be sure and keep that in mind." She must have rrealized the harshness of her tone, since her next comment was softer. "I need to talk to you about something else, while we are on this subject." She paused briefly, as though steeling herself for what was to come. She winced and spoke with her eyes closed. "I'm very sorry for slapping you today. Those interactions we had earlier today...I don't usually do that."

"I deserved the slap," he admitted, rubbing his jaw absently. "And I could tell you don't do that often," he replied as he tried to bite back a grin.

"What?" The checkmark at the top of her nose grew deeper.

"I could tell you don't normally do that. You didn't kiss like someone who does it very often."

"What's that supposed to mean?" Her voice raised an octave with outrage. Or embarrassment. He wasn't sure which.

"It means there are a lot of women out there who will wrap themselves around you and not let go until you are both done. You're not one of them. I could tell that the first time I kissed you." He was amazed to find that he wouldn't mind having her wrapped around him. Not a bit. Brody sat forward, his fingers tracing a circle on her arm. He felt the immediately need to touch her. Particularly since she seemed discomfited by his choice of words. He was an idiot. He let his finger trail up toward her elbow, until she grabbed it in a tight fist. A fist that shot straight to his groin.

She gently moved it off of her arm before she released his finger. "Just so you know. I don't do casual," Lou stated succinctly, her brown eyes meeting his steely grey.

"Casual?" What the hell did that mean? "I don't understand."

"You're the doctor. Figure it out," she tossed out flippantly as she rose from the chair and walked in her room. Brody watched the door close firmly and heard the bolt shoot home as she locked the door behind her.

Chapter Five

As usual, Lou woke early the following day and rose to help Sadie prepare breakfast. She put on her normal attire of T-shirt and shorts, socks and running shoes. She checked the mirror and noticed the dark smudges beneath her eyes, but shrugged them off as she splashed some cold water on her face. She put her long, dark hair in a ponytail, brushed her teeth and walked downstairs. She stopped short when she saw Brody standing at the stove, stirring a pan of scrambled eggs like a mad scientist might stir petri dish of germs.

"What's going on?" Lou asked, her eyebrows drawn together. She stopped on the bottom step, her gaze sweeping the room.

Brody dropped the spatula into the eggs. He reached to grab it and swore softly as he burned his thumb on the side of the pan. He lifted it to his mouth and spoke around it. "I thought you might be tired so I wanted to help."

Lou stepped around him and cautiously removed the spatula from the yellow egg mess he was scrambling. She scraped the bottom of the pan, removing what was stuck. "Oh, dear," she sighed.

"Did I mess it up?" he asked. He reminded her of Sarah when she tried to take on tasks well beyond her skill level.

Lou smiled gently and stood on tiptoe. She mockingly patted the top of his head just like she would Sarah. "Not at all," she replied. "Grab me some cheese and some salsa from the fridge."

Brody turned and gathered the items from the refrigerator and presented them to her. "What are you going to do with these?"

"Some of the eggs stuck so I'm going to scramble these in to cover up the taste. Otherwise, the whole pan will be ruined." She poured the contents of the salsa into the skillet and stirred again.

"I guess you never burn the eggs, do you?" he grumbled.

"Never," she replied stoically.

Brody grunted in return.

Lou scrambled as long as was necessary, then poured the egg and salsa mixture onto a serving platter. She then topped it with the cheese. She opened a container of sour cream and poured it into a bowl. She grabbed several packages of tortillas from the pantry and carried the food to the dining hall. Once the table was set, she rang the bell to call the hands in for breakfast. Then she turned and went upstairs.

Moments later, she returned with a bubbling Sarah who was once again streaking toward Sadie. This time, she held a brush and two ponytail holders in her hand. Sadie took the objects and Sarah sat down on her lap. Sadie created two perfect pigtails and kissed Sarah good morning.

Sarah surveyed the breakfast fare and snickered. "Did Mommy burn the eggs again?"

Jeb and Sadie couldn't hide their grins.

Lou scowled at Sarah. "Do you have to tell everything you know?" She swatted her gently on the behind.

"So you're not perfect, huh?" Brody asked with a grin, his comments directed toward Lou.

"Far from it, in fact. I just like to pretend every now and then."

John walked into the kitchen and removed his hat from his head. He hung it on the back of a chair and moved to fill his plate. He gave one to Sarah as well. He tugged her ponytails and said, "Morning, Squirt."

"Morning, John," she said as she let him fill a plate for her.

Lou picked up Sarah's backpack and a note fell to the floor. It was crumpled like the remains of yesterday's lunch. Lou unwrinkled the paper and read it. Of course, Sarah had discarded the note.

"Something the matter, Lou?" John asked quietly, coming to stand beside her. She passed the note to him. He read it slowly, looked up with a grin, and winked at Lou. He took a deep breath and addressed Sarah. "Hey, Squirt. I heard a rumor the other day that there is a Father-Daughter dance coming up in a few weeks at school."

Sarah's eyebrows drew together and her face flushed. "Yes, sir," she said quietly.

"Well, I've never had an opportunity to go to one of those dances, so I was wondering if you might let me be your date. I would hate to miss out just because I don't have a daughter. You think you might let me go with you, so I can see what it's like? I heard there might be cake and ice cream and dancing…" Begging puppies had nothing on John Wester.

Sarah's eyes grew big as saucers. "Really? You want to go to the Father-Daughter dance with me?" She came out of her chair and caught John around the waist.

"Yep. I would love to go with you. If you don't mind, that is," he added slyly.

"I don't mind. I'll let you go just this once."

Lou's eyes filled with unshed tears. She coughed to clear the emotion from her throat. "You had better finish your breakfast or you're going to be late for school."
Sarah quickly said grace and everyone sat down to breakfast.
After breakfast, Lou cleared the dishes and Sadie loaded the dishwasher. John took Sarah to the bus stop and, when Lou and Sadie were done, Lou looked at her watch to check the time. "Be back in a little while," she said absently as she headed for the backdoor.

Lou walked to the fence surrounding the corral and started to stretch, preparing for her run. She bent at the waist and stretched her back. When she braced herself to stand up straight, she was startled to find Brody standing in her path. He was wearing purple athletic shorts, running shoes, and a printed T-shirt that read "You're no bunny 'til some bunny loves you." Lou's left eyebrow rose as her eyes met his.

"What?" Brody replied innocently. "This was my bonus for volunteering at the animal shelter during Adopt-A-Bunny week. You got a problem with it?" He added a mock Mafia tone to his speech.

"You volunteered at an animal shelter?" Lou asked incredulously.

Brody replied sheepishly, "Well, not exactly volunteered. In college, I had to write a paper for psychology. I chose prostitution as my topic and I had this great idea I could get some information by interviewing a hooker."

"Wait." Lou cut him off, "Interviewing?"

"Yes. Interviewing." Brody paused to stretch and continued talking. "You know, asking questions and getting answers. I approached this hooker on Fifth Street and, next thing I knew, I was in handcuffs. I got booked and had to go before the judge. He wasn't sure whether or not he believed my story so he decided to give me community service. I had to work at the shelter so I would get the idea of "screwing like a rabbit" out of my head."

Lou could hide neither her smirk nor her laugh. She covered her smile with her hand.

"Quit laughing at me and let's run. You don't mind if I join you, do you?"

"Not at all. Think you can keep up?" she asked teasingly.

"No doubt about it," he replied. "Lead on."

Brody leveled up with Lou so he could run beside her and found a rhythm alongside her footfalls. She remained silent as they ran, her breath moving in and out in a regular cadence in time with her feet.

Lou was acutely aware of Brody as he ran beside her. Her heart pounded, and it wasn't completely because of the running. She could hear his breath blowing across his lips as he maintained the pace. Sweat broke out across his strong brow, and he lifted his powerful arm to wipe it away. It would be so easy to get closer to someone like Brody if she let herself fall for his sexuality, but he wasn't a permanent kind of man and she did not do casual.

Lou pushed herself harder than she had in a long time. She blocked out Brody's presence and picked up the pace, sweat pouring down her face like a hard rain. Her clothes stuck to her body despite the coolness of the early morning air. Brody was in the same shape. He kept the pace, but just barely. Just when Brody began to falter, her pace slowed slightly and she brought herself to a fast walk. They rounded the corner of the house about three minutes later and Lou stopped to cool down and stretch.

Brody bent and placed his hands on his knees. His breath came in gasps and raised his chin to look in her direction. "I thought you were trying to kill me," he panted at her.

"Nope. I was just trying to outrun you," Lou replied with a grin. She wiped the sweat from her brow with her forearm. Lou thought she heard him mumble something as she turned and entered the house.

Before she walked through the door, he said, "Outrun me or outrun something else…wonder which one it is, Lou." She let herself pause for no more than a second. It was better if he thought she didn't hear him, wasn't it?

Lou showered and went downstairs to go to work. She met Brody on the porch after she stopped to get a bottle of water. His hair was still wet from his own shower and hung in sandy colored curls across his forehead and his collar. He had transformed from a college kid in a printed T-shirt to Dr. Broden Wester in a matter of minutes. He wore a black polo and khaki trousers. His sneakers had been replaced with casual loafers.

"Do you want to go to the hospital with me today to see Mom?" Brody asked.

"Not this morning. I might go by later today. Sarah wants to make a card for her when she comes home from school so I'll probably go for a few minutes later in the evening."
His steely grey gaze met hers. " Thanks, Lou, for understanding."

She smiled gently and patted his arm. "No problem. She's your mother after all, not mine."

"I'll call if anything changes."

"Please do," she called out as she turned and walked toward her office.

Chapter Six

Wesley lowered the telescopic lens of the thirty-five millimeter camera and cupped it in his hand. He took a deep breath and blew it out between his closed teeth. He fished his cell phone from his pocket and flipped it open. Then he dialed the number he had been given.

"Jerry's Towing," a pleasant voice answered. The detective knew Jerry's Towing was a front for a phony business which did not and never had existed. But who was he to rock the boat?

"Yo, Wanda. Put the boss on the phone." There was no response on the other end as the call was transferred.

"You had better have something for me, Wesley," a voice snapped in his ear.

"I'm pretty sure I do, Boss. Looks like the old lady was right and it could have been her at the hospital last night. I had to do some digging, but I think I found her. I'm emailing some photos to you now."

There was no click on the other end, but the call had been disconnected. Wesley got out of the car and opened the trunk of the old sedan. He put the jack back in the trunk. Hopefully, no one noticed there had never been a flat tire. He would have to switch cars next time so no one would get suspicious.

Within ten minutes, his cell phone rang. He flipped it open. "Yeah""

"That's her. She looks just like her mama. I would know her anywhere."

"What do you want me to do?" Wesley asked.

"Keep an eye on her. Find out who she's living with. Get as close to her as you can and let her know I want my property back."

"Consider it done." He closed his phone and smiled broadly. The chase was on.

****

Brody walked through the sliding doors of the hospital and past the reception desk. He entered the elevators that would take him to the Intensive Care Unit.

Without waiting for permission, he strolled by the nurse's station and walked into his mother's room. She looked tiny reclining in the big bed with the rails raised around her. Her head was turned to the side so her cheek was exposed but the rest of her was swaddled in bedclothes.

Brody bent and picked up her chart to see if the treatment plan had changed. Her condition was still marked as critical. The notes and the suggestions in the chart were more along the lines of maintenance and comfort than rehabilitation. The doctors wanted to stabilize her condition with medication and then send her either home or to a nursing home for care until her final days.

Brody replaced the chart and walked to the side of the bed. He lowered the bedrail and bent to kiss his mother on the cheek. She stirred slightly as he slipped his hand into hers. Her eyes fluttered open and she smiled slowly at him, taking a deep breath. She untangled her arms from the covers and reached a tentative hand to brush the curls from his forehead.

"Your father always wanted you to keep your hair short and tidy, but I did so love those curls," she said slowly to him.

"Morning, Mom. Did you sleep okay?"

"Well as can be expected, I guess. Nurses came in all hours of the night to test this or that, or just to see if my old heart was still beating."

"Sure beats the alternative, doesn't it?" He forced himself to grin at her, although it was the last thing he felt like doing.

She tapped him gently on the arm and smiled back at him.

A nurse walked in behind them and began to check the fluid levels in the IV bags hanging on nearby hooks.

"Did Lou come with you?" Mrs. Wester asked.

"No. She's at home catching up on some work. She said she would try to come by for a little while tonight. Sarah wanted to make something for you so she's going to bring it by later."

The nurse broke in. "Is Lou the young woman who was here with you last night?"

"Yes," Brody replied.

"The night nurse said there was a man here late last night asking questions about your mother and the girl who was with you."

Brody released his mother's hand to turn toward the nurse.

" He started out wanting medical information about your mother. He also wanted to know about your mom and her relationship to the young lady. Of course, we couldn't release any information to him since he wasn't family." She shrugged and walked from the room.

"Wonder what that was about," Brody mumbled to himself.

Mrs. Wester was visibly flustered when he turned back toward her in the bed. A fine sheen of perspiration graced her upper lip and her breathing was labored.

"Mom! Are you okay?"

She reached for his hand and gripped it with amazing strength. "I'm okay but you have to get me out of here, Brody." She paused to take a deep breath. This set forth a series of hacking coughs. When the coughing spell was over, she took another breath and continued. "I want to go home. I want to go home today. Do you see? You have to take me home where everything can get back to normal."

"Will you calm down if I promise to take you home? Soon?"

"Today, Brody. I want to home today." She clutched his shirt from in her spindly grasp.

"Okay, Mom. I'll see what I can do." He gently took her hand in his and unwound it from his shirt, laying it into her lap.

Brody made arrangements in record time. His mom couldn't be calmed down until he promised she would be moved home that very day. He spoke with the doctor and then called the medical equipment company to have a hospital bed and other supplies delivered. He also made arrangements for an around-the-clock nursing staff to take up the slack, just in case something went wrong.

At three in the afternoon, the ambulance was backing up to the door of the ranch house and Mrs. Wester was being moved to her new bed. The nurse, Lola, a plump firecracker of a woman, fussed over the move and introduced herself to Mrs. Wester as they rolled her into the house. She took over with amazing efficiency. Brody stood back on the porch with Lou as Sadie and Lola barked orders at the medical technicians.

Lou turned to Brody and said with a light smile, "I feel like I'm in the way."

"So do I," Brody responded.

"I never thought she would come home so soon," Lou stated, worry etched across her brow. "Is she ready to be at home?"

"Probably not but she got really upset this morning and said she had to come home today. She wouldn't calm down unless I agreed."

"That's strange. Any idea what upset her?" Lou's eyebrows drew together.

"I'm not sure, but it had something to do with you…"

Lou cut him off. "Oh my God! What time is it?" She glanced at her watch. "It's three o'clock! Sarah should have gotten off the bus five minutes ago." Lou shaded her eyes with her hand and looked down the long drive. He could almost see Sarah's long, dark hair and pink dress in the distance where she was standing beside a parked car at the end of the drive.

"Who is she talking to?" Brody asked but Lou was already gone. The water bottle that had been clutched in her hand rolled across the porch.

Lou ran down the drive and Brody took off only seconds behind her. They tore down the long winding driveway, dirt flying from beneath their feet in their haste. They reached Sarah at almost the same time, just as the dark sedan pulled away. Dust flew behind the vehicle, making it impossible to get a license plate number.

Lou spun Sarah around, gripping her upper arms tightly.

"Who was that man?" she asked between broken breaths, choked by exertion.

Sarah shrugged her shoulders and looked toward the retreating car. "I don't know, Mommy. He said he was moving to a house near here and wanted to know if I live at this house. Did I do something wrong?"

"Yes! You did something wrong! You are never, never, never, ever supposed to talk to strangers!"

Brody was much more composed than Lou. He bent down beside Sarah. "Can you tell us what he looked like? Did he say anything else to you?"

"He had on a baseball cap and he smelled like cherry smoke," Sarah replied after some deliberate thought, tapping her finger lightly on her temple.

"Cherry smoke?"

"Yeah. Like that man who smoked the cigar when he came to see Mr. Jeb."

"But it wasn't the same man?" Sarah shook her head. Lou sighed and looked at Brody. "That's probably all she noticed."

Sarah looked toward the house and commented, "Why is an ambulance here? Is someone sick?"

Lou patted her gently on the shoulder. "The ambulance just brought Mrs. Wester home from the hospital."

"But I have not finished my card yet!"

"You'll have plenty of time to finish after you do your homework. She's going to take a nap now and you can see her later if Dr. Wester says it's okay."

Sarah looked skeptically toward Brody. "Do you mean him?" She squinted one eye at him, as though appraising his appearance. "He's a doctor?"

"He's a doctor." Lou grinned slightly, her eyes smiling as they met Brody's.

"Cool," Sarah stated plainly. "Can I go ahead and get my snack?"

"Yeah. Run along."

As Sarah ran quickly down the drive, Brody looked at Lou, who looked everywhere but at him. "Now why don't you tell me what the hell is going on?"

Chapter Seven

Lou turned to walk toward the house, throwing over her shoulder, "I don't know what you're talking about."

Brody rushed forward and grabbed her by the upper arm, stopping her mad march toward the house. "You damn sure do know what I'm talking about, and you are going to tell me what all this is about. There's something going on here, and I want to know what it is."

Lou jerked her arm free of his grasp. "Don't ever grab me again," Lou said calmly as she turned toward the house. Her pace quickened as she walked up the drive, Brody right behind her. She stomped up the steps and slammed through the back screen door.

Brody stopped long enough to run a hand through his hair in frustration. As he reached to open the screen door, he was stopped by Jeb's voice. "Whatcha in such a hurry for, boy?" Jeb sat in a rocker on the porch whittling with his knife on a piece of wood.

"Nothing, Jeb. I just need to talk to Lou."

"That why she's looking like a scared rabbit and you're looking like the hungry wolf that wants to eat her?" Jeb asked with a short snicker.

"That's no scared rabbit, Jeb."

"That's where you're wrong, boy. She's scared of her own shadow, most days." Jeb nodded his head slightly, indicating that Brody should take a seat. "She hides it well and you just don't know her well enough to realize it."

Brody sat down in the rocker, his elbows on his knees. "There's something going on here, Jeb. First, she has nightmares that are so loud they could shake the rafters on the roof. Then someone who thought they knew her stopped her at the hospital but she denied ever having met her. Then Mom insists on coming home from the hospital because someone was asking about Lou. Now, there's a strange man stopping to ask Sarah questions at the end of the drive, but he didn't hang around when he saw me and Lou coming. That seems a little strange to me, and I'd like to get some answers about it."

Jeb opened his mouth to respond but was cut off by Lou, who was standing inside the doorway behind the screen. She opened the door. "I'll explain it to him, Jeb."

She walked across the porch and scuffed her boot across the boards, her hands in the pockets of her jeans, her eyes focused on the floor. Her gaze rose and met his, a challenge in her eyes. "Care to take a ride with me, Brody? I want to go and check on the mare."

"Are you going to give me some answers?"

"Why don't you just come with me and we'll talk?"

Brody looked toward Jeb who nodded his head slightly, indicating he should go.

Brody rose from the chair and walked side by side to the barn with Lou. They saddled two horses and Lou grabbed two bottles of water from the barn fridge to put in a saddlebag. Then she took two carrots and placed them in her back pocket.

They rode in silence for a few minutes and then Lou asked, "You doing okay over there? I worry a little about your riding skills, with you being such a greenhorn and all."

Brody scoffed, "Greenhorn, my foot. I have been riding horses since before I could walk."

"But last time you said you were afraid to ride alone."
"Oh, I just wanted to rattle your cage and see if you would let me ride behind you," Brody replied absently.

"You did not…" Lou tried to look offended.

"Don't worry. I got the worse end of that deal. Trust me."

"Serves you right," Lou mumbled.

"What did you say?"

"Nothing." She smiled at him.

They loped along in silence until they saw the rock where they had eaten lunch on their previous ride. Lou dismounted, wrapped her reins around the saddle horn, and let the horse graze. Brody did the same. Lou looked toward the mountains and crossed her arms over her chest. "This is one of my favorite places," she stated.

"Does it remind you of where you grew up?"

"God, no. Not at all." She snorted indelicately. "I grew up in the city. We lived in trailer parks where there were dirty children, cockroaches, and traffic. I guess that's why I like it here so much, because it's so different from where I came from. We had just moved into a different trailer in the middle of nowhere the night Jeb and John found me."

"Found you?"

She took a deep breath. "Yeah. We were watching TV one night when someone knocked at the door. My mother started going crazy about it and threw Sarah into a bag and put it over my shoulder. Sarah was just a couple of weeks old at the time. Then, my mother told me to go out the back window and run like hell, so that's what I did. I heard her scream as I ran through the woods. I stopped for a second and that's when a bullet hit me."

"Bullet? Where?"

Lou lifted her bangs and showed Brody the shallow trench on her temple. He touched it lightly with his fingers, which were gentle, but firm.

Lou began to pace in front of him. "I ran through the woods and came out on a street. That's when I fell down and passed out. Jeb and John just happened to be driving by. They stopped and picked me up, the bag with Sarah in it still hanging over my shoulder. I think they were a little surprised to find a baby. Not to mention me. They brought me and Sarah here for Sadie to take care of us."

"She always did take care of all the wounded birds and children at Western Skies. She's fixed up more than one scrape that I had."

"They're the best thing that ever happened to me."

"What happened to your mother?" His eyes searched hers.

"She died." Lou heaved a sigh. "After I had been here for about a year, I stopped being afraid someone was looking for us. I just started living my life and raising my daughter. I had almost begun to believe the past was just a dream when, the other night at the hospital, we ran into Mrs. Downy. She was our neighbor when I was younger. And I did know her but I didn't want to admit it. Then that man stopped Sarah at the end of the drive."

"A stranger asked about you at the hospital, too. That's why Mom wanted to come home so quickly. She wants to be sure you're safe."

Lou's eyes met his "I had no idea. If I ever thought your family would be in danger, I would take Sarah and leave. I promise. And if it ever comes to that, I will. I love them like they're my own. I just wanted to bring you out here to explain it to you. I didn't want you to think there is some big conspiracy to keep you out of the loop."

Wringing her hands, Lou paced over to stand near the big rock and stopped. Then he heard it, the rattling sound that could only come from one source. Lou looked down at her boots and saw a rattle snake, coiled and ready to strike, about two inches from the toe of her boot. Brody saw it at the same time.

Brody bent to retrieve a large rock. "Be very still. Don't move an inch."

"Don't worry," she breathed out slowly.

From behind the rock, Lou felt a snort against the back of her neck. Then the strong body of the pregnant mare pushed her to the side and out of the way. Lou landed on her backside in the dirt as the mare startled. She stomped, hooves flailing wildly as she reared. On the second strike, her hoof severed the snake's head from its body. Its length continued to slither on the ground for a moment as the horse stilled. Brody quickly moved over to Lou and extended a hand. She grabbed it and scuttled away from the heaving mare. The horse approached Lou slowly, and Brody moved to shoo her away.

"Don't," she said quickly as she reached into her back pocket and pulled out the two carrots. She held them out to the mare. "She certainly earned these, didn't she?" Lou laughed lightly as she touched the side of the mare's face. The mare snorted and moved away from her, not ready to accept human contact, before marching off into the distance, still chewing on the carrots.

"I can't believe she did that. I think she was just coming over to get a carrot and got caught in the wrong place," Lou stated quietly. "I could have been killed." She reached out and touched Brody's forearms, her hands shaking as she did so. "Oh, God, I could have been killed." Lou's voice caught as she looked at the snake.

Brody said quietly, "You did just great. You're fine now." He gently brushed the hair away from her face and wiped a smudge of dirt from her cheek.

Lou's entire body began to shake. Her knees gave way under her and she nearly fell to the ground. She collapsed against Brody. He caught her before she hit the ground with a hand beneath her knees and one under her shoulders.

"You're going to faint on me again, aren't you?" he asked quietly as he lowered her to sit on a nearby boulder. He stood in front of her and held on to her shoulders. He placed a hand beneath her chin and forced her to make eye contact.

"I don't faint," she stated.

"Oh, yeah? Prove it."

"I don't know why I'm shaking so badly." She wringed her hands together.

"It's from the adrenaline. The body is flooded by it when there's a traumatic situation. Then it takes a moment for your body to catch up and realize the danger has passed."

"Really?"

" I'm a doctor, remember?"

"I remember. Do you hold all your patients and rub their hair when they are shaking?"

He chuckled softly. " I'm just making an exception with you."

"Thanks."

"You're welcome." He continued to rub her hair as the shaking eased, her face pressed against his chest and her eyes closed.

"You're getting way too comfortable here," he stated quietly.

She smiled against his chest. "Maybe."

She leaned back, and her eyes met his. "We had better get back."

He grabbed her hands and pulled her to her feet, yet his fingers stayed laced with hers.

"Sure you're ready?"

"Yep." She gave an exaggerated nod and lifted on tiptoe to place a kiss on his cheek. He turned his head at the last moment and her lips met his. She stilled and started to retreat, but his hand caught the back of her neck, gently holding her head still. His lips applied pressure against hers.

Brody smiled against her lips as he whispered, "I just thought I might try to scare you out of that adrenaline rush. Is it working?"

"Yep."

"Want me to stop?" Brody asked. She hesitated briefly. "Guess not. Lou, you took too long with that answer." He turned his head slightly to deepen the kiss. His lips pressed gently against hers, forcing them to open.

Her lips parted and his tongue slipped inside, tangling with hers in the most delectable way. Her breath caught in her throat. Brody lifted Lou's hands onto his shoulders, where they curled around his neck of their own accord. His larger hands moved to her waist, then dipped into the back pockets of her jeans, pulling her closer to him. He was rock hard against her belly. She pulled back.

"Sorry about that. Didn't mean to scare you that much," he breathed against her mouth. She lowered her head and pressed her forehead against his chest, her breath coming in gasps.

"Your plan worked. I'm not shaking from fear anymore." An unsteady hand patted his chest.

"Now, you're shaking from something else?"

"Sure looks like it."

"Can I help?"

"I think you already did."

He rested his chin atop her head. "Glad to hear it. Just one more," he tilted her chin up one more time. His lips touched hers gently and her hands rose to his shoulders again, one hand playing in the curls at the nape of his neck. Lou moaned softly as he deepened the kiss. His hands came out of her back pockets and encircled her narrow waist. His fingers slipped below the back waistband of her jeans. He tugged gently at her T-shirt, pulling it free from her pants where it was tucked so neatly. His hands touched the skin of her waist and she moaned. Her skin was slickened with sweat yet his warm, strong hands glided over her skin leisurely. His fingers slid around and touched the sides of her waist and then tickled her belly. Brody groaned out loud as he hands moved across her soft skin. He continued his assault on her mouth as his hands crept up her sides, sending electrical currents running through her. Her nipples tightened against the soft cotton of her bra in response.

She gasped as he cupped her full right breast and ran a thumb across her erect nipple. Her knees buckled. She leaned back against his arm, which was all that stood between her and hitting the dirt. He took advantage of her position and lifted her shirt. He kissed her stomach and traced a slow pattern with his tongue up to her breasts. He placed his lips against the thin cotton and traced a warm circle through the fabric with his tongue. Her nipple tightened even more and her hands moved to his hair. She moaned loudly.

"Oh, my God," she breathed.

His eyes met hers. "That feels good?" he asked teasingly.

"Oh, yeah," she responded quickly.

He moved and repeated his assault on her other breast, never trying to remove the lacy bra that covered her but coaxing her nipple to stand beneath the fabric. A shiver crawled up her spine.

Brody heard what he thought was his heart pounding in his ears. Then he realized the sound was getting closer. He glanced over his shoulder and saw John riding up quickly. He straightened, coughed gently, and said, "We have company."

"What?"

"John's coming."

John yelled from a distance, "Lou!"

She cried out weakly, "Yeah?"

"Hey! Did you forget that today is Girl Scout day? You have twelve little girls at the house waiting for you, all dressed in Girl Scout uniforms."

As he came closer, Brody stepped between Lou and John, blocking John's view. He whispered to her, "Better tuck your shirt in."

"Oh, God." She frantically started pushing her shirt into her pants. Brody smirked as he watched.

John pulled up closer on his horse and noticed her red face and agitation. "Are you okay, Lou?"

"Yeah. I'm fine. I just got the crap scared out of me by a big old rattler."

"No way! Where is it?"

"Over by the rock."

John dismounted and went to look at the snake. "You think the Girl Scouts might like to see this?" he asked with a mischievous glint in his eyes.

"You're not actually thinking about taking that home with you, are you?"

"Yeah! Of course I am. I can just see them now. All of them running…screaming." He guffawed at the thought of it.

"Don't even think about it."

"Oh, I won't scare them with it but I'm sure going to take it home with me." He mounted and turned his horse toward home. "You coming?"

"Yeah. We're right behind you."

"Hurry up. Sadie is feeding them cookies."

"Fantastic. Twelve little girls, all with a sugar rush."

Brody held Lou's horse as she mounted. She stopped briefly, a shy smile in the eyes that met his. He kissed her on the knee and patted her calf gently before mounting his own horse. Then the three of them headed for home.

Chapter Eight

Wesley's pocket rang and he retrieved his cell phone. He flipped it open and groaned inwardly when he saw the number displayed on the caller ID. "Hey, Boss."

"Tell me what you know," was barked in his ear.

"Boss, it's barely been twenty-four hours."

"You need longer than that? What the hell have you been doing? Sitting on your thumbs?" The tone wasn't jovial.

"No. I've been researching the problem." He almost stuttered.

"Got anything at all for me? Or do I need to get someone to come and replace you?"

"No boss. I know she's working at a place called Western Skies. It's a horse-breeding farm. Tons of old money. The old lady who owns the place is sick, just got out of the hospital. There's an old couple who takes care of the place and a couple of men who are family who live there, but that's all I know so far. It's not easy to get close to the place. They have farm hands all over. I've got some leads I'm working on, though."

"Stay on it. I want a full report within the week." He mumbled under his breath. "I want what's mine." The call disconnected.

Chapter Nine

Lou avoided Brody for days. She stayed as far from him as she could and was obviously surprised when he showed up to jog with her every morning. She made a cursory attempt at small talk but he knew it was only as a courtesy. Her tone was pleasant but she avoided meeting his eyes. After the first day, Brody thought that it might be a good thing. Maybe he could get her out of his system. But when he went to bed at night, she was all he could think about.

She continued to have nightmares, although they were not as loud as the one that occurred the first night, and they lessened in intensity as each day passed. They were quiet enough to wake no one but him, he didn't run to her room to help now that he knew what was going on. Catching her bathed in sweat, wearing skimpy nightclothes would not be a good idea at this point.

How Sarah slept through them all, he would never know. She must be a deep sleeper, or maybe it was because she played hard during the day. She barely ever sat still, unless she was minding her manners at the table or visiting with his mother. She visited once a day with a card or homemade gift that his mother always seemed to adore. She posted every last one on her vanity mirror so she could enjoy them all day.

His mother sat up a few times a day now but she rarely ever felt well enough to get out of bed. He watched the life draining right out of her eyes as she became weaker and weaker. Her breathing was much shallower and her periods of alertness were fewer and farther between.

It was just a matter of time.

****

Lou was disturbed by Brody's mere presence. She was bound and determined not to get any closer to him than she already had. She caught herself at the most inappropriate times looking for him, wondering where he was in the big old house. Then he would appear right behind her, as though he had been conjured for her discomfort.

She had given him the wrong impression. She wasn't like her mother and she never would be. She would never allow a man to use her for sex and then discard her like a piece of trash. She didn't know why every time she got close to Brody, she behaved like a harlot. She let him take liberties she normally didn't allow anyone else to take. It all felt so natural, like he'd been there forever. But he wasn't. And he wouldn't be.

To avoid the pitfalls that must come with lust, Lou drowned herself in work and her daughter. She found paperwork to do and Girl Scout schedules to adjust. She helped with homework and fought about ponytails and pigtails.

The nightmares had started to subside, although they were still troublesome. After waking in a pool of sweat, Brody's bedroom door squeaked open. She would try not to move, hoping she hadn't disturbed him. He would wait for a moment or two and then she would hear his bedroom door close again. Sometimes, she imagined she heard him blow in frustration.

She regretted disturbing him at all, but it seemed to be unavoidable. Her waking moments were filled with his presence. Was it so bad his sleep was filled with hers?

****

Brody woke on Sunday morning around nine, much later than normal. Lou's clock usually woke him as it blared music from a popular rock station. It always screamed well before dawn.

His eyes opened slowly as he glanced around and noticed that daylight had flooded the room. He squinted and rubbed his eyes, slightly disoriented. He glanced at the clock and remembered it was Sunday. He donned some lounge pants and a printed T-shirt. He then slipped his bare feet into slippers and ran a hand through his curly blond hair, all of which was standing on end.

He padded softly down the stairs and entered the kitchen. The smell of coffee met his nose. He blindly poured a cup and turned around. There sat Lou, sitting casually at the kitchen table with the newspaper, one leg dangling on the floor and the other knee up by her nose with her arm wrapped around it. She looked just as tousled as he did in a robe and fuzzy bedroom slippers with Pooh Bear faces at the toes. She looked like she had just risen from bed, too, with hair that was askew and lines pressed across her face from her pillow.

"Where is everyone?" Brody mumbled.

"Church," she replied, without looking up.

"Everybody?"

"Yep," she continued to read her paper and eat her Lucky Charms from a bowl in front of her.

"Is that marshmallow cereal you have there?" he asked, appraising the contents of her bowl.

She slurped her milk loudly. "Yep," she replied.

"Got any more?" he asked quietly.

"Maybe," was her response.

"What would I have to do to get some?"

She held out a coffee cup in response. "Get me some coffee when you go and get a bowl."

"That I can do," he said casually, as he walked to the coffeepot. "Where's the cereal?"

"Uh uh...coffee first," she sang.

"You drive a hard bargain," he grunted.

"Don't ever forget it," she mumbled.

Brody poured her coffee and held it out to her.

"Cream and sugar?" She raised an eyebrow.

"Damn, you're tough on me." He added both and held the cup out to her.

"Cereal is in the pantry, in the corner behind the mashed potatoes." She pointed her finger at him. "And don't tell anyone about my secret stash. I save it for Sundays when I'm usually alone." Her tone let him know she did not like the interruption.

"Where's Sarah?"

"Church," she said around a mouth full of Lucky Charms.

"She goes and you don't?"

"She's been going since she could walk and talk. Jeb and Sadie love it."

"I bet they do. They used to take me, too. Some of my fondest memories of them. We would all go out to eat pancakes before church." He smiled at the memory.

"They still do. John goes because no one will cook for him here and he's always hoping to pick up a girl."

Brody choked on his cereal. "At church?"

"Yep." She continued to read her paper.

"Why don't you go? Not a God-fearing Christian?"

"My mother always said that standing in church and stating you're a Christian is about like standing in a bank and claiming you're rich. It's just not the way it works. Besides, this is the one day a week I get to be all alone. Usually," she said caustically.

"Sorry I'm invading your space," he muttered, as he poured another bowl of cereal.

"Hey! Go easy on my Lucky Charms, will you?" she scolded.

"I'll buy you some more. Good grief. Can I have the sports section?" he asked quietly.

"You can have it when I'm done with it."

"Oh, come on. You're not even reading the sports section."

She growled beneath her breath. "Will you be quiet if I give it to you?"

"Try me and see."

She begrudgingly handed over the sports section, and then raised the paper to block her view of him.

They ate quietly for a few minutes and finished their coffee, newspapers and cereal. Lou folded the newspaper back up and laid it on the table in front of her.

She filled her coffee cup back up and sat down.

"Have you been avoiding me?" Brody asked quietly.

"I don't know what you're talking about," Lou responded nervously as she rose to put her bowl in the sink.

She walked by him, heading for the stairs. He gently grabbed her hand as she walked by. "I won't try to scare you into kissing me today. Promise."

She tried to pull her hand from his grasp but he held on tightly. "Thank God," she said sarcastically. "I have kissed you more in the past week than I have kissed anyone in years." She pulled again. "Will you let me go?"

"You don't have to avoid me. I promise I'll try to keep my hands to myself."

"You're doing a great job of it right now," she groaned, finally freeing her hand. "I haven't been avoiding…"

"Yes, you have. Every time I walk in a room, you leave it."

"That's just a coincidence."

"No, it's not. I think you're scared of me."

"I'm not scared of anything," she said flippantly as she turned and went upstairs.

"Tell that to those nightmares you've been having," he said loudly to her retreating back. His last view of her was her curvy bottom going up the stairs. How in the world could a woman look so sexy in Pooh Bear bedroom slippers?

****

Lou held her breath as she marched up the stairs. She flopped on the bed gracelessly and squeezed her eyes shut.

That man could be insufferable. He looked so sweet, so innocent, and so inherently male. He had enough confidence for ten men. He made her shake with anger, quake with fear and shiver with anticipation, yet she had been stupid enough to go downstairs in Pooh slippers and her hair all mussed. A sex-kitten, she was not.

Lou gave up the pretense of going back to sleep and decided to shower, dress and curl up with a romance novel on the porch for a few hours.

She put on shorts and a lightweight tank top. She left her feet bare and her hair hanging loose, and went out to porch. She sat down in the creaky rocker and pulled her knees up to her chest. She turned sideways so her feet dangled over the arm of the chair. Cradling her book in her lap, she began to read. She was quickly taken in by the romance and lost track of time.

Brody coughed gently and caused her to jump out of her skin. "What are you doing, Lou?" he asked as he sat down beside her in the other rocker.

"What's it look like?" she responded absently. She tugged at the length of her shorts, afraid she was showing too much leg.

"Looks like you are comfy with a book," Brody stated. "What's the name of it?"

"Does it matter?"

"Only if you are reading a steamy novel and don't want me to know about it," he chided.

Heat crept up her cheeks.

"I knew it!" he exploded. "You're reading a trashy novel!" He laughed uproariously.

"Oh, good grief," she blew. "It's not trash. It's romance." She arched a brow at him. "You only read the greats?"

"Tolstoy, Shakespeare…" he claimed.

" Playboy?" she goaded.

"Playboy is not trash. It's literature." He grinned slowly. "Let me see what you have." He held out his hand.

"Never," she swore vehemently.

"We'll see about that, won't we?" he said as he grabbed her foot which was still hanging over the arm of the chair. He held it firmly with his two hands and started to tickle the bottom of her foot.

She squirmed in her chair and slapped against his hands with her own. "That doesn't even tickle," she promised as she stilled, hoping to fake him out. She held her breath.

"Then how about this?" he asked as he grabbed her big toe and pulled it. She heard it pop.

"Oh, God! Will you stop?" she screamed. She dropped the book to grab his hands. When she did, he released her foot and bent to pick up the book.

"I thought that would get you," he goaded her as he opened her book.

He began to read aloud, "Chase brushed his hand against the side of her breast, making her quiver with excitement."

"Would you stop!" she screamed and covered her ears.

"It was enjoyable to you a few minutes ago." He grinned and continued. "Her breath stilled as she saw his gaze travel from her mouth to her breast."

"Enough!" She got up and opened the door to her room.

He stopped her. "Hey! Do you care if I keep this? This isn't half bad." He feigned genuine interest as he read more.

She turned toward her bedroom. "Do whatever you want," she grumbled.

"Hey, I was just kidding. Here! You can have it back." He closed the book and laid it on her chair. She bent to pick it up.

"Oh, sit down, will you?" he pouted.

"Why should I?"

"Because I don't have anyone else to talk to. Mom's asleep and Lola's watching her."

"So, I'm just here for your entertainment?" she asked.

He appraised her from head-to-toe. "Yeah." He grinned and cocked his head sideways.

She shook her head in consternation as she flopped ungracefully in the chair. She pulled her knees up to her chest and watched him out of the corner of her eye.

"Do you read a lot?" he asked calmly.

"Just on Sundays. I usually don't have time the rest of the week." she stated.

"Always read romance?" he asked pleasantly.

"No! Not always! Just sometimes." She grinned mischievously at him. "You know what they say. People who don't get to have sex can at least read about it."

After he picked his chin up off the floor, he grinned. "Point taken."

"I'll read just about anything. Where I grew up, we didn't have a lot of access to libraries. So I never learned to enjoy it. After moving in here, your mom gave me some of her books to read." She motioned with the one in her hand. "Not like this one, of course." She smiled again.

"My mom always did love to read. She would sneak flashlights to me so I could read under the covers after my dad went to sleep." He smiled fondly at the memory.

Lou heard the commotion of a car crunching down the gravel drive. Brody rose from the chair and leaned over the rail to check out the noise. "Looks like they're back from church already," he said, when Jeb's truck stopped at the back door.

They leaned over the rail together and saw Sadie turn to help John out of the car, placing crutches in his hands. Lou gasped and covered her mouth. "What happened?" she yelled down.

Jeb looked up at them and grinned. "Damn fool was watching a woman walk by and tripped over a bush beside the sidewalk. Tumbled headfirst into the bush and broke his ankle!"

"I'll be right down," Lou cried, as she turned to go in the house. Brody followed her and they met the others in the kitchen.

"You should have called me! I would have come and gotten Sarah so she wouldn't be trouble," Lou cried when she saw them all. Sarah ran upstairs to change out of her Sunday clothes.

Sadie smiled. "She was no trouble at all. She and I went to church while Jeb took John to the hospital."

Jeb shook his head. "Doctor says six weeks with no activity."

"What are we going to do about getting up the hay?" John groaned. The hay season was just about to begin. This was the time of year they cut the hay in the fields, baled and stored it for the winter. John was an instrumental part of the operation, and his shoes would be tough to fill.

"We'll just have to hire someone to replace you," Lou replied.

"It will take four men to do the work of this one," Jeb countered.

"Then we'll just have to hire four," Lou replied.

"Just hire three," Brody broke in. "I'm here. I can help."

"Mighty nice of you, boy. Been a long time since you put up hay."

"I can still do it, though."

Lou agreed. "I'll call tomorrow and get three temp helpers."

"So, what did she look like?" Brody surprised everyone by asking John. Was it worth it?"

"Seemed like it at the time. Would have been fine if that damn bush hadn't jumped out in front of me," John groaned as he raised his leg onto the pillow Sadie placed in a chair opposite him.

The room shook with laughter.

Chapter Ten

Brody wasn't surprised at all when Jeb prayed for clear skies at the morning meal. It was a family ritual, one he had been involved in for many years before he left home. Putting up hay was a tough job, with hundreds of acres to cut. But he wasn't afraid of hard work and actually looked forward to contributing.

Jeb was the only one allowed to rake the hay into windrows after Brody's first attempts to drive the delivery rake. He took a good amount of ribbing for his amateurish efforts at forking the hay into clean rows. His rows turned into zigzags, which made it harder on the person driving the baler. "Yeah, yeah, yeah... Pick on the new guy."

Brody gave up on the rake and, from that time forward, Jeb raked the hay into rows and Brody cut more pasture. As Brody finished cutting, Jeb would turn the hay and put it in neat windrows. The hay would then be left in the fields to dry and cure.

When Jeb thought the hay was dry, he would walk out the pastures and place a few stalks of hay into a small box. He added two to three tablespoons of salt and shook it wildly. If the salt stayed dry, the hay was ready to bale. John had tried to teach him new ways to test the age of the hay but Jeb's only response to it was, "Why change what works? You young'uns and your newfangled ideas."

Since they could only get two temps to help with the harvest, Lou was drafted to drive the baler. She drove down the neat and tidy rows of hay and the baler performed the task of firmly wrapping the hay and dropping it in square bundles on the ground. Each solid block of hay weighed about seventy-five pounds.

The crew then used flatbed trucks to move the hay from the fields to the hay barns. Lou and two hands could reasonably move five hundred bales of hay per day if they worked from dawn until dusk. Once one pasture was complete, they moved on to another.

The two temp laborers, Wes and Darrel, seemed to know very little about hay but they were eager to work. They showed up bright and early every morning, ready to get busy. Darrel was no more than thirty and had a pleasant smile and a good attitude. Wes was a little more subdued, wore a baseball cap and had a dark beard.

They showed up in time for breakfast each day and went straight to work. They doffed their hats, said amen to the prayers at mealtime and fit right in. They worked tirelessly alongside Lou, Brody, and Jeb. Everyone worked from sunup to sundown.

The days flew by and the weather stayed clear, right up until the last day. Jeb started out the day by saying, "Looks like we'll get some rain today."

Brody shook his head. "Not even a cloud in the sky, Jeb."

"We'll just see about that, won't we?"

Brody nodded absently.

About five o'clock, the sky began to darken and thunder rolled across the horizon. Brody parked the tractor and ran out to the flatbed Lou had parked in the pasture. He carried three huge tarps with ropes attached in his hands. He saw Darrel throw the last of the hay onto the bed. Wes was nowhere to be found.

Brody screamed at Darrel on top of the wind, "Go to the house! I got this!" Lightning struck two hundred yards from them and almost immediately the thunder burst. Darrel took off across the pasture as Brody climbed on top of the flatbed and began to cover the hay with the tarps. It would keep the hay dry long enough to get the flatbed to the barn. Lou met him on the opposite side and held out her hands, motioning for him to throw one side over to her.

"Get back in the truck" he shouted.

"Just give me one side and some rope, Brody!" she shouted back.

Realizing that arguing was futile, he tossed her one side of the tarp. She pulled it tight and attached the ropes to the trailer, hoping to keep the wind from blowing the tarp away. She continued tying rope down the length of the blue plastic until the whole trailer was covered. Just as she was about to climb down, she looked over and noticed Brody frantically trying to untie a knot in the rope on his side of the trailer. This one knot prevented the tarp from adequately covering the entire rear section of hay. Lou climbed over the trailer to his side. She took the rope from his frantic hands, put it in her teeth, and pulled the knot loose. "How did you do that?" he bellowed.

She yelled back with a grin, "You try having a daughter who can't untie shoes!"

Brody covered the remaining hay and tied the rope to hold the tarp in place. Just as he finished, the bottom dropped out of the sky.

Rain came down in a torrential downfall. They were immediately drenched and couldn't see two feet in front of them. Lightening burst over their heads and thunder clapped in appreciation. Brody jumped off the trailer and reached up for Lou. She dropped into his outstretched hands and he caught her by the waist. He swung her down and she hit the ground with a jolt. They ran for the passenger side of the truck cab and Lou slid in.

Brody followed right behind her and slammed the door. He took a deep breath.

Lou started the truck.

"What are you doing?" Brody asked.

"What's it look like?" Lou replied. "Those tarps are not going to keep it dry once the wind shifts. We need to get it to the hay barn or we're going to lose it. There's plenty of room in the south barn."

He scoffed. "Move over, then, and let me drive." He motioned for her to trade places.

Instead, she turned on the headlights and wipers and put the truck in gear.

"Good grief! Do you even know how to drive this thing?"

"Watch me," she whispered.

She expertly drove the truck through the pasture gate, driving slowly because vision was poor in the rain. She turned onto the gravel drive that led to the south barn and drove straight inside. It was a barn that was open on both ends this time of the year as they put up the hay.
Brody let out a sigh of relief. "Good job," he breathed.

"Thanks," she said sarcastically as she cut the engine and turned off the headlights. They were now in total darkness. His hand grabbed for hers. "You scared of the dark, cowboy?" she chided.

Lou opened the glove box and pulled out a flashlight. She flicked it on and shined it in his face. He blinked and held out a hand to fend off the glare. "You're just a laugh a minute, aren't you?" he taunted.

Lou turned, opened the door of the truck and slid out on the ground. Brody followed out his side. Lou walked the length of the trailer and shined her flashlight on it. "Looks like the ropes held," she said absently, as she walked toward the exit doors. "Those tarps would never have held, though, in this storm."

"I thought it might pass quickly," Brody said.

"You should listen to Jeb. He's never wrong about the weather," she flung back.

"Thanks for reminding me," he grumbled back at her.

Rain fell from the sky in sheets. Lou looked toward the house and saw that the lights were off. "Power must be out."

"Will Sarah be okay with no power in the middle of a storm?"

Lou shrugged. "She's with Sadie. There's no safer place to be."

"I remember," he smiled at her.

"They are probably roasting marshmallows in a candle flame, by now."

"She still does that? She used to do that with me. It was one of my favorite things. And Jeb would make shadow puppets in the glow from a candle flame."

"And now John tells scary stories." Lou's eyes met his and she sighed. "You feel like streaking to the house in this mess?"

He emphatically said, "Hell, no. Have you lost your mind? I'm staying right here." He sat down on a bale of hay that was already stacked yet was low to the ground. Lou climbed one level above him and sat down as well.

Brody leaned back against her bale and grunted.

"Something wrong?" she asked.

"To be honest, I'm tired as hell and more sore than I have ever been in my life." He flexed his neck muscles, trying to stretch.

"I would offer you a massage but you might take it the wrong way," she said.

His eyes met hers in the darkness. "And just what way do you think I might take it?""

"Never mind," she bit out.

"Lou, if I promise to behave, can you rub my shoulders?" He formed a temple with his hands.

"Lean back." She patted her knees and Brody scooted back on the hay bale until his back touched her shins. Unexpectedly, he pulled his shirt over his head. "What? It was soaked."

Lou looked down at his strong shoulders, shadowed in the moonlight. His neck and shoulders were tight and strong, just like the rest of him. She took a deep breath before her fingers lightly touched his shoulders and gently began to knead his sore muscles. He groaned low in his throat at her efforts.

"That feel good?" she asked, deepening the pressure.

"Oh, yeah," he hissed. Her movements became stronger and faster as she worked the muscles in his neck and shoulders. He groaned and moaned for a full ten minutes, his head finally falling over in a relaxed pose. She shook out her hands and wrung them lightly together.

"Thank you," he said as he took her hand in his. "Now your hands are sore." He lightly brushed her leg as he reached for her hand. "And cold! Good grief! You're freezing." He ran his hand up her arms, feeling the goose bumps on her skin.

Brody stepped to the truck and pulled out another tarp. Motioning for her to move, he covered the area where she had been sitting. He lay down along the length of two bales. He patted the area in front of him, holding his arms open wide. "Come on. Let's share some body heat." *I have enough to share.*

"I don't think that's a good idea, Brody." Nerves shook in her voice.

"Oh, get over it, Lou. I'm too damn tired to put the moves on you. Come on." He patted the hay again.

Lou reluctantly let Brody pull her down onto the hay. He could probably feel her hesitation as she lay down stiffly beside him. He groaned as he tucked one hand around her waist and flipped her on her side. Her bottom was tucked into his lap like two spoons fit together in a drawer. He supported the weight of her head as his arm slipped under her head.

The long work day soon took its toll and, no matter how much she wanted to fight it. She relaxed and curled into him.
Four hours later, Brody woke to total darkness. He shifted slowly, unsure of where he was. He felt a round bottom pressed against his groin and long, dark hair tickled his nose. He shook Lou gently. "Lou?"

She came instantly awake and sat up. "What's wrong?" she asked groggily.

"Nothing. I think it's stopped raining." He sat up as well and stretched. "We should probably get back to the house."

She yawned and nodded. "I'm ready when you are."

They walked side by side out of the barn. Lou stopped and sniffed the air. "Do you smell that?"

"What? The hay?" Brody could smell the clean scent of damp earth after a heavy rain. He watched her sniff for another scent she couldn't recognize.

"No. It's something else." She sniffed again. "It's probably nothing." She shook her head to clear it as they walked to the house.

Neither of them recognized the smell of cherry cigar that was carried off by the breeze.

Chapter Eleven

Brody and Lou walked through the backdoor into a dark house. The power was still off. Jeb, Sadie, and John all sat around the kitchen table playing cards by candlelight. John had one leg resting on a pillow in a chair across from him. They all looked up as the door opened.

"Well, look who found their way home!" Sadie exclaimed.

Lou asked, "Is everything okay? Where's Sarah?"

"Soon as the thunder stopped, she crawled on our bed and fell asleep," Sadie replied. "Poor thing was tuckered out."

John looked up and grinned. "What happened to y'all?"

"We got caught out in the rain getting in the last bed of hay. It was raining too hard to run back to the house, so we stayed put. We put the tarps over it just before the bottom dropped out of the sky, and then drove the truck into the south barn to keep it dry."

Lou coughed loudly. "We drove the truck into the barn?" She smiled broadly.

Brody pretended to mumble, his head hung low in false dejection. "Ok, Lou drove the truck into the barn..." He patted her on the shoulder. "And did a good job with it, too," he added for good measure.

Brody went to the pantry and took out a loaf of bread, mustard, and a jar of pickles. Then he went to the fridge and grabbed ham and cheese. Lou's stomach growled as she realized they had missed dinner. Brody heard it and laughed.

"Don't worry. I'll make one for you, too," he chided.

Jeb rubbed his eyes. "I sure am glad we got all that hay up before the rain."

"You told me this morning it would rain today and I didn't believe you," Brody replied, shaking his head.

"When you get to be as old as me, boy, you'll be able to predict the rain, too," was his only response.

"I don't think I've worked that hard in years, Jeb." Brody sighed as he pulled two of Sadie's prized dill pickles out of a jar and placed them on the plates beside the sandwiches.

"Speaking of working hard, those two fellas that helped with the hay did a real good job. We had two stable hands out with the flu so I asked them to stay on for another week. They will both be back on Monday and'll work 'til Friday," Jeb said.

"Just so you know, the next time I see John turn around to look at a pretty lady, I'm going to deck him. So, you guys be forewarned," Brody said with a venomous look in John's direction.

"Brody, if you had seen her..." John began.

"Save it, John," Brody chuckled. Then he asked, "Sadie, is Mom okay with the power out?"

"I just checked on her. Lola is sleeping in there tonight and all her machines are on battery power. She should be just fine. You could go and see her, but she would just sleep right through it."

"I won't bother her, then."

"Guys, I hate to do it, but I think I'm going to get Sarah to bed and eat my sandwich upstairs. I'm tired," Lou said as she stretched slowly. "I'll carry her up and then I'll come back for it."

Brody asked, "You said she's a deep sleeper. Will she stay asleep if I go and pick her up? If so, I'll carry her while you carry the food and a couple of flashlights."

Lou smiled her thanks and shrugged her aching shoulders. "If you don't mind, that would be great. She always feels heavier when she's asleep."

Lou followed Brody to Jeb and Sadie's room, guided by a flashlight, and pulled the covers back. Sarah stirred but didn't wake. Brody picked her up gently and held her against his chest. Her legs automatically wrapped around his waist as her arms encircled his neck. "She hangs on like a leech, huh?" he asked, slightly uncomfortable.

"If it's too much trouble, I'll carry her myself," Lou stated, her hands on her hips.

"Don't go getting your back up, Lou." He grunted as he shifted her. "I got her."

Lou brushed the dark hair from Sarah's eyes and Sarah snuggled deeper into Brody's chest. Brody followed Lou and the light back down the hallway. When they got to the kitchen, Lou grabbed two bottles of water, the two plates, and another flashlight.

"Night, guys," she called over her shoulder, as they started at the stairs.

"Night," three voices chimed back.

Lou followed Brody up the stairs, shining the flashlight in his path. "Don't drop my baby," she requested.

"If you'll keep that light on the stairs, I won't," he grunted.

Lou perfected her aim and Brody sighed his thanks.

She opened the door to her bedroom, laid the plates on her desk, and led him through the bathroom to the adjoining nursery. The room had been converted to a little girl's dream room when Sarah was four and was "too big for baby stuff." The room was now full of pink frills, princesses, and lace. It was beautiful even though it was shrouded in shadows. Ballet tutus had been sewn by Sadie and served as valances on the windows. A bookshelf donned one wall with its lower shelves full of books and the upper shelves filled with fragile trinkets Sarah loved.

Lou pulled back the covers and sheets and Brody gently laid Sarah down. She never moved but sighed loudly as he moved away. Lou pulled just the sheets up to her chin because it was a warm night and kissed her on the forehead. She placed an extra flashlight on the nightstand by the bed. She left it on just in case Sarah woke and was confused.

They walked back into Lou's room and Brody picked up his plate and bottle of water. Lou said, "Thanks for bringing her up. She's heavier than she looks."

"Tell me about it," Brody pretended to flex his back.

"You stop," Lou teased as she touched his arm.

Brody gestured to her plate that still lay on the desk. "Come out on the porch and eat with me?"

"Sure…why not?" She followed him through the door and onto the porch. They sat, side by side, in the rocking chairs. Lou dove into her sandwich with relish. Brody laughed at her antics and did the same.

"Where did you learn to be such a good mother?" he asked out of the blue, his mouth full of sandwich.

"I didn't know I was one," Lou replied, shrugging her shoulders. "I just do the best I can. It's hard for her, sometimes, not having a dad. But, most of the time, she has enough family to make up for it. I didn't know squat when she and I first came here. Sadie had to teach me a lot."

"You learned from the best, then."

"Absolutely."

They ate in silence for a few minutes.

"How long do you plan to stay, Brody? I mean...afterward."

"Not long. I have a life and work to get back to. I love it here and wish I could stay longer, but all I have ever wanted to be is a doctor. Back home, I get to be a doctor while I never could be one here."

"Why couldn't you be one here?"

"My dad wouldn't allow it. No son of his was going to waste his time doctoring when there was real work to be done. So, he took away my choice. He said I could either be his son or I could be a doctor. I couldn't let him take my choice away, so I let him take my family instead."

"Was it worth it?" she asked gently.

"I have always thought so but, being back here, I'm not so sure. I do know though that I still won't let anyone take my choices away from me."

"Having Sarah wasn't a choice I would have made for myself, either. Just so you know." She looked almost guilty as she said it. "Those first few days, I wasn't sure if I could make it. I was tired, irritable and overwhelmed. But it was all worth it. She's the best thing that ever happened to me. I'm glad that's one choice I didn't have.

It seemed like it was just thrust into my lap. Second best thing that ever happened to me was finding this family."

She munched on her pickle after the sandwich disappeared from her plate. She looked over at his plate. "You going to eat that pickle?"

"I was planning on it," he replied.

"Sure?" She ogled it some more.

"Oh, here! Good grief!" He passed it over. "Who could resist you with those sad, little puppy dog eyes?" He paused briefly. Then his tone changed. "You do have beautiful eyes, you know."

She stopped in mid-bite. "My eyes are ordinary. They're brown—plain, ol', ordinary brown. When I was young, I wanted blue eyes or glasses, anything that would make me stand out."

He appraised her from head to toe. "You stand out pretty well, already, Lou."

"Stop. I mean it. I'm ordinary."

He grabbed her chin lightly with his hand and tipped her face toward the moonlight. "In this light, they are the color of mahogany. That deep and dark wood has a ton of strength and can withstand almost anything you throw at it. That's what you remind me of."

Lou snorted. "My mother always said I had eyes the color of a beer bottle."

Brody laughed loudly. "A beer bottle? Boy, was she imaginative! That's about as flattering as comparing them to an A-1 Steak Sauce bottle, huh?" His look became more serious. "She wasn't thinking clearly. It is really what's behind the eyes that matter."

His steely gray eyes met hers. Lou looked away nervously. Brody lightened the mood by leaning back in his rocker and singing out the lyrics to Brown Eyed Girl.

Lou grinned wildly. "God, I love that song! I always thought it was written just for me."

He stopped singing momentarily. "Did a lot of laughing and running, skipping and jumping, huh? Or was it hearts a-thumping?" he joked.

"Laughing and running. I never did a lot of hearts a-thumping." *Not 'til recently*, she thought.

"I bet you danced to that song at every school dance," he teased.

"Nope. Never danced to it even once," she responded.

He got up from his chair and extended a hand to her. "We'll just have to change that, won't we?"

"Oh, no. Absolutely not!" She laughed nervously.

"Come on…I can tell you want to." He took her hand and gently pulled her from the chair. She rose cautiously and regarded him from beneath lowered lashes.

Brody started to sing quietly as he pulled her close to him. He held one hand in his and put the other on his shoulder. He pulled her close, but not close enough that their bodies touched. He swayed with her to the tune in his head.

Lou, slightly embarrassed, looked down at her feet. He touched her chin with one hand and brought her eyes back up to meet his. He smiled softly.

He saw resolution return to her face as her voice tentatively met his on the chorus.

"Now, you're getting the hang of it," he said, laughing gently as they swayed as softly and slowly as the breeze.

He stopped singing, stopped dancing. He pulled her a little closer to him and raised her hand, still held in his palm, to his shoulder. Then both of his larger hands circled her waist. "This is that awkward moment when you can't figure out whether or not to let the girl go."

"You probably should," she said quietly, her arms trembling.

"What if I don't want to?"

"You're going to go away some time soon, Brody," she groaned. "I don't want to fall for you." *Any harder than I already have.*

"You do have a point." He nodded and then raised an eyebrow. "But the best laid plans of mice and men…"

"Often go awry," she finished for him breathlessly as she stood on tiptoe and placed her lips against his.

He immediately enveloped her in his arms, as though her invitation was all he needed. His arms moved around her waist, crossing at her back. He pulled her as tightly to him as he could, as though he could pull her right into himself.

"I can't seem to get you off my mind." His lips left hers to trail across her throat.

"Same here," she said breathlessly. His lips traced a silky pattern across her collarbone. Brody bent and slipped one arm beneath her knees and lifted her from her feet.

"Brody!" she cried. He smothered her protest with another searing kiss, his lips parting hers with his tongue. Brody sat down with her in a rocking chair and placed her in his lap. Her legs hung over the arm of the chair and her bottom fit snugly in his lap.

She tried to sit up. "I'm too heavy to sit in your lap."

He grabbed the outside of her thigh and ceased her frantic retreat. His hand roamed up her thigh toward her bottom. "You're perfect for sitting on my lap." His hand moved over her hip, up her arm, and found a place under her hair to hold her neck. He smiled at her gently and said against her closed lips, "Want to relax some? I promise I won't bite."

In response, she nipped lightly against his bottom lip.

"I can't believe you did that." he mumbled.

"Sorry," she responded. "Let me make it better." She pressed her lips to his and touched his bottom lip with her tongue. She traced the line of the lower lip with the tip of her tongue and then closed her lips against his, their tongues warring desperately.

Brody grabbed her hip and pulled her closer to him. His hardness pressing against her bottom and she shifted her body in his lap. He groaned. "Careful," he whispered.

"Sorry. Did I hurt you?" she asked tentatively, one hand reaching to caress his cheek.

"Not in the way you think," he said. "I haven't enjoyed making out like this since I was eighteen." He pulled her shirt out of her jeans and ran his hand across the skin of her waist.

"I don't think I've ever made out like this."

"I know, it feels as good as the first time, huh?"

"Something like that," she mumbled.

His fingertips traced a pattern across her belly, causing the breath to catch in her throat and a flutter low in her stomach. She jumped as his fingers brushed the skin just an inch below her bra.

"This okay?" he asked quietly.

"I think so," she breathed back, her lips still playing with his.

His fingers moved up the side of her breast, touching the lacy material reverently. Her nipple stood at attention, straining against the thin cotton of her bra almost painfully, but he still didn't' touch it. Instead, he traced slow circles around her breast, working closer and closer to her nipple. She squirmed in his lap, hoping for something but not quite sure just what she wanted.

He lifted her shirt so he could see her bra and reached between her breasts to unhook the front closure. Uncovering her breast, he groaned at the sight of it. He began his lazy circles again. Lou released his lips and threw her head back, her breath coming in gasps. Brody watched her with veiled eyes as he came closer and closer to the small brown nub that stood so proudly. He bent his head and took her nipple into his mouth. She gasped and reached for his hair, holding his head with a strong grip. No longer able to keep her eyes open, she bit her bottom lip and concentrated on the sensations his touch was creating.

He gently flicked her nipple with his tongue, and it grew even harder in his mouth. He opened his lips, raising them a half inch from her skin, and took in a great gasp of air. This caused cool air to rush around her nipple and make it strain even harder toward his touch. He removed his mouth from her breast and replaced it with his hand, gently rolling her nipple between his thumb and forefinger. He repeated his lazy circles on the other breast.

When his mouth finally closed over her, she moaned and grasped his hair tightly. She pulled him against her breast. At her urging, his cool seduction became more powerful. He bit gently against her nipple. She moved wildly in his lap.

He grabbed the back of her neck and lifted her head where it hung back in abandon. He devoured her mouth as though she was his last meal.

Just then, the porch lights came on above them, flooding them in brilliant, white light. The power was back on. Lou jumped as though she had been scalded and looked down. Her naked, white skin was in stark contrast against his dark hand that still cupped her full breast. Reality hit her. She frantically grabbed her shirttail and covered herself. She sat up stiffly in Brody's lap, turning to move.

He gripped her tightly around the waist and said close to her ear, "Hold on. Be still a minute. It's still just you and me, all alone."

Her guilty conscience spoke. "I shouldn't have behaved like that."

"Like what? Like you enjoyed it? That's crazy. I love the way you 'behaved'," he added with a hint of sarcasm, still holding her close to him, still talking softly.

"I don't know how you get to me, but you do." She kissed him gently on the lips and climbed out of his lap. She sat down awkwardly in the chair beside him and took his hand in hers. She held it gently as their breaths returned to normal. "I have never felt like this before."

"Surely, Sarah's father…"

She cut him off. "That was a completely different situation. You have so much more experience than I do." She leaned forward with her elbows on her knees and held her face in her hands. She waited the length of a few breaths. Then her eyes rose to meet his, tears threatening to spill over her lashes. "I am not a whore."

He got up from his chair and knelt before her. He grabbed her chin and forced her to look at him. "You think I don't know that?"

A tear rolled across her cheek and he caught it with his thumb. He kissed her forehead and rose, pulling her to a standing position before him. He encircled her with his strong arms and squeezed her gently. He held the pose until once again she relaxed and sighed.

"Better?" he asked. She nodded against his shoulder. "Go to bed, Lou." She turned and entered her room, closing the door firmly behind her and leaving him standing under the porch light all alone.

I have a daughter, for Christ's sake. Lou changed clothes and slipped beneath the covers. The cool sheets touched her skin, which still had goose bumps from her encounter with Brody. Every nerve ending stood on end as she remembered the way his hands had moved across her body.

He must think I am an immeasurable tease, she thought as she lay on her back with one arm across her forehead, staring at the ceiling. A prick tease was what boys in high school had called her. Tonight, she had been the aggressor.

He might have asked me to dance, but then I'm the one who kissed him. And then I bit him on the lip. Oh God! She would never be able to look him in the eye again.

Lou tossed and turned most of the night but never slept deeply enough for nightmares, thank goodness. She woke the next day feeling just as unsure of herself as she had the night before. She rose, dressed, and put on tennis shoes for her morning run. She brushed the snarls from her long, dark hair and put it in a ponytail. Today was Saturday so she wasn't expected to make breakfast for the hands but still rose early. She poured a bowl of cereal for Sarah and kissed Sadie on the cheek as she went out the back door for her run.

She looked around for Brody as she stretched against the fence but didn't see any sign he was even up yet. It was probably better. He might not ever want to see her again.

She checked her watch and started jogging slowly through the winding path she always used. She found a good rhythm and then picked up the pace. The sun felt good on her body and the exertion was always good for stress. She forgot time and place, and concentrated on her footfalls and her breathing. About ten minutes into her run, she rounded a corner and came up short as she spotted a man standing in her path. She slowed to a walk and shielded her eyes with her hand, trying to see if it was Brody who had somehow gotten ahead of her.

She walked a few steps closer and got a good glimpse of the man. It certainly wasn't Brody. But who else would be out here? She walked a few steps in reverse but then the man called out.

"Why don't you stay right where you are, Mary Lou?"

"Pardon me?" she asked, certain she had not heard him clearly.

"I said, I think you need to stay right there so we can have a talk," the man said quietly. He took a few more steps forward and Lou caught the scent of cherry cigar on the breeze as he lifted it to his lips. The face looked vaguely familiar.

Ball cap. Five o'clock shadow. The temp who had helped to put up hay. Wes? Lou's thoughts dashed in mad abandon like ping pong balls set loose inside her head. She tried to grab each one as it bounced around but had no luck. He had just called her by her given name.

"Do I know you?" she asked tentatively.

"No. But you know my boss. Or at least he knew your mother. He was real sorry to hear about her passing." He took a draw on the cigar.

"What are you talking about?" Lou asked defensively.

He pulled an envelope out of his pocket and threw it at her. She caught it against her chest and opened it with shaky fingers. Photos fell out that Lou had never seen. They showed her mother, standing in front of their trailer. Her mother at work. Lou together with her mother, sitting at the kitchen table. Lou gasped as she looked through them all.

"Where did you get these?" she asked, her voice hoarse with emotion.

"We have sources," he replied.

"What do you want?" she asked, putting the pictures back in the envelope.

"Your mother stole something from my boss. He thinks you have it and he wants it back. I'm here to collect."

"I don't know what you're talking about. I left with nothing the night my mother died," Lou's voice shook with the memory.

" I know you're lying. You left with one thing. He's sure of it. You were seen with a black bag as you ran through the woods. This bag just happened to contain something that was precious to my boss. He wants it back."

Lou's heart skipped a beat. She held out the pictures. "I can't help you," she stated.

"I think you can." His face took on an even more menacing look. "I think you will."

"Or what?" Lou asked.

"Or you'll be sorry." He nodded his head toward the house. "And so will they."

"And if I refuse?" She thought long and hard for a moment. "I would be willing to pay whatever it's worth to you."

"Refusal is not an option. But we could discuss compensation."

"If you touch my daughter…" Lou started.

"She's safe for now but you need to take this seriously." The man stopped and turned his head, listening to something in the distance. Lou could hear footfalls behind them. "I'll be back. I'm watching you, so don't try to run away again." He walked into the woods that lined the jogging path and disappeared. Lou tucked the packet of photos into the back of her shorts and covered it with her shirt.

Brody came over the hill just at that moment, a big smile on his face as he saw Lou standing in his path. "You didn't have to wait for me. I could have caught up," he said smiling, already winded. "I saw you as you were leaving, but I was running late. I couldn't catch you before you left the yard."

"Well, you got me now," she responded sarcastically, her heart still thudding wildly in her chest from the encounter.

"What's wrong?" he asked cautiously. "You're not mad at me about last night, are you?"

"Last night?" Lou searched her mind. "Oh, that. No. I'm not mad about that."

"Well, are you ready to run?" he asked.

"What? Yeah. Sure. I guess," she replied absently.

"You sure there's nothing wrong, Lou?"

"Yeah. Positive." She turned and started to jog slowly, picking up the pace as she went. She felt like the run would never end. She needed to get back to the house so she could look through the photos. Lou had not seen her mother's face in seven years and had nearly forgotten what she looked like.

They finally rounded the last turn and Lou dropped to a slower pace. Brody broke in to her thoughts. "You're awfully quiet. Sure you're not mad at me?"

"No. I'm not mad at you." She managed a fake smile.

"Boy, you look sincere," he mumbled.

Lou didn't stop to stretch but walked right into the house and up the stairs to her room.

Jeb looked at him. "What did you do to her now?"

"Hell if I know," Brody replied.

****

Lou closed her bedroom door behind her with a resounding thud. She took the envelope from the back of her shorts with trembling fingers. She opened the envelope and dumped the pictures onto the bed. Emotions overwhelmed her as she looked through the photos. These were from a different time, a different place. They depicted a sullen girl who no longer existed. Lou was no longer a teenager, no longer a kid. She was a mother. A good employee. A part of a family.

Oh, God, a family! The pictures showed her old family. They showed her mother, heavily made up, big hair, smoking a cigarette. In some of the photos, she was in various stages of undress as she worked at the strip club. They showed her wearing tiny shorts and tube tops sitting on the steps of the trailer because there was no air-conditioning inside.

Then Lou thought about the family she had now. Sadie was like a mother to her and Jeb was the father she never had. Having him around, she felt safe during waking hours, like she was never alone. She had Mrs. Wester, who had financed her education and given her a job and a home. She had John, who was like a playful younger brother, and she had Sarah. Sarah was the only thing she took with her the night her mother died.

Now, someone wanted her? Who? Why? What am I going to do? She touched the photos that showed her past. And then thought about her future. The two didn't meet anywhere in the middle. How long could she run from the past before she got too tired to enjoy her future?

Lou gathered the photos together and glanced at them one more time. She placed them back in the envelope and slid it between her mattress and box spring. She went downstairs to join the family in the kitchen.

****

"Did you tell her I want it back?"

"Yeah, Boss. I told her."

"What was her response?"

"She swears she doesn't have it," Wesley responded quietly.

"Doesn't have it?" His boss exploded. His fist hit the desktop and glasses rattled. Pens danced and rolled off the table. "Of course, she has it! If that little bitch thinks she's going to use it against me, she has another think coming."

"I don't think it will come to that," Wesley stuttered. "I'm going to give her a couple of days and go back to see her again."

The boss said quietly, "She'll be sorry she ever ran from me. Just as sorry as her mother was." His meaty fist hit the table again.

Chapter Twelve

Brody spent his Saturday with his mother, reading to her and watching her sleep. She continued to go downhill and was sleeping more and more. After dinner, Lou and Sarah knocked softly on the door. Lou poked her head around the corner. "Knock, knock," she whispered, peering in at the hospital bed.

Brody touched Mrs. Wester gently on the arm. "Mom, you have company," he said quietly. Her eyes fluttered open and she smiled warmly at Lou and Sarah.

"Look who's here," she said. "Two of my favorite people." She took Lou's hand in her own. Sarah leaned over the side of the bed and presented her with a new card to add to her collection. Mrs. Wester managed a weak smile in return.

With the innocence of youth, Sarah started telling Mrs. Wester about her day and about Girl Scouts. She finally began to tell Mrs. Wester about the upcoming Father-Daughter dance at school. She told Mrs. Wester John was going to be her pretend Daddy for the night because he wanted to go and eat cake. Since he didn't have a daughter, he couldn't go unless she took him.

Lou cut her off when she heard the comments. She brushed Sarah's hair from her face and tucked it behind her ear. "You know what, sweetheart? John is not going to be able to take you because of his broken ankle. He can't even walk well with those crutches, much less dance."

Sarah immediately pouted up and tears filled her eyes. Mrs. Wester reached for Brody's hand and said, "Will you take her for me, Brody?"

"Me? Mom…I don't know if that's a good idea."

Lou broke in as well, shaking her head. "We wouldn't want to impose." Her eyes met Brody's with a look of apology.

Mrs. Wester lifted her eyes. "Broden, will you take her for me?"

"When is it?" Brody grumbled.

"In a couple of weeks. But really. It's not necessary."

"I'll do it." He looked Lou in the eye with a resolved look, winked at Sarah, and turned to his mother. "Does it make you happy?" He smiled into her eyes with the question on his face.

"You've always made me happy, son." She patted his hand absently. "Now, you'll make Sarah happy, too, which directly affects me as well."

"It does, does it?"

"Yes. It does."

Brody and Lou stood in the kitchen later that evening. Brody reached for a beer and popped the top.

"You really don't have to do it. I don't know why your mom put you on the spot like that but we won't hold you to it."

"Lou, I'm going to take her. I don't know much about kids but I think I can pull this off."

"Brody…"

"Lou!" he interjected. "Would you shut up and let me take her, please? I just promised my dying mother I would do something, and you're damned well going to let me do it."

Lou's lips compressed into a thin line. "If you say so."

"I say so," was his response as he took a swig from his beer bottle.

He pointed to his beer. "Want one?"

"No, thanks. I don't drink."

"Lou, you need to learn to let your hair down a little." He stepped over close to her and said softly. "You don't drink. You don't smoke. You don't have sex." She gasped. "Sorry," he continued with a casual shrug of his shoulders. "But it's true. You have to start living your life and stop trying to unlive hers."

"That's not what I'm doing." She crossed her arms over her chest.

"Sure you are and you do it so well." He placed an arm around her shoulders and led her outside. As they walked through the door, he whispered in her ear, "Stop pouting." She elbowed him in the ribs in response. He grunted loudly and laughed.

"What's so funny, boy?" Jeb asked, looking up from his game of checkers with John. They could barely see the game under the porch light.

"Lou packs one hell of a punch, Jeb." He rubbed his side as he sank down into a chair. Lou perched herself on the porch rail and hooked her feet through the slats. The moon was high in the sky so Sarah was already in bed. The crickets chirped a quiet song and the horses could be heard talking to one another in the distance.

"God, I love it out here." Brody broke the silence.

Sadie smiled and patted his arm. "Then maybe you'd like to stay for a while. We sure have missed you."

"Sooner or later, Sadie, I have to get back to the real world."

"It doesn't get any more real than this," Lou stated, her head flung back, wind blowing her hair gently.

"Maybe not for you, but I have to get back to the hustle and bustle of the hospital, the bright lights and the commotion."

"You can't tell me that's what you really prefer," Lou replied skeptically.

"No. I can't tell you that, but I can tell you I get to practice medicine in the city which does make it worthwhile."

The other adults were silent for a few moments. Jeb groaned as he got up and walked into the house. When he returned, he was carrying an old guitar which he handed to Brody.

Brody sat up instantly and reached for it. "Oh, my God. I have not seen this old thing in years. I can't believe she kept it all this time."

"She could never part with it, Brody, because she knew it meant a lot to you."

Brody caressed the dark wood like it was an old lover who had been absent too long.

"Think you can still carry a tune on that thing, Brody?" Jeb challenged.

"To be quite honest, Jeb, I'm not sure. But I'll give it a shot."

He spent a moment tuning the guitar and then started to play hesitantly. Lou quickly picked up the tune in her head. Sadie began to sing The Old Rugged Cross. Her deep, soulful sound flooded the porch and Lou smiled as she watched. When the song was over, everyone clapped and Sadie took a small bow.

"Let's try another," Brody said as he started the chorus of I'll Fly Away. Jeb sang along with Sadie on this one.

Brody laid the guitar beside his chair and Lou asked, "Where did you learn to play the choir music?"

"At Sadie's knee. Where else? She had me playing the guitar in church before I could even date girls. Or was even interested in girls." He chuckled loudly.

Jeb looked startled. "I didn't think there was a time when you didn't show an interest in girls, Brody."

"You might just be right, Jeb." Brody laughed. "You might just be right."

"I think that's enough for me for tonight," Jeb said as he jumped John's last checker. He and Sadie stood up. "Tomorrow comes awfully early."

"Sure beats the alternative, huh, Jeb?".

"You got that right, boy. Y'all sleep tight, now."

Jeb pointed to John. "You come on along, too, Hopalong. I would hate for you to break something else hopping around out here in the dark."

John maneuvered himself on crutches through the door, leaving Brody and Lou alone.

She slid down from the porch rail. "I had better get to bed, too."

"Oh, sit down and stay while. I promise I won't bite."

"It's not *you* biting *me* that I worry about, Brody," she mumbled in his direction.

He smiled innocently and picked up his guitar. He strummed a few notes. Lou quickly picked up the tune of Brown Eyed Girl and colored slightly. Brody looked through lowered lashes at her.

"You need to stop," she mumbled.

"Stop what?" he asked playfully.

"Stop looking at me like you are going to eat me." Her face turned red when realized what she'd said.

Brody laughed loudly. Lou couldn't figure out what to do with her hands. She reached for Brody's beer bottle and cupped it loosely, resting it on her knee. His left eyebrow rose and his smile issued a challenge.

"Living dangerously tonight, Lou?" Brody asked quietly.

She lifted the bottle to her lips. His heart sped up as she realized her lips were where his had just been. But then she grimaced slightly and frowned. "Oh, God. That's awful."

"Try it again. You might be surprised."

Lou frowned but lifted the bottle to her lips and drank more. She wiped her mouth with the back of her hand. "Nope. Still terrible. How do you drink that stuff?"

"Let me see it." He took the bottle from her outstretched hand and raised it to his own lips. Warm beer sloshed into his mouth. "No wonder, Lou. It's hot. That's a lot like drinking warm piss. Hang on and I'll get some cold ones." He rose from his chair despite her protests.

"No, Brody. Really. I need to get to bed, anyway."

He was already returning from the kitchen. "Nuh uh, Lou," he walked back through the screen door. "Your first taste of beer will not be spoiled by warmth." He held out a frosty bottle that had steam floating from the open neck. She took it cautiously and raised it to her lips.

She took a full swallow, then held the bottle up, looked at it, and said, "Not nearly as bad as the warm piss."

Brody chuckled. Then he grew serious. "Why are you drinking beer, Lou?" His silver eyes searched her own.

She halfway shrugged, breaking eye contact with him and looking at the floor. She said quietly, "I heard what you said about my mom earlier. About me not being able to 'unlive' her life."

"And?" he coaxed gently.

"And…you might be right. Just because my mom was all those things doesn't mean I will be as well."

"And that means?"

"That I can let my hair down a little. Maybe not be so serious."

And let me make love to you like I have wanted to do since I first laid eyes on you. Brody's jeans got tighter and he adjusted his pants. Her next few words were just as potent as cold water being thrown in his lap.

"That does not mean my morals have changed. I still believe the same things I did before." She glared at him.

"Point taken."

"Good," she said.

"Good."

Lou drained the rest of her beer quickly and rose to stand up. He watched her surprise as she found her world wasn't quite as steady and she stumbled slightly. She reached for the arm of the chair she had just vacated, but the arm of the chair obviously wasn't where she remembered it to be, so she weaved again.

Brody wrapped his arms around her waist as she sank against him. He said softly by her ear, "I forgot what a first beer can do to you." She tilted her head back to look up at him, her eyes veiled by suddenly weak eyelids.

"Got one hell of a kick, huh?" she asked, grinning widely.

He laughed at her antics and tweaked her nose with his thumb and forefinger. "You're awfully cute when you're tipsy."

"Tipsy? Is that what you call this?" she asked incredulously.

"Yep," he replied. "This is tipsy." He took a long, deep breath. "And this is me putting you to bed. Let's go."

"Where? To bed?"

"Don't I wish," he responded candidly.

"Huh?" was her only response.

"Never mind." He turned her around slowly and swatted her on the bottom. She yelped loudly. "Get to bed."

He opened the screen door for her and she walked slowly through it. She turned back to him. "Are you coming?"

Not tonight. No. But his response was, "Yep. I'm right behind you."

She walked slowly up the stairs, her bottom well outlined by her jeans. He watched the sway of her hips as she carefully traversed each step. Sweat broke out on his brow. He was thankful when they reached the top step so he could walk beside her rather than behind her.

She reached for the doorknob that would open the door to her room, but he beat her to it. Her hand closed over his and she smacked it playfully. "I can do it," she said petulantly.

"A gentleman always opens the door for his lady," Brody responded with a bow.

"Your lady?" She snorted. Very unladylike. And adorable.

He stood in her doorway, watching her pull the sheets and comforter back. The scene seemed almost too intimate to watch. Then her hands moved to pull her shirt from where it was tucked in her jeans. He imagined he saw the skin of her belly as her shirt fell back in place. He coughed gently. "Are you okay? I'm going to go to bed." He pointed down the hallway as though she didn't know where his room was.

She reached between her breasts and unhooked her bra. She slid her arms into the armholes of her shirt one by one and removed it without ever taking off her shirt. Brody watched in amazement. The fluttering piece of lace danced its way to the floor.

Then she was tripped up by her pants. Lou fought desperately with the button of her jeans, which would not budge. "Oh, good grief," she said, wiggling her fingers for him to see. She giggled and said, "My fingers don't seem to want to work quite right."

He walked into the room, knowing he was walking into dangerous territory. "Do you need some help?"

"With my pants? Probably," she said absently as she fell onto the bed on her back. She threw her forearm over her eyes and said, "I give up."

He sat down on the side of the bed and tried to put on his best doctor's face as he reached for the button of her jeans. "I'll get it started for you and then I'm going to go."

"How chivalrous of you," she responded, laughter bubbling out with the comment.

Brody unbuttoned her jeans, the skin of her waist warm against the back of his hand. He unzipped her pants. "Can you take it from here?"

"Can I take it? Take what?" she sat up slightly, confusion apparent on her features.

Brody groaned. "Your pants, Lou. Can you take your pants off?"

She thought seriously for a moment and replied, "Oh, yeah. I can take my pants off."

Before Brody could draw a breath, she reached to the waistband of her pants and lifted her hips off the bed. She slid the jeans over her hips and down to her ankles, where she shoved them from her feet and flung them on the floor. She lay back on the bed and covered her eyes again with her forearm.

Brody gasped and groaned as he saw her panties, narrow hips and long, lean thighs bared to his gaze. Her panties were pink lace and were no more than narrow strings on her hips. He forced himself to look away. He tried so gently to straighten her on the bed and then raise the covers over her legs. He took a deep breath and tucked the blankets around her. He moved her arm from over her eyes and she opened them slowly. His eyes met hers and he asked quietly, "Are you going to be okay?"

She grinned again and he felt his heart flip in his chest. "I'm going to be just fine."

Brody leaned forward and pressed his lips to her forehead. He lingered there and drew a deep breath, taking in the scent of her.

He sat back slightly. "Night," he said softly, looking into her eyes.

"Night," she responded. He got up and walked to the adjoining bathroom door. He verified Sarah was sound asleep and moved to walk out of Lou's bedroom. "Brody," she called out.

Sweat beaded up on his neck. If she called him back to the bed, he would be lost.

"Thanks for getting me tipsy. It was a lot of fun."

"Glad to hear it, Lou," he grumbled as he walked out the door.

Brody closed the door behind him and heard the click as the door closed, removing the temptation Lou presented. He'd thought his heart would jump out of his chest when she innocently took off her jeans, exposing hips, thighs and panties. Oh, God, those panties. They were nothing but wisps of lace that did nothing to conceal the treasures beneath. He remembered seeing her wearing her underwear that first day when he had caught her swimming with John. Even then, he had been interested and appreciative, but it wasn't like seeing her close up, so close he could feel the warmth of her body. He could probably walk right back into the room, have sex with her, and get rid of some of the frustration he had been dealing with. The woman was driving him crazy and she did it without any games or flirting or coy glances. She was just Lou. Plain old Lou.

But there wasn't anything plain about her. Brody placed his hand on her doorknob and started to turn it to walk back into the room. Then he hesitated. Who would hate him more the next day? Lou or himself? Probably both of them. He placed his forehead against the cool wood of the door and took a deep breath before he went to his room and took a cold shower.

He toweled off and pulled on a pair of boxer shorts. He dried his hair with a towel and tried not to think about the lady sleeping just twenty feet away. His imagination got the best of him as he tossed and turned for the next hour, unable to get her off his mind. Then, just when sleep was about to claim him, she began to scream.

Her terror was loud enough to wake the dead. Lou shrieked at the top of her lungs. Brody jumped out of bed, sure he would not need the baseball bat because he was used to Lou's nocturnal noises. These screams were different. She sounded tortured. He flew across the room and flung open his door. It slammed against the wall in his haste. He opened the door to her room even more quickly and didn't bother to turn on the light. Lou was still asleep. A tortured expression was on her face and screams still tore from her throat.

Brody sat down on the edge of the bed and grabbed her shoulders. He sat her up and pulled her up by her forearms. Her eyes opened and looked straight into his. Yet she was still asleep and struggled frantically to get away from him. She scrambled across the bed to the corner of the mattress and crouched there, still screaming.

"No! You can't have her!" she screamed, tears running down her face, her body wet with sweat. Her naked legs shook under her weight.

Not sure what she was talking about he started, "Lou, I don't want her." He extended a hand in her direction, hoping she would see it as a sign of peace. The screaming only grew louder.

Brody rose from the bed. "For the love of God," he muttered as he went to the adjoining bathroom and grabbed a cup of water from the sink. He walked back to the bed and threw it in her face. She sputtered blowing water from her lips. Her eyes grew wide. She reached shaking hands up to wipe her eyes.

"Brody?" she asked quietly. Realization crossed her face and she visibly relaxed. He could literally watch the tension leave her body. She crawled across the bed and deposited herself in his lap, still shaking. Her arms climbed around his neck and she burrowed her face into his shoulder. "Thank God you're here," she whispered against his skin.

He gently rubbed her sweat dampened skin as he murmured to her, "You okay?"

He felt her nod against his chest and heard a small, "I think so."

Brody looked up to find Sadie and Jeb in Lou's doorway. Sadie started to enter the room and Brody held up a hand. He said quietly to her, "I got this, Sadie."

"But…" she started.

Jeb cut her off. He took Sadie by the hand and said firmly, "The boy says he's got it, Sadie." He looked pointedly at Brody and said, "It certainly looks to me like he's got it."

"She's safe with me." His eyes met each of theirs in turn. "I promise."

Jeb tugged Sadie's hand gently. "Let's go back to bed."

Sadie frowned but allowed herself to be led from the room. Jeb closed the door behind them.

Brody cupped Lou's cheek with his hand and brushed the sweat-dampened hair from her forehead. He felt her breaths rising and falling against his chest. That was when he looked down and realized he only wore boxer shorts. *At least I slept in something tonight.*

"Do you want to tell me about it?" he asked softly against her hair.

He felt her shake her head against his chest but felt her arms loosen their strangle hold from around his neck. She visibly relaxed in his arms. He reached out and grabbed the outside of her thigh and pulled her closer to him on his lap to keep her from falling. She looked down, noticed her state of undress and said, "Boy, this is awkward, isn't it?"

"I won't tell anyone if you won't," he said. He realized there was only a slip of lace between her bottom and his boxers and he stiffened slightly. "Maybe I had better put you down." He slid her slowly off his lap and leaned back against the headboard. He crossed his arms over his chest. She started to shake again and he groaned. "Come here." He motioned with his hands she should come closer. This time, she tucked herself under his armpit and put her head on his shoulder. One hand lay flat on his chest. Slightly uncomfortable, he slid down further in the bed so they were both reclining. He pulled the covers over her bare legs and bunched them in his lap to hide the ever increasing bulge in his boxers. He took a deep breath.

When he imagined Lou trembling and sweating in bed, it certainly wasn't because of a nightmare. So, he needed to focus more on the situation and less on his needs.

"Why don't you tell me what the dream was about?"

He could feel her lips move against his skin and her breath tickled the hair on his chest as she took a long breath and then sighed. To distract himself, he used one hand to lift the heavy mass of sodden hair from her neck in hopes of cooling her down. She shifted slightly and burrowed even closer to him. "My mother always said your dreams will come true if you talk about them."

He stared straight up at the ceiling. Trying to stay focused. "And you believed her?"

"Well, I certainly don't want to chance it." He felt her smile against his chest. She yawned loudly. "Can you stay with me for a while?'

"Do you need me to stay?"

"Please?" she asked quietly.

"Sure." He tightened his arm around her shoulders and squeezed gently. "I can stay." *Not sure how long I can stay like this, but I can stay.*

She started to relax against him and her breaths became more even. The slow rise and fall of her chest moved against his. The length of her leg pressed up against his own. Her hand rested against his chest hair. He felt everything. Boy, did he feel everything.

She was fast asleep. At least one of them would be able to get some sleep. Brody closed his eyes, knowing there were not enough sheep in the world to help him get to dreamland. He kissed her gently on the forehead, tasting the salty sweat on her skin. He was in for a long night.

****

Brody woke at sunrise to a tangle of limbs. Lou's head was on his chest and her arm was wrapped so tightly around him that it was tucked under him on the other side. One leg was flung across his thighs. Lou's breath touched his chin and tickled his morning whiskers. He raised his head and looked around. He lifted his one free hand and rubbed the sleep from his eyes. The other was firmly planted under Lou and was asleep.

Brody looked down the length of their tangled bodies and noted the covers had shifted during the night. Lou's legs were once again bare and one cheek of her bottom was exposed because her panties had risen during the night. He groaned inwardly and laid his head back, staring up at the ceiling.

The woman was driving him crazy and to top it all off, she didn't even intend to. She was independent and self-assured yet she had these tiny moments of weakness like last night when she had the nightmare. She was open and honest, and she was sleeping on top of him. He groaned again. When he did, she shifted slightly. *Please don't move. Please don't move.* He looked down at her again. *Please move. Please move.* He had to get out from under her or he was going to go crazy.

Brody rolled sideways toward Lou, hoping to slide from under her without waking her. But with his arm asleep, that was nearly impossible. He rolled onto his side, causing Lou to straighten her leg that was originally across his lap. She was now stretched along the length of him, nose to nose. Lou peered at him through lids that were open a fraction of an inch. She grumbled and closed her eyes again. Brody slid his sleeping arm out from under her head and tucked a pillow under it instead. She rolled toward his body heat as he moved away from her.

"Oh, no, you don't," he whispered. "You're going to stay over there and I'm going to get out of your bed while I still can." He grabbed the covers and pulled them up to her chest and tucked them around her. He lifted himself gently from the bed, shook his dead arm, and flexed his fingers. When he could feel the blood moving again, he opened the door to Lou's room and stepped out, running straight into John.

John took one look at Brody as he tiptoed out of Lou's room and his face turned red with anger. "What the hell are you doing?"

Brody sighed. "John, it's not what it looks like."

"What it looks like? It looks like you are sneaking out of Lou's room before the sun comes up! That's what it looks like." He paused. "Are you and Lou?" He motioned with his hands while trying to balance the crutches trying to indicate they might be together.

"No, John, it's not like that." He reached to place his hand on John's shoulder and John dodged him, obviously still ticked off.

Then Brody got angry, too. "What the hell is wrong with you?" he whispered vehemently. "She had a nightmare, John. A nightmare! She had another of those screaming, wall-shattering nightmares. So, I went in to help her and she asked me to stay and 'hold' her for a few minutes. We fell asleep."

"So, you guys are not?" John motioned again with his hands.

"Not what?" Brody asked, exasperated.

"Not sleeping together?"

Brody ran a frustrated hand through his hair. "No, John. We are not having sex. Is that what you want to know?" He laughed sarcastically. "We slept in the same bed and didn't have sex. I swear to God." He held up one hand to the heavens. "And to be honest, I got a pair of blue ones the size of my head because I haven't slept with her. Do you hear me? The size of my head! But you know what? I like her. There. I said it. I like her. If I didn't like her so damn much, I would have slept with her long before now. So, go back to bed, John. Lou's virtue is still intact, thanks to me. Feel better?"

"Well…" he began.

"Shut up and go to bed, John, before I knock your crutches out from under you and leave you in the hallway."

Brody turned and went into his own room, closing out John and the rest of the world.

****

Lou lay in her bed smiling, having just heard every word that they had just said. What a great way to start the day.

A bit later, after she had already showered and had Sarah ready for church, Sadie came to get her. Sadie knocked softly on her door and then poked her head inside. Lou sat on the edge of her bed. She had Sarah between her knees as she pulled the girl's long, dark tresses up and held them back with barrettes. She patted Sarah on the bottom and said, "Go and brush your teeth."

Sadie's eyes met Lou's as she walked into the room and sat down beside her on the bed. She candidly asked, "What are you doing up so early? You usually sleep in on Sundays."

Lou sighed. "I just couldn't sleep." She shrugged her shoulders and looked down at the floor.

Sadie reached and touched her hand to Lou's forehead. "No fever." She raised one finger to her lips and pretended to think really hard. She touched Lou's cheek and grinned. "But I do think you have been bitten."

"Bitten?" Lou asked incredulously.

"Yep. By the love bug. Symptoms usually include a racing heart, rosy cheeks, and an allover warm sensation, not unlike a fever but a little more pleasant."

Lou laughed out loud. "I don't know what you're talking about."

"Sure you do. You have the hots for that fancy pants, Brody, who I happen to love like he's my own son, but he's no angel and we both know it."

"I do not have the hots…" Lou started.

Sadie cut her off. "Uh uh," she scolded, shaking her finger. "This is old Sadie you're talking to, but I'm not so old I can't remember that feeling you're fighting. My man still makes my toes tingle and look how old we are." She snorted.

"Sadie!" Lou shrieked as she stood and clamped a hand over her mouth.

"Hey, I just wanted you to know I have been where you are standing."

"And what did you do?" Lou stammered.

"Well, I married him. Do you have the same opportunity?" Sadie asked.

"Probably not," Lou replied.

"Then you need to figure out what you're doing before you do it. It's hard to make decisions that might affect your future when you're feeling all flushed and warm and a man is holding you."

Lou squeezed her eyes shut tightly. "Sadie," she moaned.

Sadie stood up and wiped Lou's bangs from her eyes. "He's got you all tore up inside?" she asked softly.

"Yeah," Lou replied, just as softly.

"You're a mother. You're a friend. Are you ready to be someone's short-term lover?"

"No."

Sadie patted Lou's arm. "Then there's your answer." She took a dramatic bow, as dramatic as her old bones would allow. "Glad I could be of service."

Sarah ran out of the bathroom, one hair bow already falling out of her hair. Lou reached to repair the damage. Sadie held up a hand and said, "I got it," as she ushered Sarah from the room.

As Sadie walked through the threshold, Lou called out, "Sadie?"

"Yeah, honey," Sadie replied, smiling softly at Lou.

"Thanks."

All she got in response was a nonchalant wave.

****

Lou walked into the kitchen and was surprised to see Brody was already up. He sat at the table with the newspaper and a box of Lucky Charms before him.

She stared at him. "Is that my hidden stash of Lucky Charms?"

He grinned broadly and tipped it over. A few crumbs fell into his bowl. "Not anymore," he said around the cereal in his mouth.

"You think it's funny to eat all my Lucky Charms?" She picked up the box and tapped him gently over the head with it.

"It was for a minute, yeah." He was still smiling. He pulled out the chair beside him, and in it sat a gaily wrapped present.

Lou's eyebrows drew together and she frowned. "What's that?" She pointed at the package.

"Why don't you open it and find out?"

She cautiously walked around the table and picked up the gift. She sat down in the chair and lifted it to her ear. She shook it gently.

"Would you just open it already?" he scowled.

"Would you wait a minute? Playing with the package before you open it is half the fun."

"Don't I know it?" He spoke again around another mouthful of Lucky Charms.

Lou raised her head. "What did you say?"

"Nothing."

Lou slid her finger under one corner of the wrapping paper and lifted it slowly.

"Good God, girl. You're killing me, here."

She used her best mother's voice, shook her finger at him and snapped, "Patience, please." Then she opened the other corner of the package. She looked inside and started to laugh. "Lucky Charms. You shouldn't have."

"Oh, it's nothing."

"No. I mean it. You shouldn't have eaten all my cereal and then you wouldn't have had to buy me another box." She lifted one eyebrow and looking at him. Then she sobered. "Thanks, though."

Brody held out his hand. "Can I open the box, now? I want another bowl," Brody asked.

"I should have known you had a motive."

"Your smile when you opened it was motive enough, my lady," he said quietly as he took the cereal from her hand. Then, more playfully, he added, "I get the toy."

"You'll have to fight me for it," she replied, snatching it back quickly from his grasp. She searched the outside of the box and saw no clue that spoke of the prize within. She opened the lid and noticed the bag inside was already open. "Hey! This bag must have already been torn." Then she saw it. A small jewelry box lying on top of the cereal. Her eyes met Brody's and he smiled. "Did you put this in here?" she whispered as she pulled the small package from its bed of Lucky Charms.

"If you like it, I did. If not, then definitely not. In that case, it was a mistake the leprechauns made."

Lou tilted the lid on the jewelry box and gasped as she saw the contents. It contained a thin, silver chain and a small charm. Lou removed the charm from the velvet lining and held it up to the light. It was a small silver circle with tiny feather charms around the outside. The inside looked like a spider's web, yet had an open hole in the center. Small turquoise beads danced around the middle.

Lou gasped. "It's beautiful! What is it?"

Brody took the charm from her fingers and lifted the necklace from the box. He began to thread the charm onto the silver necklace. "It's called a dream catcher. You're supposed to hang it over a baby's bed and it catches all the dreams before they get to the baby. The good ones go on through the center hole and float on the feathers down to the baby. The bad ones are caught in the web and held there until morning light. When the sun touches them, they vanish."

Brody took a deep breath and motioned with his finger that she should spin around. She turned her back to him and lifted her hair. He placed the silver chain around her neck and fastened the clasp. He lingered a tad too long and then bent to place a quick kiss on her shoulder. She stiffened yet still turned to him and buried her face in his chest. He lifted her face in his hands with his thumbs at her chin and his fingers in her hair. He smiled broadly at her.

"I guess you like my gift," he said, wiping the tears from her eyes with his thumbs.

"It's the most beautiful gift I have ever seen," she sniffed. She raised herself on tiptoe to kiss his cheek but then heard a discreet cough in the doorway.

"Lola, is everything all right?" Brody asked, his face marred with worry.

"Yes, Dr. Wester. It's your mother." She turned and pointed back to the bedroom.

"Is she all right?" He quickly disentangled himself from Lou and started to walk toward Lola.

"Absolutely, Dr. Wester. She's sitting up and asking for you."

Chapter Thirteen

Lou followed Brody to Mrs. Wester's bedroom and was astonished to see her sitting up in bed with a big smile on her face. She raised her arms to Brody as he approached and took his hands in her own. He bent and touched his lips to her cheek.

"How are you, Mom?" He reached and touched her forehead.

She grabbed his hand with her own and swatted him away like a pesky fly. "I feel wonderful. Better than I have felt in quite some time, actually." She spoke clearly and succinctly, eyes bright and shining. Then she noticed Lou in the room.

"You come here, too." She swiftly waved her hand in a come-hither motion. Lou approached the bed, a worried frown upon her face. "Why do you look so sour? Both of you? You both look like you've just spotted a deer with antlers on his ass."

"Mom!" Brody replied, smiling broadly. Then he sobered. "I am glad to see you feeling so much better."

"Me too!" Mrs. Wester sighed. "Now. What are we going to do today?"

"What do you mean?" Brody asked, his eyebrows drawn together.

"I mean I am tired of sitting in this bed all day and I want you to take me somewhere."

"Did you have somewhere in particular in mind, Mom?"

"Actually, I do." Her eyes met Brody's as she said, "I want to go to your father's grave."

"Mom, we can't…"

"Don't 'we can't' me, son. I'm telling you where I want to go. Now, either you can take me or I can call a cab." She pointed to her nightstand and said, "Lou, would you get the phone book out of the bottom drawer for me, please?"

Lou looked at Brody like a deer caught in the headlights.

"Don't do it, Lou." Then he turned to his mother and groaned. "You're sure this is what you want to do?"

"Positive." She smiled softly at Brody. "Why don't you two go and pack a picnic while Lola here helps me get dressed?" She motioned for Lola to get up from her chair and pointed her toward the bureau to retrieve some clothes. "Move it, son. I don't have a lifetime."

"Yes, ma'am," Brody said as he pushed Lou from the room.

In the hallway, her worried eyes met his. "Are you sure this is a good idea?"

"No," was his only reply.

"Then why are we doing it?"

"Because, when people as sick as my mom are about to die, they usually have a day or two of clarity before it happens. They usually rally right before death. They have an opportunity to take care of unfinished business and to say goodbye to the people they love."

Lou reached up and touched his cheek. "Oh, Brody, I had no idea."

He took her hand and brought it to his lips. He kissed the backs of her fingers gently. "It's going to be okay. I have been expecting this for a while but it sure doesn't make it any easier." He drew in one deep breath, steeling himself. "Let's go and make sandwiches."

They worked well in the kitchen, packing a picnic basket with sandwiches, chips, cookies, and drinks. Lou made three sandwiches and placed them in the basket. "You need to make one more," Brody said around a mouthful of ham.

"Why?"

"Because you're going with us." With the look on her face, she expected him to follow the comment with, "Duh," but he refrained.

"Are you sure you want me to come? Don't you want to be alone with her for today?"

"Nope. I want what she wants, and she's going to want you to go. I want you to go, too. Otherwise, I'll get stuck with Lola if there's a crisis." He made a face of horror, probably in hopes of winning her sympathy.

She laughed softly and then hung her head.

He reached over and tipped her chin up, looking into her eyes. "What's wrong?"

"It just doesn't feel right to laugh when your mom is so sick."

"I'll make a deal with you."

"What kind of deal?"

"While she's alive, we'll laugh. Then, when she's gone, we'll cry."

"Deal," Lou replied.

"Deal." Brody snapped the picnic basket closed and went to stow it in the trunk of the car.

****

Brody found loading the car with picnic supplies was much easier than loading his mother into the car. She was still weak and tired but her mind was clear for the first time in weeks. Brody gently lifted her from the wheelchair and lowered her just as tenderly into the backseat of the car. Lou buckled her seatbelt while Brody put the wheelchair in the trunk. Lola slid into the backseat alongside her and Lou got in front.

She turned around in her seat to look back with a frown on her face. "Are you sure you want to do this, Mrs. Wester. Are you okay?"

"I promise you, dear, that if I get tired, I'll ask to come home. This short little trip won't kill me, I'm sure. If it does, I'll go out happy."

Lou hid her smile behind her hand. They drove down the winding driveway to the main road and traveled twenty more minutes to the local Baptist church. The church sat on a hill beside a pasture and a pond, and had a fenced family graveyard next door. Brody set up the wheelchair and moved his mother over to the chair while Lola and Lou anxiously hovered. He gently tipped the wheelchair back and smiled into her eyes.

"Looks like you get to recline while we go across these rocks."

"Just get me there, son. I don't care how you have to do it," she replied.

"I've never been to the grave, Mom. Which way do I go?"

Lou caught his eye with a silent question.

"I didn't come home when my dad died," he mumbled under his breath.

"But you're here now, son. That's what matters."

The headstone was overgrown with weeds and brambles and showed a general lack of care. Brody bent immediately and began to pull up weeds and remove sticks and old flowers.

His mother looked at Lou and asked, "Lou, will you take Lola and go down to the pond? There are some nice flowers that grow down there. They would look pretty up here." She stared absently at the headstone.

"Sure. We would love to." Lou bent and placed a kiss on the old lady's weathered cheek before they walked toward the pond.

Brody sat down on the grass beside the wheelchair and looked up at her. She touched the curls on his forehead tenderly. "I remember when you were just a little thing and you looked up at me like that."

Brody rested his cheek against her knee. He looked into her gray eyes, so like his own, and said, "I'm sorry, Mom."

"For what?" She absently patted his head.

"For running away. For not coming home. For not being here for you when he died. For not being what you needed."

"You were always what I needed, Broden. Always. You were your own person. I remember when you were little and your dad got angry at me because I let you do things your way. He thought you should fit in this neat and tidy little box and we should try to keep you there. You were never made to fit in a box like that. You were made for bigger and better things." She smiled at him. "You were made for love and laughter and life. You have had all of those things and made your own way. I am so proud you are mine."

"I just couldn't make him see..." Brody started.

"He was your father. Fathers want what's best for their children. If you were on the farm, he could watch you and protect you from things that would hurt you. He did it because he thought you would never go. He regretted it every day after you left, but then he saw you were successful and happy. He was proud of you, too. You didn't need him after you left. That's hard for a father to take. Did you know he went to your graduation from college? He stood way in the back and watched you get your diploma. In a perfect world, he would have let you have your dreams and let you out of the box. He would have agreed you needed to take your licks like a man while still giving you a safe haven to come home to. But the world is not perfect. Neither was the man."

"I still loved him," Brody stated blandly.

"He knew it, dear," was her only response to his comment. She grinned broadly at him and took his chin in her hand. She shook his chin gently. "But you were mine. From the day that you were born, you were mine. I counted your fingers and toes. I looked into your eyes and I knew you were mine. You were the best baby. A fabulous child. But you were not made to be a rancher."

"But I like ranching," he declared petulantly.

"But you *love* medicine."

"I've had a lot of fun here these last few weeks. I can't believe how much John has grown."

"That one will always be a rancher and will love every minute of it."

"And Sadie and Jeb will never change, will they?"

"God, I hope not!" They both laughed. "And Lou? What do you think of her, son?"

"I think she's wonderful."

"And?" Her eyebrows lifted.

"And what? She's fabulous. She's terrific. She's...Lou. Jesus. I don't know what to say about her."

"You have to take her just like she is. Because she doesn't hide anything, Brody."

"I'm not taking her at all, Mom. Good grief."

"Okay!" She held her hands up in mock surrender. "Just remember what I say. Everything doesn't fit into a neat and tidy box. Some things are complicated. And they are supposed to be that way."

"Point taken," he said. "I love you."

"Almost as much as I love you. Now, scoot. Go and help Lou finish picking the flowers. Send Lola back up here. Then we'll put the flowers on the grave and have some lunch by the pond."

"Are you getting tired?"

"No. I'll let you know when I am. Run along. I want a minute alone, please."

"Okay." He kissed her on the forehead and started to walk toward Lou who was still gathering flowers by the pond. He motioned to Lola that she should go back up and sit with his mother while he walked over to Lou.

"Are you doing all right?" she asked quietly.

"Yeah. But we had better get home before too long. She looks a little tired."

"I'm ready when you are," Lou replied and put the bouquet of wildflowers in his hand with a smile.

They turned to walk back to where Lola and Mrs. Wester waited at the gravesite. Then they heard Lola scream. "Dr. Wester! You had better come quick!"

Brody and Lou both broke into a fast run and reached her at the same time. She appeared to be sleeping, her head hanging to one side, eyes closed, and a slight smile on her face. Brody touched her lightly on the shoulder but she did not stir. He grabbed Lola's stethoscope from where it rested around her neck and listened to his mother's heart.

He stood up and turned to grab Lou in a tight embrace. He buried his face in her hair and he pulled her close to him. "She's gone," he whispered in her ear, his voice cracking only slightly as he said it.

****

The next twenty-four hours rushed by like a fast-moving wave. Time and fatigue washed over them all as they prepared for the funeral and dealt with the emotions flying around like kites caught in a summer storm.

Lou stood in her bedroom, dressing for family night at the funeral home when the reality of the situation finally hit her. Mrs. Wester was gone. She had given Lou opportunities and chances for a good life but she had also done more than that. She gave Lou a role model, someone she could look up to. She gave her something to aspire to be. And she was gone.

Lou tucked her black silk blouse into her black skirt and slid on her dress shoes. She turned to open her door to walk out of the room and the emotions slapped her in the face.

She couldn't go through the door but returned and sat down on the edge of the bed, burying her face in her hands, letting the tears flow freely. She cried until there were no tears left. She reached for a tissue to dry her eyes and felt a gentle tug on her sleeve.

"Are you okay, Mommy?" a little voice asked quietly, similar brown eyes staring into her own.

Lou pulled Sarah into a clumsy embrace, clutching the child against her. She sniffed loudly and the tears started to fall again. Lou held Sarah against her until the child started to squirm.

"Sadie says God calls some people up to heaven, Mommy. Is that where you think Mrs. Wester is?"

Lou smiled through her tears and dried her eyes once more. She took a deep breath.

"I don't just think it, Sarah, I know it."

"But, didn't God know we wanted her to stay here with us?"

"Oh, I'm sure He knew how much we all wanted her to stay, but He has to do things on His own schedule and not on ours."

"Do you think she's happy in heaven, Mommy?"

"I do think she's happy and healthy in heaven, Sarah. She's looking down on us all, watching us."

"Well, then, Mommy, what do you think she would say about all this crying you're doing? I think she would laugh at you and tell you how silly you're being. What do you think?" Sarah asked with a cheeky grin.

Lou laughed through her tears. "I think you are probably right, Sarah." She took Sarah's hand in her own. "Let's go to the funeral home and make her proud of us. Shall we?"

Lou and Sarah walked hand in hand into the kitchen where Jeb, Sadie, John and Brody were all waiting. Brody rose from his chair at the table when he saw her approach. She was sure he could still see the remnants of her tears as he asked "Are you okay?"

"I'm as okay as I'm going to be today, I think." She sniffed loudly.

"Everyone ready to go?" Jeb asked loudly. All eyes in the room swung his way. Five pairs of shoulders straightened as they steeled themselves and they all walked outside. Jeb and Sadie turned to go to Jeb's truck. Brody's hand on Jeb's shoulder stopped him.

"Mom would want you to ride in the family car. She wouldn't have it any other way."

"If you say so," Jeb replied, nodding slightly. He helped Sadie into the back seat and then climbed in himself. Lou slid into the center row and moved to sit against the far window. Sarah sat in the middle. Brody sat on the other side. John sat up front next to the driver. Lou buckled Sarah in to the middle seat and rested her arm along the back. Brody lifted his arm to the back of the seat as well. Her eyes caught his when his fingers slid between her own. She squeezed his hand gently and smiled softly at him.

Sadie squeezed Jeb's thigh in the backseat. He patted her hand in return.

Brody and John formed the receiving line at the funeral home, ready to greet the visitors. Sadie and Jeb played host and hostess, shaking hands and giving teary hugs to friends and family. Sarah held on to Sadie's dress. Lou turned to mingle with the crowd, not sure what to do with herself.

She felt Brody's arm slip around her waist. He whispered in her ear, "Come and stand by me?" His hand slid from around her waist and trailed down her arm. He lightly tugged her hand, urging her to walk with him.

She protested, "But I'm not family."

"You were to her and you are to me. Please?" She nodded slightly and allowed herself to be placed between Brody and John. He smiled the unabashed smile of a ten-year-old. "I have to admit I need someone to tell me who all these people are. It's been more than ten years since I have seen most of them."

Friends, family, and well-wishers all came to pay their respects to the late Mrs. Wester. They sobbed, they laughed and they all spoke of what a fine woman she was. She had numerous friends and acquaintances from the charities she supported and families from the neighboring farms all visited. Lou got choked up when friends spoke of how much they would miss her, and her constant laugh and quick wit. Brody had his cheeks pinched by the old dowagers and even had his bottom pinched by an old friend from school.

Heat crept up her cheeks as Brody's eyes caught hers. He knew must have known she had seen the pinch. After the visitor had passed, he whispered, "Do you know who that was?"

"Melinda Campbell from C&C Farms. They live down the road from us," she nearly growled.

"That's little Millie? No way!" He cast an appreciative glance in Melinda's direction. "She sure has filled out. Last time I saw her, she was still in braces." He glanced over in her direction again.

"I guess she's cute if you like buck teeth and a wide behind," Lou mumbled.

"What did you say?" Brody asked.

"Nothing." She planted a fake smile on her face.

Just then, a blond bombshell strode up, legs up to her ears. Brody's grin got even wider as he reached to embrace her. "Now this is a face I remember! How are you, Liz?"

"Doing fine, Brody. I'm so sorry to hear about your mom." His hand clasped hers.

"Me too, but we all know she's in a better place," Brody replied.

"Are you staying in town for a while? If so, maybe we can go out for a drink for old times' sake?" the leggy blonde wanted to know. She reached into her purse and retrieved a business card. She pressed it into his hand. Lou read the type, "Elizabeth Patton, Party Planner Extraordinaire," over his arm before he tucked it in his pocket.

"No. I actually am going back home a few days after the funeral. I'll try not to stay away so long next time so I can take you up on that drink offer." He leaned and whispered something in her ear, causing her to twitter nervously. She kissed his cheek and moved away, throwing, "Save that 'til the next time I see you," over her shoulder.

Lou stepped away from Brody, taking herself out of the receiving line.

"Where are you going?" Brody called to her retreating back.

She kept walking. She was irritated. She was angry. She was jealous! She decided some fresh air would do her good, so she went outside to where Sarah was playing with some of the neighborhood children on the small playground beside the funeral home. Sadie had her watchful eye on the child but, she was deeply engrossed in conversation with one of the parents.

Sarah's black dress was dusty with dry dirt and leaves clung to her hair. "How do you manage to get dirty so quickly, young lady?"

"It's easy, Mommy." She grinned up at Lou.

"Are you having fun?"

"Yeah," she replied. Then paused, a serious look on her face. "Is it okay to have fun with Mrs. Wester going to heaven and all?"

Lou took a deep breath and knelt down to Sarah's level. "What do you think Mrs. Wester would want? Would she want you to stop playing? Would she want you to be sad?"

Sarah's worried frown was replaced with a grin. "She would never want that!"

"I don't think so, either," replied Lou. She stood, stretched, and turned to go back into the funeral home.

Sarah called out, "Oh, Mommy!" Lou turned to her. "A man told me to give this to you." She held a plain paper envelope in her hand. Lou reached out and took it in her own, then walked straight inside to the bathroom. She stood by the counter and opened the letter, thinking it must be from a friend of the family.

A photo fell into her hand of her mother and a teenage Lou, standing side by side.

What she read took her breath.

Mary Lou,

You and I have an important matter to discuss. You still have something I need to get from you. Don't make me come and get it. You have one week and then I'm coming to get what you owe.

Wes

Lou took a deep breath, splashed some water on her face in an attempt to wash away the worry lines. She dried her face gently and placed the letter and photo in the pocket of her skirt. She lifted her shoulders, steeled herself and rejoined the crowd. They had thinned out considerably. The viewing was almost over and most of the family and friends had paid their respects. Small groups of people still milled about. Night was falling, so Sadie stood inside with Sarah. Lou took a deep breath. At least she was safe. For the next week, she was safe.

Brody walked over to Lou, his eyebrows scrunched together. "Where did you run off to?"

"Do you really want me to tell you about my trip to the ladies' room?" she flipped back at him.

"Is something wrong?"

She sighed. *If you only knew.* "No. Nothing's wrong. I'm just tired, I guess." She rubbed her eyes with the curve of her hand.

"You ready to go home? It's been a long day," Brody asked.

"Yeah. I am ready. You?"

He extended his arm, and she only hesitated a moment before wrapping her hand through the crook of it. She let him lend her some emotional support as well as physical strength. She motioned to Sarah that it was time to go, and the little girl came running.

Jeb and Sadie met them at the car. The ride home was quiet. All the occupants of the car were pensive and tired. Sarah fell asleep with her head on Lou's lap.

When they stopped at home, Lou got out of the car and bent to pick Sarah up. Brody brushed her out of the way and scooped the child up himself. She had to admit she liked the way Sarah tucked her head into his neck and held on tightly.

They walked through the kitchen and he grabbed a bottle of water from the fridge. He kissed Sadie on the forehead and said, "Night, Jeb." He nodded in John's direction. "John."

"Night," they all responded.

Lou followed him up the stairs and she undressed Sarah, sliding her nightgown on without even waking her. Brody pulled the covers over her. Lou tugged the door shut that adjoined the two rooms.

He followed Lou into her own room. "Thanks for all the help tonight."

"You didn't need my help. You're just saying that to make me feel like I was needed."

"I need you," he breathed at her.

Her breath caught in her throat. She licked her lips.

"Why do you need me?" she asked quietly.

"Because my mother just died." He rubbed both eyes with his fists and moaned. "I am so tired. I don't even think I'm fit for company."

"You going to bed?" Lou asked quietly. Then her gaze grew more serious. "Your mother did just die. You haven't had time to deal with it yet so maybe some rest will help." She patted his arm.

"I don't think I could sleep if I wanted to. I think I'm going to go down to the bar in the study and get a bottle of Jack Daniels, and get stinking drunk all by myself. Maybe then I'll just pass out and not feel this pain anymore." He took her hand and held it over his heart. "All those years, I guess I just assumed she would always be here for me."

"She was and still is, Brody. You take her strength with you in all that you do." She removed her hand from over his heart and gave him a gentle shove toward the door. "Go to bed, Brody. You'll feel better tomorrow if you get some rest."

He surprised her by kissing her on the cheek. "'Night, Lou."

"'Night," she responded.

Brody walked out of her room and Lou closed the door behind him. She took off her clothes and walked into the bathroom, stepping beneath the spray of the shower. The heat pounded the tension from her body and eased the strained muscles of her shoulders and back. She came out of the shower feeling like some of the stress of the day had been washed down the drain. She brushed through her wet locks with a wide-toothed comb and then dressed in a tank top and long pajama pants.

Lou opened the screen door and flopped down in the rocker outside her room, hanging her hair over the back of the chair to dry. She absently chewed her fingernails.

Then she heard a sound coming from the shadows. Then she heard it again. The catch of someone's breath? The rocker squeaked and then there was a sniffle, followed by someone loudly blowing his nose.

"Brody?" The squeaking rocker stopped. "Brody? Is that you?"

A muffled voice called back. "Yeah. It's me."

"Are you okay?" she asked nervously.

"I'm on my way to being okay."

"What's that supposed to mean?"

"Nothing, Lou," he sighed. "Just go to bed."

She got up slowly and walked across the porch on bare feet. She could see him sitting in the shadows, tears pouring down his face, a full glass in his hand.

"What are you doing?" she asked quietly.

"Getting stinking drunk, just like I told you I was going to do."

"How much have you had so far?"

"Just one glass as of this moment." He extended the full glass in her direction. "This one is number two." He wiped his face with a handkerchief.

"Drunk yet?"

"Hell, no."

"Close?"

"Not even."

"Want some company?" Lou asked as she sat down in the rocker beside him.

"Do I get a choice?"

"Do you want one?"

"Not really," he admitted.

"What are you drinking?"

"Jack Daniels." She looked at him blankly. "Whisky," he explained.

"Oh," was her only reply. "Do you want me to leave you alone so you can go back to crying?"

He sniffled twice and a tear fell from his left eye. "Looks like I can cry just fine with you, here."

"It's perfectly natural, you know. Crying when your mother dies. I cried for weeks when my mother died."

"But you're a girl."

"Pardon?" she tried to look offended.

"Woman." He waved one hand in air. "Whatever. Girls are supposed to cry."

"And that means you can't show emotion when your mother dies?"

Her question caused even more tears to fall.

"Oh, Brody, I'm so sorry." She stood up in front of him. "Would a hug help?"

"Yeah." He set his glass on the porch and reached one arm around her waist. He drew her down into his lap and turned her sideways so her back was pressed against the arm of the chair, her legs draped across his.

She squirmed in his lap. "This wasn't exactly what I had in mind."

"Just be still and humor me, will you? Can I just hold you for a second?"

Her movements stilled and she placed one arm around his neck and the other hand on his chest. She laid her head on his shoulder.

He took a deep breath. So did she.

They sat that way for a few minutes. Lou felt herself relax more and more, and then something changed. Brody's thighs tensed under her own and his arms clutched her closer. He rubbed her cheek with the back of his hand. She sat up a little more.

"You feeling better now?" Lou asked right before he touched her chin and lifted her lips toward his.

His lips breathed against hers, "Much. Thank you."

Her heartbeat quickened. "Brody?" she gasped right before his lips touched hers. They were firm, yet soft and she could taste the whisky on his breath. His tongue flicked lightly against her lips, daring them to open. They did. His tongue slipped inside and met hers in a frantic tangle. His hand slid into her hair and he tugged gently, breaking contact.

He looked her in the eye and said, "Unless you want me to make love to you, you had better go to bed now." Her eyes narrowed as they stared into his. She scooted closer to him in his lap and put both arms around his neck, her lips finding his. He groaned loudly and stood up with her in his arms. He turned and strode toward her bedroom. She reached out and opened the door so he could carry her inside. He dropped her legs and let her slide down his front until her feet hit the floor. His mouth devoured hers and she responded just as passionately.

"God, I want you, Lou. I need to know, though, do you want me?"

She nodded against the pressure of his lips. "But hang on." She walked through the bathroom and locked the door, just in case Sarah woke.

Brody kicked off his loafers as she started to unbutton his shirt. Her fingers trembled as the buttons slid through their holes. He broke the kiss long enough to pull the shirt over his head. Her hands tentatively touched the hair on his chest and she ran her fingers through it. Her hands shook. He clasped them both in one of his.

He asked quietly. "You can still tell me to go away if you want."

"I don't want you to go away." She looked him in the eye as she said it.

"Good, because I don't want to go." He slid his hands beneath her bottom and lifted her feet off the floor. He turned toward the bed and they tumbled onto it. His weight rested on his elbows. His knee pushed her legs apart and he rested between them.

"God, I'm scared," Lou said, her hands in his hair, stroking him gently as he gazed into her face.

"No need to be scared. I won't hurt you." His lips touched her shoulder softly. "This hurt?" he mumbled against her skin.

She shook her head no.

He kissed his way down her throat. "This hurt?"

She shook her head again.

One of his hands cupped her breast as his thumb slid slowly across her nipple. A breath hissed out between clenched teeth.

"Now, I know that didn't hurt."

"Maybe just a little," she gasped.

"Well, then I had better try it again." His thumb slid across her nipple again and she arched her back, trying to get closer to his touch.

"Much better," she whispered.

"I think I can do better." He bent and placed his hands at her waist, tickling her lightly as he lifted her shirt. He went slowly as the fabric passed over her breasts and she heard him groan before he pulled the shirt over her head.

He cupped one full breast in his hand and said, "You are so beautiful. Your body is perfect." He began to stroke one breast with his tongue, lightly flicking against her hardened nipple. She gasped. His other hand still cupped her breast, so he began to rub across her nipple with his thumb.

The sensations rocked through her and she moved her hips against his, startled to feel his hardness pressed against her belly. Her eyes grew wide. He moaned. She moved again. He moaned louder. "You had better stop that or this is not going to last nearly as long as I want it to." She moved her hips against him again. He broke contact with her and stood up to remove his pants. He lifted her hips and slid his hand inside the waist of her pajama bottoms. He kissed her lightly beneath her belly button as he lowered her pants.

Butterflies flittered in her belly as he took off her pajamas. He slid them ever-so-slowly over her thighs and over her feet. They landed in a heap at the foot of the bed.

Realizing she was completely naked to his gaze, she covered her breasts with her hands.

Brody settled himself to the right of Lou. "Don't you dare cover yourself." He licked around her fingers with the moist tip of his tongue. He lifted her fingers playfully to gain access to her nipple. The sensations were overwhelming.

Brody drew small circles on her flat stomach with his hand. Lou's stomach flipped as he ran his hand over her hip and cupped her bottom. His fingers returned to her stomach and then dipped into the auburn curls at the juncture of her thighs. She stiffened. His mouth caught hers and kept it occupied while one finger slid down through her curls and into her heat. He sighed against her lips. He slid one finger to the entrance of her core. She moved slightly against his hand. He moved from the center of her to the little nub that was her pleasure center and rubbed it slowly. She moved against his hand. He drew another circle. Her hips lifted from the bed.

Brody raised himself up on his elbows and settled himself between her parted thighs. She tipped her hips up toward him and squirmed. She would surely explode from all the sensations that were shooting through her body.

He insistently pressed against her center, gritting his teeth as he slid inside. His arms shook. She moved a little beneath him, urging him to go deeper. He did. He plunged into her.

She tensed when he entered her, crying out softly at the pain of it. He stopped and looked into her face. Small tears fell from between her clenched eyelashes.

"What the..."

She reached up and pulled his head down to hers, capturing his mouth in a fiery kiss.

He tore his mouth from hers and placed his forehead against hers, taking great gulps of air. He kissed the tears away from the corners of her eyes. He stayed still inside her, giving her time to adjust to the size of him. Then he started to move slowly. Her breath caught. He lifted her knee and whispered, "Put your legs around me."

She locked her feet around his back. The sensation suddenly changed. She met him, thrust for thrust. She felt the tension building and she reached for it until it finally found her. Great waves of pleasure pushed her over the cliff. Brody fell with her as she went over.

Brody lay with his head on Lou's chest, her legs still tangled with his, his breaths trying to catch up with his heartbeat. He lifted himself to his elbows and touched his lips to hers softly. Her gaze avoided his. He kissed her lips again. She did not respond.

"Lou?"

She sighed wearily. "Yeah?"

"Please don't tell me you hated every minute of that. "His uncertainty was her undoing.

She touched his cheek, her eyes finally meeting his. "No…I didn't hate any of it. Couldn't you tell?"

"I certainly thought so. But there was that one moment…"

She pushed his shoulders, urging him to move from on top of her.

"I don't know what you're talking about," she said as he slid from between her thighs. She sat up in bed and swung her feet to the floor. She walked across the darkened room, naked, to the bathroom, and tied her hair in a clumsy ponytail. She turned on the shower and waited a moment, then stepped in and pulled the shower curtain. Within seconds, a cool breeze blew across her skin as he stepped in with her and then his warm body enveloped hers.

"Brody!"

"Lou!" he mocked her tone.

"Would you get out!" she whispered vehemently at him.

"Nope. I need a shower, too."

"You do not. Get out." She pushed his chest away from her. He pulled her closer to him, his arms locking behind her.

"Do so. Do you want to see?" She felt his hardness against her belly. She shook her head. "Guess not." He shrugged his shoulders. "If you were to take a look, you would see I am wearing the same blood that's all over your thighs." She gasped. "But, now when I think about it, that might be a little painful to look at. Know why?" He felt the tip of her nose brush against his chest as she shook her head no. "Because, if you acknowledged it and I acknowledged it, that would mean we have to discuss it."

"D-Discuss what?" she stammered.

He pushed her back under the spray and lifted one leg so that her foot rested on the side of the tub. He picked up the soap and lathered a wash cloth, then gently started to wash her inner thighs. "That would mean we would have to discuss the fact you were a virgin."

"I don't know what you're talking about."

"Don't lie to me, Lou. It's been a long time since I've been with a virgin, but I haven't forgotten the way it feels. The proof is all over you...and me." He rinsed the washcloth and started to clean himself. Lou stood completely still.

"Does it matter to you?" she asked gently.

"Of course it matters to me." He kissed her gently and reached behind her to turn off the water. "It would have mattered to me a lot more if I had known ahead of time. I would have been gentler."

He opened the shower curtain and grabbed a towel off the rack. He wiped her face with it gently and then dried her arms and legs. He wrapped the towel around her and tucked it between her breasts. Then he grabbed one for himself and rubbed it across his hair and then tied it around his waist. He pushed her gently into the bedroom where he stripped the blood stained coverlet from her bed.

He tugged gently on the edge of her towel where it was tucked between her breasts. It fell from her body. He removed his own and slid between the sheets on her bed.

He tugged her fingertips until she joined him. They lay facing one another.

"There's just one more thing I need to know." He fiddled with the hair that hung over her forehead.

"What's that?" Lou asked quietly.

"Unless Sarah was some kind of Immaculate Conception, she's not your daughter." She tensed.

"She is my daughter!" Lou attempted to sit up and move away from him, but he grabbed her around the waist and pulled her back in bed. He pulled her back against his front, her bottom cradled by his thighs.

"Lou," he sighed and spoke close to her ear. "She's your daughter now, but you didn't give birth to her. That much is obvious." He reached around her hips to the skin above her womanly curls. Her belly flipped. He searched her flat stomach with his fingertips. "No scar. No cesarean. Who's her biological mother?"

"Oh, Brody." Tears welled up in her eyes but she refused to let them fall. She took a deep breath. "Can we enjoy the rest of the night and discuss this tomorrow?"

"You promise we'll come back to this topic?"

"Yeah, I promise."

He pulled her closer to him, one arm beneath her cheek as the other stroked her back. "Yeah. We can talk about it tomorrow. You care if I stay for a while?" He pulled the sheet up over them both.

"You had better," she responded as her eyes closed.

****

Wes's cell phone rang in his pocket. He put down his cue stick, reached for it and flipped it open, "Yeah, Boss?"

"Did you get it yet?"

"No. Not yet." He heard a growl on the other end of the line and loud curses. "I told her she has seven days to produce what you want. I gave her a little scare because I sent the note by way of her daughter." He laughed maliciously.

"Good thinking. Hit her where it hurts."

"She'll give you what you want. She would hate for something to happen to that pretty little girl."

"I want what's mine. Get it." The phone clicked off.

****

Lou woke at dawn, as usual, and sat up quickly in bed. She clutched the sheet to her naked body. Naked! Oh, my God! The pillow beside her own was still warm and smelled like Brody. She buried her face in his pillow and sniffed deeply. She smiled broadly but the smile was quickly replaced by a frown.

What had she done? She'd had sex with Brody. Wild and crazy sex. Fabulous, mind blowing sex. And now he knew. He knew her secret. She had kept it hidden for so many years. Jeb, Sadie, John, and Mrs. Wester were the only ones who knew her secret. Now there was one more person. He knew! He knew Sarah wasn't truly her daughter. She wasn't her biological daughter, at least.

Lou swung her legs over the edge of the bed and winced. She was sore in places she didn't know she had. She dressed quickly and put her hair into a ponytail. She put on her running shoes, even though she did not feel like running.

This was the day of Mrs. Wester's funeral with the service and internment at noon. She wasn't required to make breakfast because most of the hands were off for the day, but she could still fry bacon and eggs for Jeb, Sadie, and John. *And Brody. Don't forget about Brody. How can I forget Brody?* Just one thought of him made her pulse race as she remembered him from the night before. She flushed as she recalled the way his hands had moved across her body and the tender way he held her as she went to sleep. She shook the distraction from her mind like a dog shakes after a bath and walked downstairs.

She walked into the kitchen, prepared to find Sadie and Jeb sitting at the kitchen table reading the paper and drinking a cup of coffee with John. But they weren't there. Just Brody. Only Brody. Brody lowered the paper and peered over the top of it. She only saw his eyes but she saw them darken as his glance focused on hers. Light gray turned to steel as his eyes raked over her body from head to toe. He stripped her naked with just one glance.

Lou took a deep breath and turned to pour herself a cup of coffee. Strong arms moved around her waist and he placed a light kiss on her neck. She jumped and then leaned back into him. The awkwardness was quickly forgotten. "Good morning," he murmured as his lips traveled across her shoulder, his hands pressed firmly to her belly.

"Morning," she said quietly, her head thrown back on his shoulder. Her pulse began to quicken.

"You sleep okay?" he asked against her throat.

"Like a baby," she responded.

"No nightmares?"

"Not a one."

He turned her around in his arms. Her hands automatically went around his neck. Her eyes smiled into his.

"That's amazing. That must be the first full night of sleep you've had in weeks."

"Amazing doesn't begin to describe it. How did you sleep?" she asked.

"I had this lovely lady with her bottom in my lap all night. Coupled with memories of devouring her just moments before, how do you think I slept?"

"Poorly?"

"Nope. I woke up a few times," his lips touched tenderly to hers. "I wanted to ravish you again but I didn't. I am such a gentleman."

"Why didn't you?"

"Why didn't I what?"

"Why didn't you ravish me again?" she asked quietly. "You don't want me anymore?"

He pressed his forehead to hers and took a deep breath. He reached around and put his hands in her back pockets, pulling her fast and hard against him. She could feel his arousal against her belly.

"Does it feel like I don't want you anymore? I want you more than I want to take my next breath. But I thought you might be sore." He flicked her nose playfully.

Heat crept up her cheeks.

"It's just one of those things that happen."

"Yes, sir, Dr. Wester." She saluted him smartly.

He kissed her on the lips again and then they heard boots moving across the porch. They bolted apart like two wayward children caught stealing cookies.

****

The funeral service was a huge affair. The church overflowed with friends, family and business associates. Lou was relieved when it was finally over and glad when the house came into view from the limo ringing them back home. They pulled up to the house and got out of the car. Lou turned and walked into the house after Sadie and Jeb. Brody walked slowly behind her. Then he heard the limo driver call out. "Dr. Wester?"

"Yes?"

The driver held out a plain paper envelope to him. "I found this in the limo last night. I thought one of you might have dropped it."

Brody took the note from his outstretched hand and read it slowly. His eyebrows narrowed together. Then he looked at the picture enclosed.

"I know who this belongs to. I'll be sure she gets it. Thanks for bringing it for her."

"No problem, sir. My condolences on the death of your mother."

"Thank you." Brody clapped him on the shoulder and stuck the envelope in his suit pocket. He walked into the house.

Chapter Fourteen

Everyone changed clothes and lingered over a long lunch at the kitchen table. The mood was somber. The farm was quiet. Most of the hands had the day off and were spending the time with family or friends after the funeral. Lou was looking forward to being alone with Brody the way that someone might look forward to going to the dentist. One thought of the way he kissed her had her face filling with heat. And other places. But one thought of having to explain Sarah's parentage made her ice right back up.

Lou strolled out to the barn and looked over the stall door at one of the new foals. The gangly little one was just getting steady on his feet, toddling around the stall. The brood mare hung her head over the stall door and nudged Lou's pocket, looking for a piece of peppermint or a sugar cube. Lou smirked and produced one. "Girl, I know you so well. I think you would sell that baby for a piece of peppermint." She unwrapped the peppermint and held it in the palm of her hand. The horse ate it hungrily while Lou stroked her face.

"Mrs. Wester would have been really proud of you today, girl," Lou said. "That's one healthy looking baby you have, there."

The horse nudged her pocket again. "Sorry, girl, that's all I have." Lou held up both hands in surrender and stepped away from the door.

"Good thing a Boy Scout always comes prepared," John said as he hobbled up behind her. He was no longer on crutches but he still had to wear a walking cast for four more weeks.

He pulled a peppermint from his own pocket, unwrapped it, and held it out to the mare. "Do you know this one was bred with Wester's Folly? So that's a little champion we have there."

"I don't think you're supposed to be out here, are you?" Lou asked him, shaking her motherly finger at him.

John sighed long and loud. "Lou, if I have to stay cooped up inside for one more minute, I'm going to lose my mind. I love Sadie to death but she's driving me nuts." He puffed his chest out like a strutting rooster and grinned. "Sometimes, a man's just got to act like a man." Then his chest deflated.

Lou laughed out loud at his antics.

"What are you doing for the rest of the day?" John asked shyly.

He was plotting something. She just didn't know what. "I don't have any specific plans. Why?" He would drop some sort of trouble in her lap without even thinking about it twice.

"There's a stallion two counties over I want to go and take a look at. He's still a young'un but I think he would be a great sire. He has great bloodlines. Today is the only day I can go and look at him. The bank is foreclosing on the property and they are selling all the horses at auction. If I can sneak the stallion out before they do, I have a chance at getting him."

"So, why don't you go and look at him?" Lou asked. "Doesn't Jeb usually go with you for things like that?"

"See, Lou, that's the problem. This one is going to be mine. I have some money saved up and I want to get my own stallion. I want to train him, work with him, and stud him out. I want to see if I am any good." He kicked up sawdust from the barn floor with the toe of his cast. Then he pointed at it. "But, see, this thing is in my way. I can't drive." He put on his best little boy's pleading face and gracelessly dropped to one knee. "Will you, please, please, please be my…"

A third voice broke in, "I swear to God, John. If you ask that girl to marry you, I'll knock you flat on your ass."

John whispered the last word so that only Lou could hear it, "…chauffeur?" Then he smiled broadly and rose to his feet. They both turned to look at Brody.

His grey eyes flashed as his cheeks reddened. "Just what the hell is going on here?"

John rushed to explain, "Brody, I was just asking Lou…"

"No need to explain, John." She touched his arm gently. "I accept your proposal. Why don't you go inside and see if Sadie can watch Sarah and then we'll go."

"Go where?" Brody growled through gritted teeth.

Lou pushed John toward the door. "Go ahead." She shooed him with her pointed finger.

Brody grabbed Lou's elbow and spun her around as soon as John was outside of the barn. "And just where do you two think you're going?"

"Why is that any of your business?" Lou threw back at him.

He grabbed both of her arms and pulled her to him. "Do I need to remind you why it's suddenly my business?" he said, his mouth inches from hers.

Despite her anger, Lou felt her pulse begin to quicken. She pushed it down and let the anger rise back to the surface. "How dare you manhandle me?" She shrugged her arms out of his grasp and stepped away from him. "Don't ever grab me like that again." She stomped out of the barn and toward the house.

****

Brody watched her through the barn door as she walked to the house, spoke to Sadie, grabbed her purse, and kissed Sarah on the head. She slid into the driver's seat of John's pickup truck and John got in on the passenger side. Brody watched as John turned to Lou and smiled. Damn them. Where the hell were they going?

Brody's mood became more and more disturbing as the day wore on. He sat on the front porch, tapping his foot on the wooden planks, his muscles drawn tight as guitar strings. Jeb walked through the screen door and sat down in the chair beside Brody's.

"You look nervous as cat sitting in a room full of rocking chairs, boy," Jeb said quietly, talking around a toothpick.

Brody stopped thumping his foot long enough to shoot Jeb a heated glance.

"You waiting for her to get back with John?" Jeb asked pointedly.

"Who? Lou?" Brody chewed his fingernails.

"Who else?" Jeb chuckled. "I doubt it's John who has your tail in such a twist."

"Actually, it's both of them. They just took off and didn't say a word about when they would be back. I had hoped to get to talk to Lou before I leave to go home tonight. I wanted to talk with her about something important."

"How important?" Jeb asked.

"I'm not sure, Jeb." Brody sighed and reached into his back pocket, retrieving the envelope Lou had dropped in the limo the night before. He held it out to Jeb. "Do you know what this is about?"

Jeb accepted the envelope and opened it with his weathered old fingers. "This looks like it's her business, Brody."

"Not any more, Jeb. I want it to be my business now." He drew in a deep breath. "I had hoped to get to talk to her about it before I left today. But then I acted like an ass and she took off with John."

Jeb chucked again and adjusted the toothpick in his mouth. "That happens to all of us sometimes. What are you in such a hurry to get home for?"

"Work, Jeb. I have a lot of work to catch up on." He ran a hand through his hair in frustration.

"Is that really what you want?" Jeb asked candidly.

Brody sighed. "I don't know what I want, Jeb."

"I think you need to figure it out. Quickly," Jeb replied. He waved the envelope. "But don't you worry none about this. I'll see what's going on."

"My flight is at eight tonight, Jeb. Can you give me a ride to the airport?"

"If that's what you need, I reckon I can."

Brody got up from the chair and went inside to pack his suitcase.

****

As Lou and John pulled out of the drive, Lou reached over, pulled her sunglasses from her purse and put them on. Her hand tapped against the steering wheel.

John sang out, "Somebody's got a boyfriend..."

She looked at him out of the corner of her eye. He continued to grin at her boyishly. It was hard not to laugh at John sometimes, no matter how stern she wanted to be.

"I bet he's seeing red right now because you just drove off with me." He patted his chest proudly, a feigned show of bravado.

"He was seeing red before I drove off with you," Lou mumbled at him.

John soberly replied, "Jealousy is a hard emotion to deal with, Lou."

"He doesn't have any reason to be jealous. It's not like he's staying or anything. We don't even have a relationship."

"Sure looked like a relationship to me, with the way he was clinging to you at the funeral."

"He wasn't clinging," Lou protested.

"Yeah, right." John snorted.

"You think he was clinging?" she asked shyly.

"Well, yeah," he said sarcastically, rolling his eyes.

"Maybe he was a little," she said quietly.

John snorted.

The afternoon passed quickly after the mood shifted. Lou and John pulled up outside around six o'clock with John grinning from ear to ear, having just purchased his first stallion. He sat down beside Jeb to tell him all about it.

Lou got out of the truck. Her legs stuck to the seat of the truck and her skin pulled tight as she slid across the seat after the long ride home. She was hungry, irritable, and still more than a little ticked off at Brody. She sighed long and loud as she looked across the driveway and saw him stomping toward her across the graveled drive. She put one finger up and halted him with just one word.

"Don't." She walked around him, creating a wide circle. He stepped in front of her and blocked her path. She avoided looking at him and just walked around him again.

He huffed. Then asked quietly, "Would it help if I said I was sorry?"

She finally stopped and looked at him. She crossed her arms against her chest and tapped one foot, looking him in the eye. "Sorry for what?" She probably shouldn't goad him, but it was hard not to.

"Sorry for acting like a jackass?" he asked with a questioning look on his face.

"Brody Wester, if you don't know why I'm mad, I'm certainly not going to tell you!" She stepped around him again. He blocked her again.

"Damn it, Lou," he groaned. He sighed deeply and said with a straight face. "I am sorry for acting like a jackass this morning."

She crossed her arms across her chest again. "Then why did you?"

"Jesus," he whispered. Then louder, "I don't know. He stepped close enough to her that only she could hear him. "I spent the most amazing night making love to you. Then I had to get up and leave you all alone in bed before the sun even came up."

"And that put you in the foul mood?" she asked sarcastically.

"Yes. Well. No. Not exactly. Then I got to kiss you in the kitchen but we had to spring apart so no one would see. Then I walked into the barn and John was on his knees in front of you."

"He wanted a favor, Brody," she confessed. "He was begging. John does that all the time because he knows it works."

"Well, it looked different than that," he declared like a six-year-old.

"So, you were jealous?" she asked.

"So jealous I couldn't see straight, Lou. I know I have no right to be, so I apologize." He kicked at the dirt with the toe of his shoe.

"No right to be?" she asked quietly.

"Can we take a walk and discuss this privately?" Brody asked.

Lou placed her purse on the edge of the porch and walked with him toward the barns and the pond.

"You were saying you have no right to be jealous," Lou prompted.

"Well, yeah. I can't put a big stamp on you that says 'Brody's Property' like I want to. Because I have to go home."

"But you want to? You want to put a big stamp on me that mark me as yours?"

Out of sight of the house, Brody pulled her close to him and said, "Oh, yeah. I want to put a big stamp right here." He punctuated the statement with a kiss to her forehead. "And I want to put a big stamp right here." He kissed the side of her neck. One hand moved up to cup her breast. "And I particularly want to put one right here." His thumb moved across her nipple. She could feel his hardness pressed against her belly. She stilled his hand with her own, even though her hands were shaking.

"But you won't. Because you have to go home." She stepped back, out of his embrace. She took a deep breath and then dove right in. "What are your plans for the farm, Brody, now that your mom is gone? For me? Do you plan to keep me on? I get to keep my job?"

"Is your job what you're worried about right now?" Brody asked, his steely gray eyes flashing with anger.

"That and other things. I guess I just want to be sure I'll still be needed, still have a place to live, still have a job." He kicked at the dirt with his toe again. "Actually, I don't know what I'm going to do with the place, yet. I have to meet with Mother's attorneys in a couple of weeks. They'are putting together the estate now."

"You're not thinking of selling, are you?" Lou snapped at him.

"I don't know what I'm thinking, yet, Lou. I don't even know what my mother's plans were yet. She might have everything tied up in a nice and neat little package. She might not give me any choices."

"And you just hate that, don't you? Having your choices taken away?" Lou snapped at him.

"Yes! I do hate that. I hate to have my choices taken away. I hate to give in. I'm a doctor, for Christ's sake, Lou. That's what I always wanted to be."

"You enjoyed the past month here." Lou stated blandly.

"Yes. I did. I enjoyed it very much but I didn't even break ground. Running this place is a big operation."

"You could always do what your mother has done." Lou said quietly.

"What's that?"

"Leave it to the people who know how to do it."

"Why are we even discussing this right now?" He practically growled at her. "I wanted to walk with you so I could apologize."

"You already did."

"I must have missed it. Did you accept, Lou? Trying to talk to you is like trying to make a chair out of a cactus. It's painful no matter how you look at it."

"I accept your apology for acting like a jackass this morning."

Brody grinned. He tried to hide it. But he failed. "I'm not sure that's an accurate description of my actions."

"Oh, I'm sure," Lou replied blandly.

He touched her hand and brought it to his lips, a slow smile spreading across his face. He turned her hand over and kissed her palm. When he did, turned her hand to look at the face on her watch.

"Damn. I have to go." Brody said.

"Go where?" Lou asked.

"Home, Lou. I told you. I have to go home."

"When?"

"My flight leaves at eight."

"Today?"

He nodded. "Yeah. Today."

He took her hand and started walking back toward the house. This time, they did not spring apart or hide. He held her hand all the way up to the back porch, then he held the door open for her and ushered her in.

Lou was startled to find a packed bag beside the back door with old airline tags attached. She pushed it to the back of her mind.

Sadie had the kitchen table set and had dinner served. Lou perfunctorily ate some meatloaf and made idle small talk with Sarah. John couldn't stop talking about his new horse and how he couldn't wait to bring him home. Jeb and Sadie sat quietly watching the emotions that were flying around the room.

After dinner, Brody sat his napkin in his plate and rose from the table. "I guess it's time for me to get going." Jeb wasn't quite finished with his meal. He started to rise from his chair, anyway. "Stay there, Jeb. You're not even done yet. I'll just call a cab and take it to the airport."

Lou broke in. "There's no need to do all that. I'm done. I can take you."

"You don't mind?"

"Not at all. And waiting for a cab out here might make you late."

"If you don't mind, I would appreciate it."

Lou got her purse and met Brody at the Jeep. He rolled up the plastic roof to open the interior to the night sky and the breeze. "You don't mind some wind, do you?"

"No. I love it," Lou replied.

Brody threw his bag in the back of the Jeep and slid into the driver's seat. Lou got in the passenger's side and turned on the radio. Brody backed out, gravel flying behind them as they hit the main road. They traveled a few miles in silence and then Lou felt the Jeep begin to slow. She looked around absently, not quite sure where they were.

Brody pulled down a long and winding driveway to the back of an old barn and stopped the car. He turned the key backward so that the radio stayed on. He leaned his seat all the way back and gazed up at the stars.

"We don't have stars like this at home," he said blandly.

"You wanted to stop and look at the stars? What is this place?"

"This, my lady friend, just happens to be where I used to go parking with the girls when I was in high school. I was quite a catch. A whole lot of necking went on behind this barn."

Lou laughed. "I bet you had some smooth moves back then."

"Back then? You make me sound like I'm ancient." He chuckled. "I still have some smooth moves, thank you."

Brody sat up and leaned across Lou. He pulled the lever that caused her seat to recline and she was suddenly on her back, looking up at the stars.

"Was that one of them?" she laughed.

He leaned over her and scratched his chin thoughtfully. "Now that I think about it, I believe it was. But I always got farther with a different one."

"Which one was that?" Lou asked breathlessly.

"That would be this one." Brody sat back in his seat and looked up at the stars again. Lou sat up in her own seat and looked at him speculatively.

"I don't get it," she said blandly. Then Brody grabbed her arm and flipped her over, effortlessly, so she was lying on top of him, face to face. He kissed her temple. "Put your head on my shoulder. And just breathe with me for a minute, will you?"

Lou did as he suggested, taking a deep breath. It felt good. "This is how you got the girls to go parking with you?"

"Nope. I've never done this with anyone else. I just wanted to feel you stretched out on top of me. I think I like it." He touched his lips gently to hers. She kissed him back. He deepened the kiss, his mouth slanted against hers, their tongues warring. Lou broke the kiss.

"You're going to miss your flight." She tried to sit up. He pulled her back down.

"Nope. I called before we left. My flight has been delayed by one hour." Then he whispered. "So I have one hour to make love to you. If you want me to."

Did she want him to? Lou nodded against his chest. "Would it be terrible if I said I do want you to?" she asked softly.

"Not for me," Brody said, unbuttoning his shirt. "It would be like heaven." He opened his shirt and laid her against his chest. She brushed her fingers in his chest hair and absently stroked his nipple.

"Not fair. You have too many clothes on," he complained.

Impulsively, Lou sat up in his lap, her thighs straddling his and pulled her shirt over her head. Her actions left her in a slinky pink bra through which he could probably see her nipples plainly. But she didn't care. God, what was she becoming? Brody cupped a breast in each hand and toyed with her nipples. She threw her head back and

drew in a ragged breath as Brody reached between her breasts and unhooked her bra. He pulled it off her shoulders and laid it on the seat beside them. Sitting up slightly, he captured one nipple in his mouth, lathing it with his tongue, and biting gently with his teeth. Lou's heartbeat sped up and sweat broke out on her brow. Brody reached for the button on her shorts and unfastened them. Then he unzipped the zipper. The noise was amplified in the quiet.
Lou stiffened.

"It's okay," he soothed, now paying attention to her other breast. "It's just that damned zipper."

Lou reached down between her thighs and grabbed his belt buckle. She maneuvered the leather out of the buckle and unbuttoned his pants. He stilled her hands and patted her leg. "I'll finish this. You figure out a way to get these off." He tapped his fingers on her leg.

Lou scooted away from him and instantly felt the cool night air surround her. She lifted her bottom and slid her shorts and panties off, kicking her shoes off as she did so. When she looked back over at him, he had pushed his pants down to his ankles and his manhood was displayed proudly. She flushed.

Brody tore open a small package with his teeth. She watched as he rolled a condom over his length. "I forgot it last time." He looked at her sheepishly.

Sensing her discomfort, he picked her up and set her back over his lap, one leg on each side of his. He pulled her face down for a searing kiss, toying with her breast as it hung over him. Lou groaned low in her throat.

"God, I want you," Brody breathed.

Lou bit her bottom lip. "We can't do it like this."

"Oh, yes, we can." He whispered in her ear, "I want you to ride me."

"Brody!" she protested. But she was intrigued. "I don't know what to do."

He grabbed her hips and lifted her over him. She felt him at her entrance, hot and hard against her. He pushed in slightly. "Tell me if I hurt you."

"Doesn't hurt yet," she whispered. She sank lower over him, feeling the gentle glide of him into her wetness. A muscle in his jaw ticked. She stopped moving. "Are you okay?"

"Oh, much better than that," he mumbled, capturing her mouth with his.

He grabbed her hips and lifted her slightly. He slid out, hovering at her entrance. She gasped. Then she sank down on him again. She quickly found a rhythm and kept it, his tongue in her mouth and one hand manipulating her nipple. Her legs began to shake and he whispered in her ear, "Sit up." She did and she felt all of him. She threw her head back in abandon and moved up and down as he cupped one breast in each hand. He flicked his thumbs across her nipples. Her movements became jerky, her breathing labored. She continued to rise and fall against him. He reached between them and found her pleasure center. She gasped, sank down on him and a million stars exploded behind her eyes. Brody shuddered beneath her as she collapsed against his chest.

Lou lay on top of him for a few long moments, drawing in deep breaths that matched his own. Then she started to move away from him. He pulled her back down. "Don't go yet."

She sat up on her elbows, her dark hair hanging in her face. He tucked it behind her ear and kissed her gently. "I could look at you like this all night."

"You could, but you're not going to." She moved away from him, feeling him withdraw from her body. She opened the door of the Jeep and stepped out, naked, her clothes in her hand, completely unashamed. She began to dress. "You can't because you are going back home and I'm staying here."

"You knew that's what I was going to do, Lou." He sighed.

"Yes. I did," she stated calmly.

"Then why do you seem disappointed?" he asked calmly as he lifted his rear and pulled his boxers and pants up.

"I'm not disappointed." She replied calmly. *Let him think it's not about us.* "I'm worried."

"About?"

"About what's going to happen to the farm. To our jobs." To you. To me. What have we started?

"To us?" Brody asked quietly.

"I'm not worried about what's going to happen to us."

"You're not?"

"No." *Liar!* her inner voice screamed. *You're such a liar!* "There is no us."

Brody gritted his teeth. "I already told you I have to talk with the attorneys to find out what my mother's plans were for the farm. She could have deeded it to a charity, for all I know."

"You never asked her?" Lou asked incredulously.

"Lou, I just came home for the first time in years. My mother was dying when I got here." He ran his fingers through his hair in frustration. "I certainly wasn't going to say, 'Hey, Mom! Long time, no see. What are your plans for all your assets?'"

Lou rolled her eyes.

"When you find out, will you let me know?" Her voice was quiet. So choked with emotion that she was ashamed of herself.

"You'll be one of the first people I tell." He crossed his heart with his fingers. "I promise."

Lou tucked her shirt into her pants and climbed back into the Jeep. She adjusted her pants and said, "I couldn't find my panties. Help me find them, will you?" She looked under the seat. Brody reached into his pocket and withdrew a lacy slip of fabric.

He held them out, "Do you mean these?" He grinned wolfishly at her.

She reached for them and he pulled them out of her grasp, grinning wildly, stuffing them back in the pocket. "You'll just have to do without. Because those are going home with me." Lou shook her head reproachfully.

She looked around, picked up the condom wrapper from the floor and tucked it into a discarded Coke can on the floor. "I'll certainly never look at this Jeep the same way again."

Brody reached over and grabbed the back of her head. He pulled her in for a quick kiss. "Neither will I," he replied, laughing quietly.

She kissed him back.

He started the Jeep and reached over to take her hand.

"You know what, Lou?"

"What?"

"We never did have that talk you promised?"

"What talk?" She tried to play dumb.

"The one where you explain why you were still a virgin yet you have a daughter."

She flinched. "I don't want to discuss it now," was her only reply.

"When would be a good time?"

"Never?" She made a job of twirling a piece of hair around her finger.

"Not good enough," he replied.

"Ok. How about this? I'll tell you my secrets when you call me to tell me what your plans are for the farm."

"Deal," he answered.

"Deal," she agreed.

Chapter Fifteen

Lou dropped Brody off at the airport and was surprised when he grabbed her by the waist and pulled her in for a long, slow kiss that stole her breath. Her knees shook and tears hid behind her eyelids as she pulled away from him and climbed into the driver's seat. She dared not speak and she couldn't look back as she drove away.

She drove home with the wind caressing her cheeks and making her hair fly haphazardly around her face. She sang along with the radio until a sad country song had her feeling as forlorn as the love-stricken subject of the song must have felt. Tears rolled from beneath her lashes and drenched her face like a torrential storm. She finally pulled over onto the side of the road when the sobs took her breath and her vision blurred from the assaulting tears.

She dropped her face into her hands and let the tears fall. For years, she had devoutly sworn she did not possess the girly emotions that make one fall prey to the pains of the heart. But now she realized the truth. She had sworn off tears and heartache because she had never been in love. And what an emotion to have missed for so long!

Lou sat on the side of the road with her head in her hands until the shaking subsided. Then she took a deep breath, wiped her face with her shirttail, and put both hands on the wheel. She started the Jeep and turned to look for traffic before pulling out into the street. Seeing headlights approaching, she waited for them to pass but noticed they slowed as they approached her. A dark four-door sedan slowed and pulled off the road in front of the Jeep. She froze as she saw a tall gentleman get out of the car. The baseball cap immediately made Lou jump and put the Jeep in gear.

His crisp, clear voice rang out. "I wouldn't do that if I were you, Mary Lou."

Lou froze where she was when he reached for the holster under his jacket. She took a deep breath and lifted her chin. "What do you want?"

He placed one hand on the roll bar behind her seat and the other on the frame of the windshield, effectively boxing her in. He smiled a smile that did not reach his eyes. "You seem like such a smart girl, Mary Lou." He raised a cigar to his mouth and bit the end off of it. He took his sweet time lighting it and then blew a stream of cherry smoke into Lou's face. "I want you to give me what I asked for."

"Right now, you're asking for a black eye, but I doubt that's what you really want," Lou tossed back at him with more bravado than she actually felt. Her knees shook as her eyes met his.

"Oh, you are so funny!" he said mockingly. He absently picked up a lock of hair from her shoulder and ran it between his fingers. "You remind me of your mother. She was all piss and vinegar, too. She was smart, a lot like you."

"I am nothing like my mother," Lou spat back at him.

"You're more like her than you want to admit," he responded quietly. Then his voice was suddenly loud and abrasive. "I don't think you understand the kind of pressure I'm under. My boss wants that little item your mom gave to you."

Lou's voice was just as loud, despite the tremor that escaped with it. She punctuated each word. "I. Don't. Know. What. You're. Talking. About!"

"Black bag, Lou. I want what was in the black bag. Then I'll walk away and never darken your door again." He smirked at her.

"What if I can't give it to you? What then? What will you do?" Lou sat forward and steeled herself. "How much do you want for it? The contents of the bag? What would make you happy?"

"Well, well. Little Miss High-and-Mighty has some money to throw around, huh?" He took another draw from his cigar.

"I have some savings. Tell me what you want." She sounded surer than she felt. "I can get it."

Lou relaxed visibly when he stepped back from the car.

"I'll check with my boss and find out if there's an amount that would be suitable. Then I'll be in touch."

"How long?"

He appeared to mull it over. "I'll come and see you soon."

He didn't wait for her response but turned to go back to his own car. He tapped the back fender of the Jeep as he walked away.

Lou started the Jeep with a trembling hand and pulled out into the street. She drove home as fast as she could safely go and slammed on brakes in the driveway, throwing up a shower of gravel as she did so.

She jumped out of the Jeep, ran to the kitchen door, and walked in. Sadie, Jeb, and John were sitting at the kitchen table and were surprised by her entrance. She walked over to the table and sat down, looking each of them in the eye in turn. Calmly, she stated, "We need to talk."

Lou recounted her experience to the only three people in the world who knew her history and where she came from. As they talked, Jeb admitted he was already aware something was going on as he pulled the last correspondence from Wes out of his pocket.

"Where did you get this?" she asked pointedly.

"You dropped it in the limo. The driver gave it to Brody and he gave it to me. I told him I would take care of it."

Sadie rose to her feet and squared her shoulders. "That does it. I have been wanting to go and visit my sister. This seems like just as good a time as any." She met eyes with Jeb across the table. "We'll all go, take a little break, and get away for a while."

Lou reached out and grabbed Sadie's hand. She said softly, "That sounds like a grand plan, but I can't run from this anymore. I have to stay here and see this through."

John spoke up. "Well, if Lou stays, I'm not going. I'll stay right here and take care of her." They all looked down at his broken ankle that was even now propped on a pillow. "Well, I can at least offer moral support." He blushed. "Besides, I have three mares all ready to foal and there is no way I can leave them," he added with conviction.

"Then it looks like Sadie, Sarah, and I will be taking a short vacation," Jeb said, smacking the table top lightly with the flat of his hand. Lou nodded solemnly, her only concern that Sarah should be as far from the farm as possible.

Sadie nodded, worry lines etched across her forehead. "We'll leave on Sunday morning, if that plan is okay with the rest of you."

"He won't be back before then."

"Then it's settled," Jeb stated.

"It's settled," Lou agreed, as she walked from the room.

****

As soon as Lou was safely out of earshot, Jeb removed his wallet from his back pocket and took a card from the sleeve. He picked up the phone and dialed. He said, "Brody, I know you probably aren't even on the plane but give us a call when you come in. I need to discuss something with you." He hung up and gazed solemnly at Sadie and John. "We might just need that boy's help."

"He was away for a long time and left just as fast. What makes you think he'll want to come back so soon?" Sadie questioned.

"I think he has more that's tying him to this ranch than just his mother. "

"And if it's not?" Sadie wrung her hands.

"Give the boy some credit. He was brought up to know what's important, even if he forgot for a while. He can't run from everyone who loves him."

****

Lou walked around in a fearful trance. The most taxing thing she did over the next few days was help some of the ranch hands herd the wild mare into a foaling pen. Her delivery date was quickly approaching and Lou was afraid for her to foal in the wild because of animals that would pose a threat to the new foal. They were able to move her with enough riders on horseback that they didn't even need to rope her. They just herded her into a fenced area close to the barns.

During the day, Lou jumped at non-existent shadows; at night, she fought demons that clutched at her throat and stole her breath. Between the bad dreams, she also fought the memories of Brody that crept across her skin like a gentle breeze.

On Saturday afternoon, Sarah woke and wanted to go play outside. Lou wouldn't let her out of her sight, so she grabbed a book and went to sit on the front porch so she could watch Sarah play in the yard. The child could entertain herself for hours on the swing set or in a pile of dirt. John came out and joined Lou on the porch.

He sat down in the rocker beside her and asked quietly, "You doing all right?"

Lou responded absently, "Fine."

"Why don't I believe you?" he asked, his hand covering hers.

Lou felt the tears threaten to spill over her lashes and dashed them away with the back of her hand.

"You know she's going to be just fine, Lou. She's going away from here with Jeb and Sadie. No safer place she could be."

"I know. I've just never been away from her before," Lou pouted.

"You need to stop," he cajoled gently.

"Can you watch her while I go and wash my face?" Lou asked as she got up from her chair and reached for the screen door.

"Sure thing. Won't take my eyes off her." He made the Boy Scout sign with his fingers. "Scout's honor."

Lou went into the house to the bathroom and splashed some cold water onto her face. She took a long look in the mirror and was surprised by the dark circles under her eyes and the frown lines. She rubbed her cheeks to add some color and fluffed her bangs. She tightened her ponytail and went back outside. As she stepped through the screen door, she raised a hand to shield her eyes so she could block the sun's glare and get a better look at the car throwing up dust as it came down the long driveway.

The red convertible stopped in front of the house and the driver turned off the vehicle. Beautiful feet in strappy, high-heeled sandals hit the ground first, followed by legs that were a mile long. John whistled low under his breath as the driver bent over to retrieve something from the passenger seat, her black miniskirt rising to an almost indecent height.

The beauty stepped up onto the porch and extended a hand to Lou as she swung her head, causing her long, blond, perfectly sculpted hair to fall back over her shoulders.

"You must be Lou," she said boldly as Lou reached to shake the offered and.

"Yes, I am. I think we met at Mrs. Wester's funeral, although your name escapes me." Lou tried to sound just as haughty and well put together, but failed miserably.

"Elizabeth Patton. Brody and I grew up together." She snickered delicately behind her hand and whispered as though it was confidential, "We actually did a little more than just grow up together."

"Boy, did they," John said under his breath. Lou shushed him by slapping his arm.

Lou tried to keep her composure. "Well, what can we do for you, Miss Patton?"

"Actually, I'm here to see Brody. We have a date to prepare for."
"A what?" Lou asked.

"A date?" Elizabeth sounded almost like she was asking the question herself when she looked into Lou's eyes. She tried to sound polite. "I guess no one told you Brody went back home. He's not even here at the farm anymore." Lou thought she could one-up Elizabeth. She failed at that, too.

"He just called me this morning. It was a kind of a last minute thing." Elizabeth twittered her hands in front of her, clutching a clipboard. They both heard the car coming up the drive at the same time and Elizabeth turned and pointed.

"See. There he is now."

"Sure enough," John said. "There's a cab."

"I see that, John. Thanks." Lou ground her teeth together.

The cab stopped and Brody got out of the car and turned to face them, smiling and waving. He had two suitcases and a bag thrown over his shoulder.

John mumbled, "Oh, here we go."

"Would you shut up?" Lou hissed at him.

Brody walked up the steps and took both of Elizabeth's hands in his. He kissed her on the cheek, lingering a little too long. Then he stepped back, still holding her hands and spread them wide. "Damn, you look good."

At least she had the grace to blush as she punched Brody playfully on the shoulder.

She practically bubbled with enthusiasm. "Brody, I'm so glad you called me. I brought some things I want to show you before the date."

Brody dropped his bag off his shoulder and onto the porch. "Well, let's just grab those first so we can take a look at them, why don't we?"

Lou sat down beside John on the porch, her fists clenched in her lap. She brought her hand to her mouth and began to nervously chew her fingernails. John ambled out into the yard to play with Sarah.

For twenty minutes, Lou tortured herself and her fingernails as she sat on the porch. Sarah still played on the swing set. Lou sat and fumed.

How dare he walk right by me and not even acknowledge my presence. How dare he bring his slut to my house? Okay, it is truly his but I live here, too. He just breezed past me like I don't even exist.

She could hear them giggling as they came back out onto the porch. Brody walked with the long-legged freak back to the car. *Guess it is time for their date*, she sneered in her head. Brody reached out and opened the driver's side door. Then the blond bombshell leaned over and placed a kiss on his lips. Just a peck, mind you, but a kiss, nonetheless. She slid into the driver's seat and Brody shut the door. He bent over and she whispered something in his ear. He laughed out loud. She started the car and backed out of the parking space. He waved to her as she drove away without him.

Brody walked slowly up the steps. He stood in front of where she was slumped in the chair, her jaw so tight her head was hurting from the pressure of it. He grabbed her by both elbows and pulled her to her feet. She stepped back and glared at him.

"Nice to see you, too, Lou," he said quietly.

"How dare you?" she snarled.

"How dare I do what?" he asked innocently.

"How dare you bring her here? I can't believe you would do that to me." She sniffled indelicately.

"You're mad at me because Elizabeth was here?" he asked quietly, his eyebrows arched.

"Never mind," Lou grunted and tried to walk past him to go inside the house.

He grabbed her arms and spun her around. "Oh, hell, no, you don't. What's gotten in to you?" She tried to look away but he raised her chin with one finger and forced her to look into his eyes. He stepped back from her and appraised her even more closely. "Oh, God! You think Elizabeth was here to…" He ran a frustrated hand through his hair. "You think she was here for…"

Lou sniffled again. "She said you had a date," she said quietly.

"Jesus, Lou." He muttered. Then his voice grew louder. "I do have a date. But it's not with Elizabeth." He took a deep breath. "It's with Sarah, for Christ's sake."

Lou looked dumbfounded. "With Sarah? Why would you have a date with Sarah?"

"Father-Daughter dance? Remember? I promised my mother I would take her. You forgot, didn't you?" Brody asked.

"The dance? That's w…why you're here?" Lou stuttered.

He grabbed her hand and dragged her through the door. On the kitchen table were piles of items. He picked up a beautiful little sequined dress and held it up in front of him. "I sure as hell can't fit in this." He reached for small shoes and held them up. "And these might pinch my feet just a little." Then he reached for a beautiful wrist corsage. "And I would look pretty silly in this."

"Where did all this come from?" Lou asked quietly.

"Elizabeth brought it. She's a party planner, Lou, so I called her and told her to get whatever it would take to make it a perfect night for a little girl."

Lou covered her mouth with her hand and gasped. "Oh, God, I thought you were going on a date with the girl-so-beautiful-she-could-be-a-model." Then she remembered the kiss and narrowed her eyes. "She kissed you and whispered in your ear." She pointed her finger at him.

He had the nerve to laugh out loud. "Do you want to know what she said?" Lou nodded slowly, her eyes meeting his. He stepped closer to her, taking her hand and laying it on his chest. "She said it really pissed her off I had picked someone twice as pretty as she is. She said it really sucked and she wanted to know if she kissed me really quick if it would make you jealous." He grinned wildly at her. "I guess she was right, huh?"

"I'm not jealous," Lou pouted, as he pulled her closer.

"Liar."

She held her thumb and forefinger about an inch apart. "Maybe just a little." She tucked her head into his chest in shame. "I am so sorry," she mumbled against his shirt.

"How sorry?" he asked, smiling over her head.

"Really sorry?" she answered.

"You had better be.." He pointed to his cheek with his index finger. "Kiss me and tell me hello."

Lou moved to kiss his cheek and he turned his head at the last minute, capturing her mouth with his for a long and tender kiss. His arms wrapped around her like he wanted to draw her into himself.

Lou and Brody heard boots walking across the porch and the sound of a little girl's laughter. As they sprang apart, his look told her they would definitely come back to it later.

Sarah came through the door and Lou gasped at the sight of her daughter. She was covered in dirt from head to toe. "Just what have you two been doing?" Lou scolded.

John and Sarah both looked at her sheepishly. "Playing," they mumbled, looking at the floor. Sarah even had tear tracks through the dirt on her face from where John had tickled her so much her eyes leaked, she complained.

Sarah reached out to touch the sequined dress lying on the table but Lou quickly moved it from her reach. "No way, little lady! No grubby fingers will touch these things!" Lou grabbed Sarah's packages from the table and swatted Sarah on the behind. "Off you go. Upstairs. Bath time." She shooed Sarah toward the stairs.

She turned back and whispered to Brody, "You had better get yourself ready, too. The dance is at six."

Brody grabbed his own packages and went to his room to get dressed.

Lou scrubbed the mud from Sarah's hair and face, turning the water murky by the time that she was done. "You had better get out or Dr. Wester will be taking one little prune to the Father-Daughter dance," Lou chided gently.

"Mommy, do you think any of the other girls will have a date who's not their dad?" Sarah asked as Lou wrapped her in a towel.

"I feel sure some girls will have their stepfather or a granddad as their date. Don't you think so?" Lou asked, as she drew a wide-toothed comb through Sarah's tangled locks.

"Yeah. Probably." Sarah worried her lower lip between her teeth.

Lou turned on the hair dryer and dried Sarah's hair until it flew around her face in a big brown cloud. Then she combed it flat and got out the curling iron. She piled some of Sarah's hair on top of her head to keep it out of her face and secured it with studded barrettes from one of the packages. The rest she rolled into delicate ringlets with the curling iron and sprayed them to keep their shape. She turned Sarah toward the mirror and said, "Tah dah!"

"Wow," Sarah breathed. "I look beautiful like you."

Lou swatted her on the tail again and said, "Let's get you dressed."

Elizabeth had included new panties and tights, so Sarah wiggled into those with some laughter and squeaks as Lou helped. Then Lou pulled the sequined dress over her head, careful not to muss her hair, and adjusted the narrow straps on Sarah's shoulders. Further searching through the packages produced a matching shawl to keep Sarah's shoulders warm. Lou handed her the shoes, made to look like glass slippers, and Sarah stepped into them gracefully.

Lou stepped back and surveyed the whole package. "You are so beautiful," she said and embraced her daughter. "You ready to make your grand entrance?"

Sarah giggled with delight. "Yep!" she shrieked in little girl fashion.

"You wait here for a minute while I go down and get my camera. Plus I'll make sure everyone is ready to see how you look."

Sarah nodded her head, dancing in place, a huge smile on her face.

Lou skipped down the stairs and saw John, Jeb, and Sadie were sitting at the kitchen table. Then she saw Brody, standing beside the table in a sport coat, casual pants, white shirt and tie. He looked amazing. She walked over to him silently and adjusted his tie for him. She gazed up at him softly and whispered, "Thank you."

He bent and kissed her on the cheek. He said loudly with a wink to all, "And just where is my date? I hope she isn't going to stand me up."

Just then, Sarah came bounding down the stairs and landed at the bottom, arms held out wide, her shawl on her shoulders and a grin as big as all outdoors. "Here I am!"

Brody picked up her corsage, walked over to her, and bowed low before her. "How beautiful you look, my lady. I have never seen anyone so beautiful as you." He slipped the wrist corsage, which matched her dress, over her wrist and spun her around.

Jeb and John whistled and Sadie clapped. John tried to look chagrinned. "Does this mean you aren't my girl anymore?" he asked with a pretend frown.

"Oh, John," Sarah said. "I'll always be your girl." She pointed to his cast. "But you can't dance."

John nodded sadly and said, "Maybe next time."

Lou ushered the couple out into the sunshine so she could take some pictures. Brody posed good naturedly with Sarah and smiled. Lou walked over and whispered to him, "You won't let her out of your sight, will you?"

"Nope," he whispered back. "She'll be stuck to me like glue."

"Why did you do all this?" Lou asked quietly.

"Because my mother asked me, too," he responded candidly. "I make a good date." He winked at her. "Maybe you should try me out some time."

"I thought I already did that," Lou tossed back at him. His cheeks grew rosy and his eyes darkened for a moment.

Brody opened the door of his mother's old car, and seated Sarah. He buckled her in and said, "Ready to go cut a rug?"

"Well, what would we want to do that for?" Sarah replied, her eyebrows drawn together in a frown. "I thought we were going dancing."

Brody laughed out loud. "We are. I promise. That's just an old saying people use when they're going dancing."

"Oh, okay. Let's go cut a rug." She grinned.

Brody kissed Lou on the forehead as he walked around the front of the car. They pulled out of the driveway with Sarah waving.

****

They parked in the school parking lot and Brody walked around to open the door of the car for Sarah, trying to be the perfect gentleman. Truth be told, he had no idea what he was doing because he had never spent much time with children. He figured he could wing it as he took her hand, smiled, and escorted his little date across the parking lot.

They entered through the gym and Brody looked around at all the balloons and tables laden with snacks. Music played softly in the background. He leaned down and said to Sarah, "No matter what, you have to stay with me in here at all times."

"Why?" she asked innocently.

"Because I don't know anyone here and I don't want to be left all alone," he lied.

"Oh, I won't leave you. Promise." She took his hand in hers.

Several parents walked up, the dads extending their hands and introducing themselves. The moms, who had volunteered to chaperone and keep the food and punch stocked, exclaimed over Sarah's dress and her curls and he saw her puff up with pride. Job well done, he thought. He would have to thank Elizabeth and Lou for the extra effort.

He bent down to her left so she could hear him and said, "What would you like to do first? Get a drink? A cookie? Or have a dance?"

Sarah looked mortified. "Oh, I can't drink yet. No way." She whispered to him, "I might spill something on my dress."

"Ahhh…" Brody replied. "Dancing it is, then." He whisked her out onto the dance floor and suddenly found himself at a loss as to what to do.

"You do know how to dance, don't you?" Sarah asked shortly.

"Of course I do," he replied. "Why don't you tell me how you want to dance and that's what we'll do?"

"But you're supposed to lead, Dr. Wester."

"Why don't you call me Brody?" he said to her to buy some time as he looked at what the other dads were doing. Then he took her hand and placed it on his waist. He clasped her other hand firmly in his and told her to watch his feet. She quickly caught on and they danced in circles around the floor. When the music stopped and everyone clapped, Sarah said, "That was fun. Can we do it again?"

"We can do it all night, if that's what you want," Brody replied honestly.

After a few more dances, Sarah claimed she was thirsty and needed to take a break. They walked to the refreshment table and two other little girls bustled up to Sarah. They whispered to one another and then Sarah turned to Brody with tears in her eyes. Puddles of tears threatened to spill over her long brown lashes. "I think I need to go to the bathroom."

"Uh, oh. I didn't plan for this part of the night." He hadn't planned for the bathroom or for the crying. Just then, Elizabeth Patton came out from behind the punch bowl like an avenging angel.

"Could you use some help?" she asked, as she took one of Sarah's hands in her own.

"What do I do?" he whispered.

"Come on." She nodded her head toward the bathroom.

Brody stood outside while the Elizabeth went in with Sarah. He wrung his hands together until they came out about five minutes later. Sarah's tears were dry and her frown was replaced with a half-smile. He bent down to her level.

"Do you want to tell me what happened?"

"I told those stupid girls you had bought me this dress and the pretty clips in my hair and everything else and they said that it didn't count because you're not my real dad." She sniffled.

"Oh. They were just being mean, Sarah. You know what the difference is between those 'real' dads and me?"

"What?" She asked as she wiped her nose with the back of her hand. He reached into his pocket and pulled out a cotton handkerchief and handed it to her. She blew her nose loudly and gave it back. Brody took it and put it back in his pocket without saying a word.

"The difference between them and me is those dads are here because they have to be here. And me?" He patted his chest. "I'm here because I want to be here." He smiled at her.

Her face lit up like the Fourth of July. She grabbed his hand and led him back out onto the dance floor, with him laughing all the way behind her.

They danced almost every dance, drank punch with no spills and Brody could honestly say it was one of the best nights he had passed in quite some time. Sarah was a charming child. She was smart, thoughtful, independent, adorable, and a free thinker. She was quick to laugh and even quicker to make someone else laugh with her.

Sarah was exhausted when the dance was over at nine. Brody danced the last dance with her against his chest, her head on his shoulder, and her feet not even touching the ground.

The night had not been a disaster. *I actually pulled it off and had a great time doing it.*

Her breath blew against his chin as she raised her head. She grabbed his face in her two small hands and looked into his eyes. "Thanks, Brody, for taking me to the dance. This was the best night of my life. I'm really glad your mom made you do it."

Brody chucked lightly, slightly taken aback by her candor and the serious look on her face, her two hands commanding his full attention. He bent and put her feet on the floor. He bowed low before her and said, "The pleasure was all mine, my lady. Are you ready to go home?"

She nodded her head, "Yeah. I just need to go to the bathroom first."

Brody looked around and didn't see Elizabeth behind the punchbowl.

"I'm old enough to take myself to the bathroom, you know," she scolded, her eyebrows drawn together, terribly affronted by the fact he might think she was a baby.

"I know you are, Sarah." Brody looked around and saw many of the parents were leaving. He walked with Sarah to the ladies room and stood outside the door. "Go ahead. But come straight back out."

Sarah rolled her eyes dramatically and went through the bathroom door.

Brody stood outside the door for a moment, tapping his foot with impatience. He jumped as a hard edge of a table pressed into his leg.

"Hey, you," one of the dads called out. "Grab the other end of that table for me, will you?"

The slightly overweight father was huffing and puffing while rearranging the tables, so Brody grabbed one end and lifted. "Where are we going with it?"

"Just over by that wall." The dad pointed with his chin in the direction he wanted to go.

Brody walked backward until he was told to stop and deposited the table on the other side of the room.

"Thanks, man," the hefty father said.

"No problem," Brody replied, turning to walk back to the bathroom. Just as he reached the door, Elizabeth walked out. He stopped her with a hand on her arm.

"Do you know what's taking Sarah so long?"

"Sarah?" Elizabeth questioned. "There's no one else in the bathroom, Brody."

"What?" Brody barked as he pressed by her and barged his way into the room. He pushed open the stall doors, one by one, the noise bouncing off the walls of the small room like gunshots.

Elizabeth ran into the bathroom behind him. "What's wrong with you, Brody?" she barked, becoming agitated herself.

"Sarah!" he called loudly as he ran out of the room. He turned to Elizabeth. "I only took my eyes off her for a second." He frantically scanned the dispersing crowd, looking for her sequined dress and dark hair.

Sarah was gone.

Chapter Sixteen

Brody ran around the gymnasium, his fingers shooting through his hair in frustration as he searched for Sarah. He called her name. No response. The other parents noticed his plight and walked over. Over the heartbeat drumming in his ears, he heard Elizabeth say to them, "It's Sarah. We can't find her."

Sarah's teacher said, "Oh, I'm sure she's here somewhere. She probably just wandered around the corner."

"Sarah can't wander," Brody cried in frustration. "She's supposed to stay with me. The whole time. God, I can't believe I lost her!" He ran out the gymnasium door and scanned the parking lot.

Then he saw it. He saw a tiny flash of sequins as he heard a shrill, "No!" Brody's heart jumped into his throat as he recognized Sarah's tiny form being carried across the parking lot. She struggled in the arms of her captor, biting into the flesh of his hand as he tried to cover her mouth. The man cursed as he jerked his hand from her mouth and lost his hold on her. Sarah fought, kicked, and screamed with all her might.

Brody streaked across the parking lot toward them as the man put his hands on Sarah again, trying to throw her over his shoulder. Her assailant adjusted his hold, but Sarah continued to struggle.

Brody could feel his heart beating in his chest. Blood filled his face as anger overtook him. If not for Sarah's struggling, they might have gotten away. Instead, Brody overtook them and crashed with all his strength into the man who held Sarah so unkindly. The man stumbled and dropped Sarah to the ground. Sarah scrambled away on her hands and feet like a crab as Brody spun him around, his fist connecting with the meaty jaw of the dark haired man. He fought back, striking a blow to Brody's eye and one swift jab at his belly, which caused Brody to double over. Sarah sobbed gently behind him and straightened back up.

The skin of his knuckles tore as he connected with the man's teeth. The injured man sank to the ground. Brody stood over the fallen one, putting himself between Sarah and her captor. "Who are you and what do you want?" Brody ground out.

The man stood up slowly. His five-foot-ten frame was dwarfed by Brody's. But he quickly took the upper hand when he reached into his jacket and pulled out a pistol. Brody realized what it was as soon as he saw the black barrel. He took two steps back and raised his hands.

"I want the girl," the man said, spitting out a mouthful of blood onto the asphalt.

"She's not going anywhere," Brody stated calmly.

The man waved the pistol at him, indicating he should move from in front of Sarah, but Brody held his ground. "Not on my watch," he said. "You'll have to kill me first."

They heard the sirens at the same time. Brody looked up to see two police cars racing down the street. Recognition dawned on the other man's face. "Next time, you won't be so lucky," he said. The man jumped into a black SUV and quickly drove away.

"There won't be a next time," Brody grumbled as he turned and scooped Sarah up into his arms. Her hands were bleeding from her mad scramble across the parking lot and her gown was a filthy mess. Her curls were disheveled and her face was streaked with tears. Her feet were bare and her stockings torn. Brody pulled her close to him and said gently, "I told you to stay with me the whole night, remember?"

Sarah hiccupped and wiped her nose. "I came out of the bathroom and you were gone. I thought you left me," she sobbed.

"I would never leave you, Sarah," he said, kissing her gently on the forehead.

Two police officers walked up to them and said, "Do you want to tell us what happened, sir?"

"Hell, I don't even know what happened," Brody replied honestly. "I was trying to find Sarah. I came outside and this guy was carrying her across the parking lot." He reached up and wiped a trail of blood that ran from his eye down the side of his face. "I…" He was cut off mid-comment by screeching tires as the Westers' Jeep flew into the parking lot.

Lou jumped from the car, John hobbling behind her, and ran over to Brody, snatching Sarah from his arms. "What happened?" she barked, dropping Sarah to the ground and kneeling in front of her to look over her injuries.

"How did you…?" Brody began.

"I called her," Elizabeth said, pointing to her cell phone. "Right after I called the police."

"Good thinking," he threw over his shoulder as he approached Lou. "She's okay, Lou. I caught him before he could hurt her." He placed one hand on her shoulder but she violently shrugged him off.

"That's not what it looks like to me, Brody!" Lou snapped. "Look at her! All you were supposed to do was keep her safe for one night." She shook a finger in his face. "That's all I asked you to do, Brody! One night!"

"I did, Lou," Brody pleaded. "I did keep her safe. Damn it! I did more than that!" he yelled back at her.

Lou snarled a curse at him as she picked Sarah up and put her in the Jeep. She buckled her seatbelt and got in the driver's side. She addressed the officers. "I trust Dr. Wester can fill you in on any details you might have missed. I am taking my daughter home."

Brody had never felt more like an outsider than he did when walked into the house after talking with the police for an hour. Jeb and Sadie sat at the kitchen table, sipping coffee.

He walked through the backdoor, allowing the screen to slam behind him. "Where's Lou?" he barked.

Sadie rose from her chair, quickly taking in the bloodstains on his shirt and the cut above his eye. "Oh, my Lord. You're hurt." She wet a cloth in the sink and reached to raise it to his eye.

He caught her hand in his own and stopped her movements. "Where's Lou?" he asked, looking directly into her eyes.

"She's upstairs with Sarah, child. But you had better give her some time…" Her voice trailed off behind him as he ran up the stairs.

The door to Lou's room stood open so he stepped inside. He heard noises coming from the bathroom and stepped through the open door. Lou sat on the side of the tub, casually splashing water on Sarah, who was covered from head to toe with bubbles. John sat on the closed toilet lid, quietly teasing them both.

Brody brushed past them both and kneeled in front of the tub. Sarah grinned at him from amid the bubbles.

"You okay, kiddo?" he asked.

"I'm fine, Brody. Mommy let me have a lot of bubbles."

"I see that. You look like you are having a great time. Let me see your hands." He held out his own. Her small hands landed in his large ones, palms up. Brody grimaced when he saw the abraded flesh. "They don't look too bad," he mumbled. "Do you hurt anywhere else?"

"Nope. I'm fine. You look much worse than I do." She reached her bubble-laced fingers toward the bruised flesh around his eye. He flinched as she touched it and moved back out of her reach.

John stood up, grabbed a towel off the counter, and wet it in the sink. "You have blood on your face, Brody." He held the towel out to him and Brody took it in his hand, holding it up to his eye, wiping gently.

John pointed to his face, "Uh, you missed a spot, there."

Brody turned toward the mirror and assessed the damage. "I look like one scary guy, huh, Sarah?" he joked, turning back to Sarah.

"Not nearly as scary as that man was." She shook her head vehemently.

He leaned down to the tub and kissed her soapy forehead. He sighed deeply. "I had a great time tonight. Thanks for letting me take you to the dance."

"Thank you for saving my life," Sarah replied stoically.

"Any time, kiddo." He turned to walk out of the room. His eyes met Lou's. "Can I talk to you, please?" he barked in her direction.

"No," was her only reply. His flinty eyes darkened with anger. He grabbed her arm and swung her around.

"Yes!" he said quietly but forcefully. "John, watch Sarah. We'll be right outside."

"Won't take my eyes off her," John said.

"Where have I heard that before?" Lou asked sarcastically, pulling her arm out his grasp.

He grabbed her again, dragging her through the doorway and out onto the porch. She stumped her toe going across the threshold and fell against him. He looked down into her upturned face. She placed two hands against his chest and pushed with all her might. He stumbled backward.

"What is wrong with you, Lou? Damn it, will you calm down?"

"What do you want, Brody?" Lou asked quietly, her brown eyes flashing a challenge.

"I want to know if she's all right, Lou," he said, his face suddenly tormented. He ran his fingers through his hair in a frustrated motion, wincing as his hand brushed across his temple. "I have never been so scared in my whole life as I was when I thought I lost her," he breathed.

"How could you lose her, Brody? How could you?" Tears filled her eyes and ran down her cheeks.

"She went to the bathroom, Lou. She went to the bathroom and when she came out, I was moving a table and she didn't see me. So, she walked outside to see if I was out there. That's where he grabbed her. I heard her scream. I saw her kicking. I was afraid I couldn't get there in time. I fought like hell, Lou. I swear to God, I did. I would have let him kill me before I would let him have Sarah."

"You would?" she asked. "Why?" Tears streamed down her cheeks, falling onto her shirt like raindrops running down a window.

"Because she's a kid, damn it. I was taking care of her. And I did, Lou. We had a great night." He smiled slowly, remembering her antics, her smiles, and how happy she was for an evening. He grabbed Lou's forearms and pulled her close to him, despite her protests. "And because she's yours. You would never let me speak to you again if something happened to Sarah."

"What makes you think I'm going to speak to you now?" she asked childishly.

He took her chin in his hand and forced her to look at him. "Because you know I did my best and got her back. I would do it again—for you as much as for her."

Lou confessed, "I was so scared when Elizabeth called. All could think of was that you had let someone steal my baby." Lou sobbed into his shirt, great heaving sobs that rocked them both.

He held her until the sobs subsided and she wiped her nose with the back of her hand. He held out his towel to her, "Do you want my towel?"

"Oh, God. Your eye." She reached up and touched the cut above his eye. He flinched.

"What is it with you women who have to touch us while we're hurting?" he groaned.

"Does it hurt a lot?" She took the damp towel and rubbed his face gently, washing away the blood. "You might need a stitch or two. You definitely need some ice."

"I'll settle for a kiss." He bent slightly, and she stood on tiptoe and kissed his temple softly.

"Are you still mad at me for almost losing Sarah?"

"No. I'm thankful you saved her life." She snorted indelicately. "You also gave her a fine evening of dancing," she said sarcastically. "Are you mad at me for acting like a shrew?"

"Nope. I probably would have felt the same way. Hell, I do feel the same way. I wanted to kill the son of a bitch."

Lou and Brody both turned when they heard Sarah call, "Mommy?"

Lou pulled herself out of Brody's embrace and turned toward the door. He pulled her close one more time and whispered to her, "Can we finish this conversation later?" He nuzzled her hair, breathing in the scent of her.

"The only person sleeping in my bed tonight will be my daughter, Brody. I'm sure you understand." She went through the door and closed it tightly in his face. He heard the bolt shoot home as she locked it.

"Guess I'll go and lick my wounds all by myself," Brody mumbled as he went back downstairs. Sadie and Jeb were still sitting at the kitchen table. Brody sat down heavily in a chair and groaned, grasping his side, remembering the punch he had taken to the middle.

Sadie rose as quickly as her ample girth would allow, got an ice pack from the freezer, and held it to the bruised skin over his eye. He flinched.

"Geez, Sadie. That's cold," he said but he took it and held it over the area that was already swollen and tender. "But thanks."

"How are you doing, boy?" Jeb asked, his dark eyes full of concern.

Brody sighed heavily. "I'm fine." He gratefully accepted the cup of coffee Sadie sat before him and smiled gently at her. "He came out of nowhere, Jeb. I'm glad you're leaving tomorrow with Sarah."

"I just wish we could talk her mama into going with us, too," Jeb replied.

"If she went with you, you would all just have to deal with this again when you get back. Those people are not going to go away until they get what they want, whatever that may be."

"You'll take care of Lou while we're gone?" Sadie questioned him.

"To the best of my ability," Brody said truthfully.

"Guess that's all we can ask you for," Sadie added. "Just don't let her try to tackle this herself."

"I promise. I'll be with her as much as she'll let me," Brody assured her even though he had no idea what he was up against.

Jeb rose from his chair. "We had better get to bed. We have an early start and a long ride tomorrow."

"How long will you be gone?"

"As long as it takes," Jeb responded. He reached over to the kitchen counter and pulled out a thick envelope. "That lawyer of your mother's came by today and dropped this off. He said he needs to meet with you next week but he wanted you to look this over before then."

Brody accepted the envelope and placed it before him on the table. Sadie leaned over and kissed his forehead. He winced again.

"It pains me to see you so beaten up." She whispered to him. "It would have broken my heart if anything happened to either of you tonight."

"So, you're glad I'm still alive?" he teased gently. "Just so I can take care of Lou while you're gone."

"Mind you, child, taking care of her is all you do to her while we're gone," she playfully chastised him.

"I promise not to defile, demoralize or otherwise molest her." He chuckled at the look on Sadie's face.

"Mind you she doesn't get hurt. That means the heart...and the body." She patted his shoulder. "I'm counting on you."

"I know you are," he squeezed her hand as she walked by.

After he heard their bedroom door shut, Brody opened the brown paper envelope. A letter from the attorney topped the stack of papers and Brody skimmed it quickly. It listed the contents of the envelope and requested a meeting the following week to discuss his mother's will. It also contained a list of valuables that were inside the home at the time of her death—antiques, paintings, collectibles and jewelry were all listed. The note explained his mother had a safe over the mantle in her sitting room, hidden behind a painting. Any jewelry that wasn't in the safety deposit box at the bank would be in the safe along with titles, deeds and any other paperwork he might need in the future.

The lawyer's letter continued.

As you may have guessed, your mother left all of her worldly possessions to you. She was a little more creative with the business and other assets and has prepared a will to let you know her wishes in this regard.

Prior to our meeting, I would encourage you to go through the contents of the safe and familiarize yourself with these items so you will know what is and is not rightfully yours.

Brody rubbed his forehead as it was really beginning to throb.

So, she was creative with some of her assets. *I hope she made provisions for Jeb, Sadie, John, and Lou.*

Brody pulled the list of jewelry from the file and saw that each piece and its appraised value were listed. Brody could remember his mother dressing for social events when he was a child and donning herself with the most fabulous diamonds, emeralds, and rubies. He smiled slowly at the thought. He searched through the envelope until he located the combination to the safe. He gathered up the lists and carried them with him to his mother's suite of rooms.

He stopped when he walked into the room and breathed deeply, his mother's scent still lingering in the air. The hospital bed and equipment had long since been removed so it was nearly back to normal. He lovingly touched her lap quilt that was still flung over the back of her favorite chair. Her reading glasses rested on the end table.

Brody lifted the painting from the wall over the mantle and gently set it on the floor. The hard, gray steel of the safe seemed almost foreboding as he turned the knob, counting out the numbers along with left and right turns. When the last number was dialed in, the tumblers inside the lock rolled into place and he pulled the door open.

The safe was neatly stacked with papers and documents, titles to cars and lineage for the horses they raised. At the bottom of the safe lay a long, wooden jewelry box. Brody gently removed it and laid it on the coffee table, sitting on the couch so he could open it easily.

Dozens of jeweled pieces winked up at him from inside the velvet lined box when he removed the lid. Brody immediately noticed an emerald necklace and touched it reverently. Every piece had a story. This particular one had been passed down from his paternal grandmother to his mother as a wedding gift. Brody checked the list and noted that it was included, even going so far as to have a photo of the item and its last appraised value. All of the other pieces of jewelry were accounted for in a similar fashion.

Brody placed the top back on the wooden box and slid it back in the safe. He searched through papers absently, noting his mother was as efficient about keeping records as she had been about everything else. His eyes filled with tears when he searched through one stack of papers and found they included awards he had won at school from kindergarten all the way through graduation. *Never had any idea you saved all these things, Mom.*

On the middle shelf in the back of the safe, his fingers brushed against a black canvas bag he had never seen before. He pulled it from the back of the shelf and unrolled it. He unzipped the long, metal zipper and was surprised to find cash inside. His mother had never been one for keeping cash in the home. He thumbed through the stacks of green dollars, absently counting in his head. $50,000 dollars? That was an awful lot to keep at home in a safe.

Beneath the cash, lay a flat brown jewelry box, about seven inches square. Brody removed it from the bag and gave it a quick shake. He opened the box and saw the biggest clear stone he had ever seen before, nestled in a bed of black silk fabric. He whistled softly to himself, "I didn't know they made diamonds that big."

He checked the list of jewelry and couldn't find any documentation for this piece. He ran through it again. Still nothing. His eyebrows drew together. Someone must have forgotten to put this on the list. He closed the jewelry box and put it back into the bag. Monday, he would have to get an appraisal and find out why it hadn't been accounted for. Must have been an oversight. But it certainly needed to be added to the estate.

He reached into the safe and pulled out one last thick envelope. Across the front, written in his mother's handwriting, was just "Lou." He took the envelope back to the end table and dumped the contents. He unfolded several newspaper clippings, all from a nearby paper and gasped as he saw the headlines.

Woman Dies in Fire—Identity Unknown

Charred Remains Found—Police Suspect Foul Play

Information Sought on Inhabitants of Mobile Home

He read through each article, touching the photos reverently on each page.

He searched through more paperwork, including background checks for one Miss Mary Louise Smith. His mother had thoroughly investigated her. She had nothing that stood out except student records from high school and employment records from a few part-time jobs.

He then found birth certificates, first Lou's own and then one for Sarah. Sarah's birth certificate listed Lou as the child's mother. He had already proven that theory to be false. Then he found copies of letters from his mother to her own personal physician, asking for a birth certificate for an indigent girl and her child whom she had taken in. Then the pieces started to fall together.

"I'll be damned," he muttered to himself. "My mother obtained falsified birth records for Sarah and took care of Lou after she checked her out." He shook his head with wonder, finally understanding all that had taken place. He placed the documents back together in their envelope and returned them to the safe.

He closed the safe and spun the tumbler. He replaced the painting on the wall and sat down on his mother's chaise lounge. He wearily pulled her lap quilt over himself and breathed in the scent of her perfume, missing her more than he had since the day she died. He closed his eyes and quickly fell to sleep, comforted by thoughts of his mother and her personal things that surrounded him.

Chapter Seventeen

Brody woke the next morning to the feeling of small breaths rushing against his face. He slowly opened his eyes and jumped as he found Sarah just inches from his nose, her finger poised in the air, about to touch his eye. He pulled back slightly, still half-asleep and unsure of where he was.

"Sarah?" he asked groggily, stretching slowly. "What are you doing in here?"

"What are *you* doing in here?" she threw back at him saucily, placing her hands on her hips, her brown eyes dancing with a smile.

"What are you talking about?" he asked as he sat up and looked around, surprised to find he had spent the whole night in his mother's room in her chaise lounge, surrounded by blankets that smelled of her. "Oh," he replied, running his hand through his hair. "I must have fallen asleep. Where is everyone?"

"In the kitchen," Sarah replied, still looking at his eye. She reached a small finger out and touched it, quickly drawing it back when he winced. "Does that hurt a lot?"

"Only when you do that," he warned.

"Oh. Sorry." She giggled quietly.

"You sure sound like you're sorry," his sober expression turned to glee as he grabbed her and pulled her into his lap, tickling her sides.

She laughed out loud and squealed, "Stop it!"

"Stop what?" he asked dramatically, tickling her more. "Do you mean stop this?" he continued his assault.

Then he heard footsteps running down the hall. Lou ran through the doorway, a look of panic on her face. He and Sarah froze as she snapped at them both.

"You almost scared the life out of me." She breathed rapidly, her hand over her chest. Jeb and Sadie ran into the room right behind her, looking equally as worried. Jeb was quite the sight, carrying a fire poker.

Brody tapped Sarah. She looked him in the eye. "Looks like you're going to get me beaten up again." He shoved her playfully from his knee and she hit the floor. She came up rubbing her bottom.

"That wasn't very nice," she pouted.

"Keep that in mind the next time you wake me up and then get me in trouble with your squealing, young lady." He grinned at her. She grinned back and went to stand beside Lou. Lou touched her gently on the top of her head, rubbing her hair back from her face.

She spoke to Brody. "I'm sorry she woke you. She was in the kitchen just a minute ago." Lou ground out the last few words at her child, Sarah looking like the kid who stole a cookie from the cookie jar.

"She came to check out my shiner." Brody pointed to his face, turning so she could see it.

"Oh!" she gasped, walking closer to him. "That looks terrible!"

"Don't touch it. It hurts. Just ask Sarah." Brody nodded in her direction.

Jeb and Sadie ushered Sarah from the room.

Despite the warning, Lou reached a hand toward his eye. He caught her hand in his and said, "See! I warned you. I'm going to have to punish you just like I did her."

"You wouldn't dare," she challenged.

"Want to bet," he said quickly, grabbing her and pulling her into his lap.

She struggled against his arms but he held her firmly. He tickled her side lightly and she squirmed in his lap, kicking his shin. He grunted in pain and spun her around, laying her back in the chaise lounge, his body covering hers. He pulled her hands above her head, clasping them in one of his own. "I still think I can take you."

"Take me?" she asked.

He pondered that for a moment. "Well, I want to do that, too." He laughed and ground his hips into hers. She gasped as he pressed himself against her belly. "But I'll settle for winning right this second." He kissed her lips lightly. "I want to kiss you better, but I haven't brushed my teeth yet." He looked at her with his boyish grin and she couldn't help but smile back.

They heard a cough from the doorway and they both looked over. Lou was still beneath Brody on the lounge with her hands clasped in his, above her head. John stood in the entry of the sitting room, looking decidedly uncomfortable. "Would you guys knock it off? Jeb and Sadie are ready to go." He turned and walked out of the room.

Brody released her wrists and her hands came up to push against his chest. "Let me up," she said impatiently.

He kissed her on the cheek and moved off of her, sitting up and heading for the bathroom, adjusting his pants as he went. Lou straightened her clothes and looked at herself in the mirror before walking out of the room.

Brody walked into the kitchen a few minutes later to find Lou kneeling before Sarah, both of the child's small hands clutched in her own larger ones. He heard her remind Sarah, "Now you be a good girl and listen to what Jeb and Sadie say. Stay out of trouble and mind your manners. Don't get dirty every time you go outside. Try to stay clean for once."

Tears hovered over Lou's dark lashes like a dam ready to overflow. She blinked them back. Sarah said, "I promise to stay clean. I'll say please and thank you and be a good listener." She threw her arms around Lou's neck and squeezed tightly. Lou squeezed back until the child yelped. "You're hurting me, Mommy," she grunted.

Lou loosened her hold and placed her on the floor. "Sorry," she mumbled.

Sadie came to stand in front of Lou and said, "I'll take care of her, but I'm still worried about you."

"It's okay," Lou whispered to her loud enough Brody could overhear, "I have a plan. It's all worked out. I just have to pay them what they think I owe them and we'll be done with this." She shrugged. "No big deal, really. As long as Sarah is safe, it will be just fine. Promise." She kissed Sadie on the cheek and moved to embrace Jeb.

Sadie walked to stand in front of Brody. He grunted. "Why does she get lovely words of devotion and you look at me like I'm the cat that ate the canary."

"Because I happen to know you, Brody, probably better than you know yourself. If my memory serves me correctly, you have never had to go out of your way to find trouble." She leaned in and whispered, "Take care of her, please."

"Why do you think I'm here?" he whispered back, a smile on his face.

John hugged them both as well and yanked Sarah's ponytail. "I'll miss you, Squirt."

"I'll miss you, too, John." He squatted so she could climb on his back and he carried her out to the truck. Lou walked alongside them and buckled Sarah into her booster seat.

She stepped back and waved as the truck roared to life. Sarah turned around and waved all the way down the drive.

Lou placed her fingers over her mouth, trying to stifle the choking feeling that came with tears. Then she felt John's strong arm around her shoulders as he pulled her into his chest. She pushed back at him with her hands. "No. No," she said with confidence despite the tears that rolled down her face. "I can handle this." She took a deep breath through her nose.

"Glad to hear it," John said. "How about if you comfort me, instead?" She gratefully moved into his brotherly embrace, his strong arms around her shoulders, her arms clutching his waist.

Brody coughed loudly and dramatically from where he stood on the porch. They both looked up. "So, which one of you is going to make breakfast?"

Chapter Eighteen

John decided to forego the Lucky Charms and left to hit the local diner for a real meal while Lou and Brody talked over their bowls of marshmallow cereal and coffee.

"What are you going to do today?" Brody asked casually, his mouth full of cereal.

"I don't have any plans. I have a book I want to start and I was thinking of taking a nap. I haven't been sleeping well." She rubbed her neck and flexed her muscles in an attempt to relieve the tension. She covered a yawn behind her hand as she placed her bowl in the sink. "But first I want to go out and see the new foal. Wester's Fancy Lady finally delivered last night. We were starting to think that baby would never come." She started walking toward the door.

Brody took another bite of cereal and laid down his paper. "Why don't you wait a minute and I'll walk with you?"

Lou took a deep breath. "I knew this was coming." She pointed her finger at him. "Let's get one thing clear. I do not need a babysitter."

Brody smiled and raised his hands in mock surrender. "I just wanted to go and see the new foal, Lou. Not stay stuck up under you all day." He waved his spoon at her and grinned. "Although that does sound like even more fun than seeing the foal."

Lou groaned. "No pun intended, I'm sure," she muttered. "I'm just going to the barn. Alone. I'll be right back."

"If you say so." He motioned for her to continue.

Lou walked out the door and felt the cool morning breeze caress her face. Fall was approaching so the mornings were not stiflingly hot like summer mornings. The days still were just as warm so Lou was dressed in jeans and a T-shirt.

She walked into the barn and it took a moment for her eyes to adjust to the change of lighting. Each stall had a turn-out pen so the mares and foals could enjoy some time outside. Many of them nickered to her as she walked by their stalls.

Lou patted her shirt pocket. "No peppermint today, guys. Sorry." She stopped by the barn fridge and picked up two thick, orange carrots and approached the stall of the new mom and foal. She quietly looked over the stall door and smiled when she saw Lady standing up, the babe suckling from her breast. The colt was steady on his feet and appeared to be pretty sturdy. Lou dared not walk into the stall with a colt so young, because she was unsure of how the mare would react. Instead, she reached over the top of the stall and offered Lady a carrot, crooning softly to her all the while. The horse greedily ate it with no signs of stress that could have been caused by Lou's approach. She let Lou smooth her hand over the top of her head, comfortable and relaxed. Then she suddenly changed. Her ears were pinned back close against her head and she moved so she stood between the stall door and the baby.

"What's the matter, girl?" Lou asked cautiously.

"Looks like her senses are keener than yours," a masculine voice said from behind her.

Lou spun around quickly and jumped when she saw Wes, the former farm hand who helped to put up the hay, standing behind her in the barn. Lou walked backward until her back hit the wall. She jumped.

"What are you doing here?" she asked calmly.

He held a cigar in his hand and raised it to his lips. "I came to see you," he said after expelling a puff of smoke.

"You can't smoke in h...here," Lou stammered.

"Looks like I can do just about what I want," he replied, raising the cigar to his lips again.

"You're going to set the whole place on fire. There's too much hay in here for sparks," Lou protested as he flicked his ashes on the cobblestone-lined walk that ran down the center aisle of the barn. She stomped them soundly.

"Set the place on fire. Now there's a great idea," he replied as he ground the cigar out with the bottom of his shoe. He sighed sarcastically. "But not today."

"What do you want?" Lou asked with more bravado than she actually felt. "How much?"

"All of it. I want all of it." He spread his hands wide. "My boss is not willing to bargain. He will accept no less than $50,000 in cash and that other little item."

"That other little item is not here. You tried to get that last night and failed. So, it's in a safe place."

"What are you talking about?" He stiffened.

"You tried to steal my daughter but you failed."

Lou heard footsteps outside the building at the same time Wes did, if his reaction was any indication, along with the soft whistle of a man. Wes quickly disappeared into the shadows of the barn and slipped out the back door just as Brody walked in through the other end.

Lou leaned over the stall door again, pretending to be talking to the mare.

"How's she doing?" he asked casually as he walked up behind her, placing his hands on her shoulders.

"They both look great. See." Lou managed to keep the tremor out of her voice. "Healthy as a horse." She rubbed her neck again, her brow scrunched.

"Do you have a headache?" Brody asked quietly, gently rubbing her shoulders.

"Boy, do I ever," Lou moaned.

"Well, come on. I'll get you something for it. You could probably talk me into a neck rub, too, if you ask me nicely."

"Aw, shucks. I have to ask you nicely?" She covered his hand with hers and turned to walk to the house. He slipped his arm around her shoulders and pulled her close.

"Hey," Brody said. "What's that smell?"

"What's it smell like?" Lou asked.

Brody sniffed again. "Cherries?"

"Oh. Must be those new mints John buys. I just gave a couple to Lady."

"Oh, that must be it," Brody replied.

****

Wes snuck out the backdoor of the barn, careful to keep to the shadows as he skirted the two hay barns. The path around the barns led to the trail through the woods that would take him back to his car. As soon as he was out of earshot, he pulled out his phone and dialed.

"Jerry's towing," a silky voice answered.

"Let me talk to the boss," he said, his voice quivering slightly.

"What do you want?" the voice snapped in his ear.

"I just paid a little visit to Mary Lou. Did you send someone to try and take her daughter?" His breath rushed out as his pace quickened at the very thought.

"You weren't getting anywhere, so I sent Gary," the voice snapped again.

"Gary? But he's one hateful son of a bitch, boss." He took a deep breath. "You told him to steal the girl?"

"We needed a bargaining chip."

"She's just a kid, boss," Wes replied.

"He almost had her. Then Lou's boyfriend came out of nowhere and broke two of Gary's teeth and his jaw."

The man must have been running on pure adrenaline to get one over on Gary. "Then what happened?"

"Someone called the cops, so he had to get out of there."

"He didn't hurt her?" Wes asked.

"I don't give a damn if he hurt her or not," the boss said gruffly. "Why do you care so much?"

"You just should have told me your plan. That's all." Wes stammered, suddenly at a loss for words.

"I want results," the boss bellowed into the phone. "I don't care who gets them or how it's done."

He heard a click on the other end and the call ended.

Wes ran a frustrated hand through his hair. "Shit."

Chapter Nineteen

Brody walked back to the house with Lou, his arm around her shoulders. He sat down in the long porch swing and patted his lap. "Put your head here and I'll rub your neck."

Lou wrung her neck muscles again with her hand, hearing her pulse beat a steady rhythm in her ears. "I'm okay. I'll just go and lay down."

She walked past him to the stairs and into the house, heading straight for the stairs. She walked into her room and kicked her shoes off, falling heavily onto the bed and tucking the pillow beneath her head. Brody walked into the room just moments later.

"Hurts that bad, huh?" he asked quietly.

"Yeah," she moaned.

He walked to her side and lifted the covers. "Sit up and take this." He held out two pills in his hand and a glass of water.

"What is it?" she asked cautiously.

"Just some Extra Strength Tylenol. Unless you want something stronger?" he asked.

"No. This will be fine." She popped the pills into her mouth and washed them down with water.

"Lay on your stomach," he said, pointing to the bed.

"Brody, I don't think…" she started.

"Just shut up and do it," he threw back over his shoulder as he walked into the bathroom. He came back carrying a bottle of lotion from her medicine cabinet. He squirted a good-sized amount into his hands and rubbed them together, warming the lotion. She moaned when he laid his warm hands on the skin of her neck and started to knead the stiff muscles.

"What happened to make you so tense?" he asked quietly.

"I don't know," she muttered against her pillow. "Just a combination of last night, today, and the past couple of weeks, I guess." She gasped as he found a particularly sensitive area by her collarbone. He concentrated on that area until it relaxed and then moved his hands beneath the neck of her T-shirt.

"This isn't going to work. Sit up for a second." He patted her bottom and she rose slowly. He grasped the end of her shirt and lifted it slowly over head, exposing her lacy white bra beneath.

"I don't think..." she started to say.

"You don't have to think." He stopped her. "It's just a massage. Sexy as you look in that bra, even I would not try to take advantage of you when you're hurting." He pointed to the bed again. "Lay back down."

She did, moaning as his hands ran over the muscles of her back. He gently attacked each muscle, working until he felt it relax.

"Do you tell Sarah stories as she goes to sleep?"

"Yeah. Sometimes. Why?" she asked against her pillow.

"I'm going to tell you one, now. While I have a captive audience," he replied.

"You can do anything you want as long as you keep doing that," she said, gasping as he found a sensitive spot by her shoulder blade.

Brody started. "Once, in a different place and time, there was a little girl named Lou. Lou lived with her mother, who was too wrapped up in her own addictions to properly care for Little Lou. Lou's mother had no education and no family to help her, so she did what she could to take care of her daughter to the best of her ability. Despite this fact, Lou still felt misplaced and unloved because they moved from place to place, never having one true home to call their own. Lou did the best she could, getting good grades and working part-time jobs to buy groceries and gas.

"She hated the men her mother brought home from the clubs and the way they would leer at her. But they never stayed very long. Then, when the rent was past-due and the lights turned off because no one paid the electric bill, they would move again.

"Then, when Lou was nineteen, her life changed. Someone gave her a baby."

Lou rolled over and looked at him. "Her mother gave her a baby," she supplied. "Lou's mother asked to be driven to the clinic for the abortion she had scheduled. Lou refused. Lou begged and begged for her to keep the baby. She wanted a little sister, you see. She made a deal with her mother. If she would just carry the baby to term, Lou would raise the baby and be responsible for her care. Lou threatened and stomped and told her mother she would leave if the baby was aborted. Lou's mother needed the income Lou brought home to pay the rent."

Lou's tone changed to one of sorrow, but she continued. "Little did I realize at the time that my mother would be forced to quit her job when she started to show. She was a stripper after all, and men just didn't want to see a pregnant stripper."

Brody nodded thoughtfully, urging her to continue.

"My part-time job couldn't pay all the bills. We were sitting there with no lights, no food, and no dignity. Then, one day, my mother came home with groceries. The rent had been paid and the lights were back on. She had bought new clothes for both of us and she'd had her hair and nails done. I had no idea what she did to get the money but I noticed she had a new, haunted, look in her eyes. She was constantly looking over her shoulder. We moved again to a tiny little trailer out in the middle of nowhere.

"She went through the pregnancy and was healthy. She even stopped smoking and drinking. She was clearer than she had ever been." Lou smiled. "Then Sarah was born. I was there in the delivery room and was amazed when they placed her in my mother's arms. I was even more surprised when she passed her to me and said, 'I hope you're ready for this, 'cause she's yours.' From that moment on, she was. I woke up at night to feed her and to take care of her."

Lou shivered just a bit as she continued. "Then one night, these men came to the trailer and started beating on the windows and doors, trying to get in. My mother looked defeated. She threw Sarah in a bag and told me to run like hell which I did." Lou's eyes met his. "You know the rest. John and Jeb found us, and we have been here ever since."

Lou lay on her back, her head on her pillow and her forearm over her eyes. She used her arm to wipe the tears away and looked up at Brody.

"How's your headache?" he asked softly.

"Better, actually." She sighed and rolled over, facing away from him. "I'm going to take a nap, though."

She felt him slide in behind her and pull her close to him. She snuggled closer and put her head on his arm, his chin resting on the top of her head. His legs twined with hers.

"Me, too," he said.

****

Lou woke slowly and stretched languidly in his arms, her body lengthening against his own. His hand splayed against her naked belly, still clad only in her lacy bra. She could wake up like this every day and wouldn't complain.
"What time is it?" she muttered.

"Who cares?" Brody asked as he kissed the back of her neck and her shoulder.

She reached back and patted his thigh. "We need to get up."

"Why?" he asked, his mouth tracing her collarbone.

She smiled into her pillow, feeling her pulse quicken. She turned over slowly to face him. He nuzzled her forehead and breathed in the scent of her. "Because we just should," she whispered.

His kisses trailed down her hairline to her ear. He grasped her earlobe firmly with his teeth and tugged. She giggled and brushed him off with her hand. She felt him smile against her skin. His trail of kisses continued down her jaw until they reached her chin. Then his lips touched hers, firmly. He captured her mouth in a kiss that had her reeling.

He moved so his head was above hers. He supported himself on one elbow and reached the other hand to trace a slow line along the lacy edge of her bra with his fingertips. His kiss deepened as he used his tongue to trace her lower lip. He drew it into his mouth and sucked lightly. Her tongue raised and met his. They tangled in her mouth until she lightly caught the tip of his tongue between her teeth. She sucked the tip of it gently and felt his hand begin to shake on her breast. She released her hold and softened the kiss, her lips firmly yet softly slowing against his own. His mouth lifted from hers and they touched, nose to nose. They both breathed heavily.

"How's your headache?" he asked quietly.

"Much better," she sighed, her breath warring with his as he hovered over her.

"Glad to hear it," he mumbled against her skin as his lips moved down to graze her neck.

Just then, a loud rap sounded on the door. John called out, "Lou! Are you in there?"

Lou whispered frantically, "Oh, God!" She shoved against his chest. "Get out!" she said vehemently against his ear.

"Where am I going to go, Lou?" he whispered back. "He's outside the door."

She shoved at him again. "Go out the other door."

"He'll hear me if I do that."

Lou grabbed the covers and threw them over him, tossing a few pillows haphazardly around him as well. She picked her T-shirt up and slid it back over her head.

John rapped on the door again. "Lou!" he called out.

"Yeah," she answered weakly.

"Can I come in?" John asked.

"I really don't feel like…" Lou started as she heard the doorknob turn, "…company," she finished as he peeked his red head around the door.

"Are you okay?" he asked, his brows drawn together. "You look a little peaked."

"Yeah," she responded, her voice shaky. "I just had a headache so I took a nap." She wiped the sleep from her eyes with the tips of her fingers.

"You have company. Elizabeth Patton is downstairs and wants to see you and Brody. Have you seen him?" A slow, sneaky smile spread across John's face.

"What does Elizabeth Patton want?" she asked absently. "Never mind," she waved off his further comments. "I'll go downstairs and see. I'm sure Brody's around somewhere."

"Oh…." John smiled broadly. "When you find him, tell him he might want to cover his toes next time he's hiding under your covers."

Lou gasped as she looked toward the foot of the bed. Sure enough, Brody's feet were sticking out from under the covers. Lou picked up a pillow and lifted it to fling it at John's head. It hit the closed door instead as John slipped through it and shut it tightly. She heard his laughter all the way down the hall.

Brody uncovered his head and laughed out loud. "No one ever accused that boy of being stupid," he said as he stood up. Lou tossed a pillow at him, too. He ducked and caught her around the middle, pulling her close to him. He kissed her quickly on the lips and walked into her bathroom. He ran her brush through his hair and said, "You want to fix your ponytail and meet me downstairs in a minute?"

She just nodded a response, tucking her head into his neck as he pulled her close one more time. He kissed her cheek, still smiling, before he walked out of the room.

Lou walked down the stairs and entered the kitchen to find Elizabeth sitting at the kitchen table quietly. Brody stood at the sink, pouring sweet tea into Mason jar glasses. Lou took a glass from Brody's hand as he held it out. He handed one to Elizabeth as well. Elizabeth stood as Lou walked close.

"My dad wanted to come and see the new foal that was born to Lucky Lady. I wanted to drop by and be sure Sarah's okay. We were all worried about her last night," Elizabeth said. "Sarah and my daughter go to the same school."

Lou indicated she should sit by pointing to the kitchen chairs around the table. Then she took a chair on the opposite side.

"She's doing just fine. She left this morning for a short vacation with Jeb and Sadie," Brody replied. He reached to touch his eye. "She actually fared a lot better than I did. She won't have any lasting scars," he said. He looked out the screen door. "I'm going to go out and talk to Mr. Patton. Be right back." He nodded at them both.

A pregnant pause filled the space in the room. "Well," Elizabeth said slowly, taking a deep breath. "I just wanted to see if she was all right. You guys sure gave us a scare last night. Never had that kind of drama at a school dance before."

Lou reached over and covered Elizabeth's nervous hand with hers. "I appreciate what you did, Elizabeth." She squeezed her hand before releasing it. "I hear you called the police right before you called me." Lou's eyes filled with unshed tears. "I appreciate all you did."

"It's Brody you should thank. He fought like a madman."

Lou's eyebrows drew together.

Liz nodded. "Really." She covered her heart with a hand. "I've known Brody for a lot of years but I've never seen him like that. He's always been strong and powerful but I've never seen him fight before. Ever. He went after that man like he was fighting for his own life."

"I'm sure he would have done the same thing for anyone else." Lou replied, taking a sip of her tea.

"No, Lou." She shook her head vehemently. "He wouldn't. He did it for Sarah because he feels something for her."

"What do you mean?" Lou asked.

"You don't see it, do you?" Elizabeth asked. "She's an extension of you. It's you he would have hurt if something had happened to her. That's why he fought the way he did. You don't get that desperate look on your face unless you really care about something."

"I fail to see…"

Liz cut her off. "And you won't see until you feel the same way he does."

Brody breezed back into the house, John beside him and Elizabeth's dad bringing up the rear.

"We better get home if you want to go out tonight, Liz."

"Oh," Elizabeth took one last sip of her tea. "I almost forgot about that. I'm going dancing at The Pour House tonight."

Brody smiled. "The Pour House, huh? That place is still open? I haven't been there in years. Do you remember that time we…" Brody's voice trailed off as he caught Lou's curious look. "Never mind," he muttered.

Lou crossed her legs and regarded him coolly. "No. Please continue."

"We went there a lot the last year before I left." He chuckled again. "Boy, those were the days."

She pointed to Liz and then to Brody. "You guys went there together?"

"Well, yeah," Liz replied uncomfortably. "That was a long time ago."

"Yes, it was," Lou agreed.

John piped in. "Well, I'm going. That's where all the good-looking ladies end up on Sunday nights." He grinned boyishly. "You guys know how much I like to follow the ladies."

"You can barely walk, much less dance."

"I sure can sit a bar stool just fine." John puffed his chest out. "I might just get some sympathetic attention." They all laughed.

"Did you want to go, Brody? For old time's sake?" Liz asked hesitantly.

"Only if Lou goes, too." He regarded her quizzically.

"Oh, no. You guys go ahead. I have some things I need to get done here," Lou said.

"What kind of things?" Brody asked.

"Just some work," she lied.

"I guess we'll have to take a rain check, Liz. Lou's a fraidy cat," Brody provoked her.

"I am not!" Lou protested loudly.

Liz stood up and walked toward the door. "It was good to see you again, Lou."

"You, too, Liz. Thanks again for last night."

"No problem. Someone might need to help my daughter like that someday. You guys are sure you don't want to go tonight?" Liz asked one more time.

Lou heard him say to Liz quietly. "Lou's not like you, Liz. She's a quiet sort of girl."

Lou felt the anger boil up inside her with that comment. Men never picked the quiet girls. They went for the boisterous, beautiful girls with outgoing personalities, like Liz.

"You know what?" Lou stood up straighter. "I think I do want to go."

"Really?" Brody and John both asked in chorus.

"Yeah, really," Lou said sarcastically. Lou stepped closer to Liz and asked quietly. "What should I wear?"

Liz whispered back, "Something sexy and daring."

Lou nodded seriously, having no idea what that meant.

"Do you want me to bring over something you can wear?" she whispered in Lou's ear.

"Would you?" Lou whispered back.

"Six o'clock," Liz said as she got into the truck with her father.

****

Lou relaxed most of the afternoon, second-guessing herself about going out for the evening. She couldn't begin to compare to the knockout, Liz, and was feeling completely uncomfortable about spending the evening walking in her shadow. However, Brody had thrown down the gauntlet and she had picked it up. Now she had to make the best of it. Brody knew what she looked like, in and out of bed. *Would he still pick me if there are other women within his reach? Would he still be just as interested? Or would he pass me over and move on to someone else?* Only one way to find out.

Brody knocked on her door at suppertime. She opened the door a crack. "Yeah?"

"Hey. John just burned some chicken on the grill. Want to come down and eat?"

She glanced absently at her watch. "Is it that late already?"

"Yeah. Liz will be here in about thirty minutes. Come on down and get something to eat."

He reached to put an arm around her shoulders and she sidestepped, avoiding him, walking ahead of him down the hallway instead. "Something bothering you?" he asked.

She spoke around the fingernail she was chewing. "No. Why would anything be wrong?"

"Is your head still hurting? We can cancel tonight if you don't feel like going out."

"Oh, no," she breathed. "We're going out. With Liz," she added as an afterthought. She shook the thoughts away. They would get her nowhere. But she wanted to know so badly. . "Tell me one thing?"

"What?"

"What kind of relationship did you have with her all those years ago?"

"We grew up together. We were best friends. Then, in high school, we were boyfriend and girlfriend."

"What kind of boyfriend and girlfriend? Casual? Or serious?"

He stopped her in the hallway and put his arms around her, pulling her close. "What kind of question is that?"

"It's the kind of question you ask someone who you've been sleeping with," she snapped at him.

"Do you want to know if we had sex, Lou? If you do, just ask." It was almost like he was daring her to do just that.

"Never mind," she bit out. "I really don't want to know. I just want to know how many memories I'll be up against tonight.

"If you change your mind, just ask me."

"I won't change my mind." She pushed against his chest. He turned her loose.

They ate supper in relative silence. John prattled on about various topics, not oblivious to the tension. After dinner, they cleared the table and loaded the dishwasher. Then they went and sat outside on the porch.

About five minutes later, Lou saw a cloud of dust coming down the winding drive, created by the red convertible that belonged to Liz. She had the top up this time and Lou realized why as soon as she stepped out of the car. She punched John's arm as he whistled softly under his breath. Liz was beautiful. Her long hair fell in waves against her bare shoulders. Her tube top looked stunning rather than gaudy, showing off her perfect breasts.

"She didn't have those back when I knew her," Lou heard Brody whisper to John. Her black jeans hugged her thighs and rode low on her hips. Lou saw the dimples at the small of her back as she bent over to retrieve a bag from the backseat of the car.

Lou shot Brody a scathing look. Then she smiled a fake smile at Liz and rose from her seat.

Liz cocked her head to one side and regarded Lou's ponytail, shorts, and T-shirt with a small smile. "You ready?" she asked.

"Ready as I'll ever be." Lou held up two hands as though surrendering.

"Then let's get started," Liz said, walking through the screen door. She motioned for Lou to follow her. "Get moving," she snapped playfully. "We don't have all day." She turned to Brody and John. "I know you both have a certain level of adorability at all times but you need to go and get ready, too." She snapped her fingers.

They both hopped out of their chairs and headed for their rooms as well.

Liz followed Lou up the stairs, chattering the whole way.

They walked into Lou's room and Liz turned her around slowly, silently appraising Lou's figure. "You got some mighty fine assets, lady. Easy as pie. Go get in the shower while I get things ready here." She shooed Lou with her hands, slowly prodding her.

Lou stepped into the shower feeling defeated. She showered and washed her hair quickly. She shaved her armpits and legs and applied scented lotion to her whole body. She wrapped her hair in a towel, turban style, and tied a towel around her body. She stepped back into the room, feeling like a teenager back in the locker room. "Okay, let get started," Liz began.

Lou cut her off, holding up one hand. "Wait." She took a deep breath. "I need to talk to you about something first."

Liz sat down on the edge of the bed. "I was wondering when you were going to get around to it?" she grinned.

"Get around to what?" Lou asked, biting her lip.

"Let me make it easy for you, Lou. Brody and I were 'a thing' when we were young."

"How serious?" she asked, biting her lip again.

"All the way serious," she replied. Lou groaned. "But that was when we were young, Lou."

"You were old enough for it to be 'all the way'," Lou tossed at her.

"All the way in the way teenagers do, Lou. Not adults. It was over before he ever left town and neither of us wants to strike it back up again."

"You don't?" Lou asked hesitantly.

"Hell, no, Lou. Anyone can see he's crazy about you. Anyone but you, that is. He certainly doesn't want me. To be quite honest, I'm one hundred percent in love with my 'baby daddy'." She laughed out loud at her own choice of words. "We've been dating for years. I got pregnant and we tried to make it work. We never got married because he just wasn't interested. So, a few months ago, I kicked him out on his ear and told him not to come back until he had a ring in his hand." She sighed. "So far, he hasn't shown up. But, he's going to be there tonight. Why do you think I dressed like this?" She pointed to her attire. "It sure as hell ain't for Brody. I could be standing butt naked in front of him and he would see right through me, looking for you."

"I don't see it that way," Lou replied.

"Of course you don't. You're on the inside looking out. Things can be a little distorted when you're looking from that direction. Trust me, you've got that man wrapped around your little finger." She dumped the bag she brought with her on the bed. "Now let's get started. Sexy starts on the inside." She dug through Lou's underwear drawer until she found a pair of black thong panties. "Put these on."

Lou clutched them in her hand. "You have to be kidding me. I have never worn these before."

"Nope. If he sees a little string of lace above your waistband, he'll be thinking about them all night long. Trust me."

Lou stepped into the panties and pulled them up, wiggling as they settled into place. "You'll forget about them in a few minutes," Liz said. Lou nodded.

She opened Lou's underwear drawer again and sifted through her bras. "Your breasts are bigger than mine. I'm jealous." She pulled a black bra from the drawer and tossed it to Lou. It was one of the smallest and sexiest ones she had. Lou turned her back and put it on, dropping the towel. "Damn, I wish I had an ass like that," Liz said. "Do you work out?"

"I run," Lou replied, uncomfortable with the appraisal.

"I could run all day and not get an ass like that," Liz stated.

Lou shrugged. "But you have great legs."

Liz waved her off. "We all have something we want to change. Besides, you have great legs, too." She fished amongst the pile of clothes again and pulled out a tiny jean miniskirt. "I think this will look fabulous on you."

"I don't know, Liz," Lou said, holding the miniscule piece of fabric up to her body. It fell just six inches below her crotch.

"Oh, try it on and see how it looks."

Lou put it on and tugged the miniskirt's hem southward but was unable to get any extra length.

"It's not going to grow on you. I promise." Liz picked up a modern version of a hippie tube top and handed it to Lou. It was light blue with complimentary streaks of color that danced across the fabric, completely off the shoulder. "If you wear this one, you'll have to lose the bra."

Lou clutched her bosom. "I can't go out without a bra."

"Lou," she said gently. "You have got a rack most women would kill for. Or pay a lot of money for, like I did."

"Your boobs aren't real?" Lou asked incredulously.

"Nope. I was born flat as a board."

Lou laughed out loud.

Lou put on the top and surveyed the effect in the mirror. She unhooked the bra and took it off. The gathered tube top clung to her breasts and gentle folds of fabric poured around her hips in a jagged edge. She had to admit that the effect was stunning.

She turned and faced Liz. "What do you think?"

"That's the one," she replied, nodding her head. "Now for the hair and makeup." She expertly applied foundation, powder, eyeliner, eye shadow, mascara, and a touch of lipstick. Liz sat her on the closed toilet lid and flipped her head upside down, drying it while she was inverted. Then she sat her up and ran her fingers through, fluffing it. She picked up a warm curling iron and rolled small ringlets of the hair around her face. Then she piled some of the hair on top of her head and secured it with a clasp. She stepped back, surveyed her work and sprayed the finished product lightly with hairspray.

Lou turned and looked into the mirror. She gasped and said, "Damn, you do good work."

"It's hard to mess with perfection, Lou. I just enhanced what you already have." Lou stepped into the room and surveyed herself in the full dressing mirror on the back of her door.

"Will this get Brody's attention? Better yet, will it keep his attention?" she muttered.

Liz heard her anyway. "Let's go and see, shall we?" She held out a pair of thong sandals to Lou and offered her some accessories. She took the sandals and pulled them on her feet. She turned down the accessories, opting to wear the silver necklace Brody had given her instead.

The two women walked down and the stairs whispering. "Are you sure this skirt's not too short?" Lou asked breathlessly, her heart fluttering in her chest.

"Positive," Liz said as she pushed her through the doorway into the kitchen.

"Jesus Christ," Brody breathed, standing when he saw her for the first time.

****

She walked through the doorway and Brody felt his pants tighten as he looked her up and down. She usually possessed such a subtle beauty that Lou all made up was somewhat shocking. He started down at her feet, appraising the leather thong sandals that fit between her perfectly manicured toes. His gaze moved up her ankles and calves, taking in her thin yet defined shin muscles. He moved past her knees to her long, firm thighs. Her tiny jean skirt barely left anything to the imagination. Yet that imagination was running wild. Damn, it was going crazy.

Silky, nearly transparent fabric floated around her hips. A tight fitting top hugged her breasts like a second skin. Her nipples tightened as his gaze ran over them. He licked his lips.

His gaze traveled up to creamy shoulders that were left bare. Her dark hair tickled those shoulders. His gaze lingered as he saw her reach up to finger the dream catcher necklace he had given her. He took in her hair, partially piled atop her head, as it touched her face. Liz had brought out the color of her eyes and made her lips look perfectly kissable. That was all he wanted to do. He wanted to kiss her. He didn't want to go to The Pour House. He didn't want to be in a room with other people.

He wanted to be all alone with Lou so that he could drink in the sight of her and appreciate her in the way he wanted—completely naked.

This was a totally different side of her. Everyone knew Lou was beautiful, but you usually noticed her inner beauty first, her laughing eyes, kind nature, her quick wit. Now, all he could see were legs stretching on endlessly, heavy breasts he ached to touch, and a perfect mouth he wanted to kiss. Her hair begged to be let down from its clasp atop her head.

John finally broke the silence by stating loudly, "Well, daggum, Lou! You look purtier than I've ever seen you!" He walked over and picked her up, spinning her around. The skirt rose up dangerously high.

Lou scolded John, putting her hand on his shoulders and smacking at them. "Will you put me down?" she shrieked, laughing.

She stepped back and took in John's appearance. "You don't look so bad yourself." John wore jeans, a button down shirt tucked into those jeans, one cowboy boot on one foot, and his cast on the other.

Her gaze moved over to Brody, similarly attired, including the hat that rested on the top of his head. He thought his bruised face gave him a rakish appearance. His hat was pulled low over his forehead, somewhat hiding his gaze from hers, which was probably a good thing. If she could have guessed what he was thinking, she would have been scared out of her britches. Which, come to think of it, didn't sound like a bad idea.

"You guys ready to go?" John asked, extending his arm to Elizabeth. She took hold of it with a smile and tapped the front of his hat. "You feel like riding with me, cowboy?"

"Why, yes, ma'am. I would be honored." He followed her out to the car and opened the door for her. She slid in and he went around to the passenger's side. John didn't like riding shotgun, but his cast still prevented him from driving.

"Try not to muss her up too much, Brody," Liz called from the open car window as they pulled away.

Lou licked her lips as Brody approached slowly. He lifted a lock of her hair and rubbed it between his fingers, regarding her from beneath lowered lashes. She licked her lips and fidgeted as his eyes surveyed her from head to toe again. She took a deep breath, her jaw quivering slightly. "You look amazing," he breathed. "Any chance I could talk you into just staying home?" he asked as his mouth rested on her bare shoulder.

"And miss my very first date ever?" Lou asked. Was she excited about tonight? "This is a date, right?" Yes, she was excited.

Brody remembered their discussion at the hospital when they had first met. She had confessed that, even at her age, she had never been on a real date. She looked a little let down that he would even suggest staying home, and he realized that she was anticipating the evening for more than just the thought of going out and having a good time. She was creating a memory. A first date. And he got to be her lucky beau with whom she would share it.

He suddenly sobered. "Yes, ma'am. This is one hundred percent a real date." He held his arm out to her in the same manner that John had with Elizabeth.

They walked out to the Jeep together and Brody held open the door for her. She slid into the seat, unaware that she was showing a good bit of the creamy skin of her inner thigh as she did so. Brody looked away and caught his lower lip between his teeth, biting hard to take his thoughts off Lou's thighs. Damn, but he was in for a long night.

Chapter Twenty

Walking into The Pour House took Lou back to the days when she would visit the strip clubs with her mother. She had to wait back in the fitting rooms and entertain herself with games and other activities while her mother danced. Sometimes, though, she would peek out at the crowd when no one was looking.

This club had the same kind of atmosphere but it didn't feel dirty in the least. Ladies stomped across the dance floor in their cowboy boots, their men trailing close behind. People told loud stories while sitting on tall stools around even taller tables. They held drinks in one hand, peanuts in the other. Women smacked their gum and men tried to outdo one another.

Lou stepped across the threshold and felt Brody's hand slip into hers. She raised her gaze and smiled into his eyes. Her sandals crunched across peanut shells spread around the floor.

Brody pointed out John and Liz seated at one of the tall tables. They had saved seats for them both. Lou sat down next to Liz and smiled tentatively, not quite sure what to do with her hands.

"Why don't you go and get her a drink to hold on to, Brody?" Liz shook her own glass in his direction and chinked the ice cubes around. "Grab me another while you're at it, won't you?"

Brody looked at Lou. "Do you want water? Soft drink?"

Liz broke in. "Hell no, she doesn't want water or a soft drink," she said with a smile.

"Lou?" he asked.

"Just get me whatever you're having," she said quietly to Brody.

"I'm driving," Brody said. "But I'll get something you'll like."

"Hey," John said, tipping his own bottle up. "Don't forget about me." He set the empty beer bottle on the table.

"Who could forget about you?" Brody muttered as he walked away.

Liz immediately scooted closer to Lou. Lou leaned over and spoke in her ear. "Is he here yet?" she asked, wondering if the object of Liz's affection had arrived.

She nodded. "Yeah." She pointed with her eyes to the man sitting two tables away. Lou turned to look in his direction. "Don't look!" she yelped in Lou's ear. "Or he's going to see you."

Lou laughed, feeling like she was back in high school. "Is he alone?"

"He had better be," was Liz's only response.

Brody came back to the table carrying one drink in a glass with ice and three beers. He passed them out and took a seat beside Lou, dropping one arm around her shoulders.

Lou heard the twangy sound of country music as the song changed and the sound of the footsteps on the dance floor took on a new beat. She tapped her foot in rhythm with the song. She lifted the beer to her lips and felt the cool glass as it pressed against them. The bitter liquid poured over her tongue and she grimaced. Liz reached into her own glass, plucked out a lemon wedge, and forced it into the rim of the bottle.

"There. Now try it." She encouraged Lou to raise the bottle again.

"Better," Lou stated, nodding her head.

Liz was totally focused on the man, the object of her affection.

"Mary Gordon just sat down next to him. The little hussy," she breathed.

Lou casually looked over and waved a hand in the air in dismissal. "She has nothing on you."

"You don't think so?"

"I know so," Lou replied. She had never had a girlfriend in her life, but was enjoying the camaraderie. "What's his name?"

Liz breathed on a heavy sigh, "Dave."

Liz gasped as she saw Dave get up and lead Mary Gordon onto the dance floor. "That's it." She smacked her hand on the table. "I need someone to dance with." She looked hesitantly toward Lou. "Can I steal your man for just a few minutes?"

Lou thought hard about it for a moment and said, "I would love to share my man with you, for the sole purpose of dancing, that is. However, I would like to dance the first dance with him myself." She looked at him beseechingly after draining the last drop of her beer.

He choked on soda. She patted him on the back, laughing. "You want to dance?" he sputtered out.

"Well, not if you don't want to." She pretended to pout.

"Oh, no," he laughed back. "If the lady wants to dance on our first date, the lady gets to dance." He stood up and pulled her from her chair, gently tugging her fingertips.

He led her onto the dance floor and quickly showed her how to do a lively two-step. Alan Jackson set the rhythm and Brody kept it. Lou followed along surprisingly well.

The sound of Alan Jackson slowly tapered off and everyone on the dance floor stopped briefly to clap.

Then it was time for the next one. Barely a breather and Lou felt Brody slide his arms around her waist and pull her close. Her arms rose up around his neck where her hands tickled the fine curls that hung over his collar.

"I had no idea you could dance so well," she said in his ear.

"You're not so bad yourself." He smiled into her eyes, as though they were the only two people in the world.

Lou felt his hands slide under her shirt to rest on the skin of her back. His hands moved along the waistline of her skirt and then he frowned. One finger slipped below the lacy fabric of the thong she was wearing which rode just a little higher than her skirt.

He took a deep breath. "Is that what I think it is?" he spoke close to her ear.

"Uh huh." She nodded. Suddenly out of breath herself, heat creeping up her cheeks. "You don't like it?"

"Well…" Common sense obviously warred with his true thoughts, "I haven't seen it yet."

"And just what makes you think you're going to see it tonight?" she asked pertly. "Do you usually sleep with women on the first date?"

"You wouldn't dare." He groaned.

"Try me," she replied.

"Well, that's what I'm trying to do, Lou. Good grief," he joked, nuzzling her neck.

Just then, the slow dance ended and Lou heard the quick beat of a Taylor Swift song begin. She felt a tap on her right shoulder and heard a kind voice speak to her. "Is this gentleman going to take all your time tonight? Or do you think you could steal a minute for an old man?" He must have been in his fifties and Brody knew him immediately, smiling and shaking hands with him.

"This old fella taught me geometry, Lou." He addressed the older man. "Anyone but you and I would have to say no," he laughed. "But if the lady agrees…" He motioned that they should proceed. Lou nodded enthusiastically.

As her new partner led her away, she yelled back to Brody, "Go and get Liz." He nodded back at her, heading in that direction.

Lou went through two more partners before Brody found his way back to her. His arms slipped around her as he nuzzled the side of her face with his evening scruff. "Having fun?" he asked.

She nodded slowly. "I'm having a great time. Thanks so much for bringing me." He brought his head down to kiss her softly and quickly on the lips.

"You see what I did?" he asked Lou, nodding to a place over his shoulder. Lou looked and saw Liz pressed close to Dave. They looked deeply into one another's eyes, as though they were made for each other.

"Bet I can guess who she'll be going home with tonight," Lou replied. "How did you do it?"

"Best way to get a man's attention is to give yours to someone else. That little green-eyed monster will get 'em every time." Brody laughed.

"Have you seen John?" Lou asked.

"Last time I saw him, he was, indeed, getting sympathy credits from a lady at the bar. He was sitting that stool pretty well."

The song ended and he led her back to the table. "I'll be right back," he said to her as she sat down and he handed her another beer. "Got to find the little cowboy's room." She nodded, raising her beer to her lips.

As soon as Brody was out of her sight, she felt a hand on her shoulder and looked up. She jumped as she realized it was Wes.

He said quietly, "Don't say a word." He held up a hand to stop her. "I just need to talk to you. Things are not what they appear to be. Call me when you can talk." He pressed a folded note into her hand, his eyebrows raised in question.

He blended back into the crowd. She unfolded the note and the only thing written on it was a phone number. She slid it into her back pocket and took another sip of her beer. She pasted on a big smile for when Brody came out of the bathroom, although her heart was still pounding.

He placed another beer in front of her and sat down on the high stool, his knee touching hers intimately before his hand reached out and lazily grazed across the sensitive skin of her thigh. She lifted the beer to her lips and regarded him from below lowered lashes.

"Just what do you think you're doing?" she breathed, her hand covering his under the small table.

"It's a lot better that you asked me what I'm doing and not what I'm thinking," he chuckled. Heat crept up her cheeks.

Liz and Dave made a huge commotion as they slid into the seats across from them, laughing. Liz immediately stood back up and grabbed Lou's arm, giggling like a schoolgirl as she said dramatically, "Come on. I need to go to the lady's room."

Lou shrugged at Brody and set her beer on the table. "Be right back," she mumbled as Liz led her away. Lou saw two doors, one labeled "Pointers" and the other "Setters." They walked into the ladies' room and Liz turned to her with a huge smile on her face.

"He wants to come home with me tonight," she announced, her arms waving in excitement.

"What are you going to do?" Lou asked, just as breathlessly.

"Lord, girl! We've been dancing cheek to cheek. He smells so good." She inhaled deeply. "I want to take him on home with me."

Lou thought for a moment. "Are you sure you want to make it that easy?"

"What do you mean by easy?" Liz stopped breathing and listened intently.

"I mean the man doesn't value you for more than one night at a time. Do you want more than that?" Lou asked thoughtfully.

"Of course, I do!" Liz shrieked.

"Then make him work for it, Liz. Make him want you and then make him go on home alone. I bet he'll be knocking on your door tomorrow wanting to spend some time with you."

"You think so?" Liz asked cautiously.

"I do think so," Lou replied.

Liz's eyes drew together. "What about you and Brody? Is that what you're going to do?"

"My situation with Brody is different. I've known all along it's only temporary." Lou turned to the mirror and applied fresh lipstick, casually. "That's okay with me." She pasted a fake grin on her face. "But you have a daughter with Dave and want him in your life forever. He obviously is drawn to you. Now you just need to get him to the point where he can't do without you. Let him be into you for a while instead of you being into him."

Liz groaned. "But it will be so hard telling him goodnight at my door."

"Oh, no!" Lou laughed. "Don't even let him take you home. You say goodnight here and then we'll take you home. We'll take away the temptation that way." Lou held out her hand for a handshake. "Deal?"

Liz gripped Lou's hand firmly in her own. "Deal."

"Good. Now let's go out there and drive him crazy just a little longer. Then you leave him panting as you drive away." It was a nice having Liz for a friend.

Brody and Lou danced a few more dances, Brody keeping her close by his side. He was the designated driver so he switched to Coke after that first beer.

Lou drank lightly but still had a serious buzz when it was time to go home.

Brody's lips grazed her exposed shoulder. "Would you stop that?" she scolded. "We're in public."

"Stop what?" His mouth trailed up the side of her neck.

She shrugged him off playfully.

"Can we go home now?" he mouthed against her ear. She shivered.

"Uh huh," she nodded.

"Now?" he asked as his teeth gently tugged her earlobe.

She stepped back from him slightly and took his fingertips in hers. "You go and get John and I'll get Liz."

Brody pouted. "Awwww. Do I have to? Can't we call them a cab?"

"That would just be rude," she replied as she marched off to find Liz. She finally found her in a dark corner, her head barely visible as she was overshadowed by Dave's larger frame. Lou stepped close to them and coughed loudly.

"Uh, hum," she coughed. Then she repeated it a little louder. Liz looked up, her eyes hazed with passion. Lou could see she was almost lost.

"Are you ready to go, Liz?"

"Go?" Dave and Liz both said in unison. But Liz recovered quickly, her eyes meeting Lou's with a sparkle.

She disengaged herself from Dave's embrace. "I do have to go, honey." She patted his cheek softly as she stepped away from him.

"But, I thought I would take you home." He gave her a knowing look.

She bent and kissed his forehead. "I wish I could, but I have to meet with a client tomorrow, first thing." She winked at Lou. "Maybe some other time," she threw back over her shoulder as they walked away.

She grabbed Lou's arm and whispered, "Did I do okay?"

"You did great!" Lou whispered back, just as Brody caught them with John in tow.

Brody looked over at Dave, silently stewing in the corner, and laughed out loud. "Poor fella doesn't know what hit him."

Lou and Liz both laughed.

John said, "What did I miss?"

Liz pointed toward Dave.

"Poor sucker should have seen that one coming," John said with a chuckle. For good measure, he put his arm around Liz as they went out the door.

****

Brody put the top down on the Jeep and Lou felt the wind blow through her hair. She removed the combs holding the hair piled on top of her head and let it fall freely over her shoulders. Brody took her hand and held it casually on the ride home. They dropped Liz off at her door and watched her until she was safely inside.

They drove slowly under the Western Skies arch at the end of the drive, Brody taking in the sights and sounds of the night and the farm with a deep breath and a glance around the property. His eyes met Lou's and she smiled. He knew she felt the same way about the place as he did.

Brody drove slowly up to the house and cut the engine, hearing the creak of the gravel beneath the tires. Lou got out and met him at the front of the Jeep. She looked at him with affection and said, "Thanks so much for such a wonderful first date." She rose on tiptoe and kissed him lightly on the lips.

"Oh, no, you don't. It's not over until I walk you to your door." He spun her around and patted her bottom. "Get a couple of bottles of water and I'll meet you in the kitchen."

Brody turned to John who lingered uncomfortably. "I'm planning on sleeping in Lou's room tonight," he stated directly. "Do you have a problem with it?"

"Does she?" John asked quickly.

"I'm about to find out," Brody answered.

John was just drunk enough to say, "You treat her right or I'll kick your ass." He pointed his finger to accentuate the words.

"If I don't, I deserve it," Brody replied.

John nodded and clapped Brody on the shoulder. John went to his room to go to bed.

Brody caught Lou bent over in front of the refrigerator and slipped in behind her, his hands gripping her hips firmly as he pulled her back against him. By her gasp, he knew she felt the swell of him against her backside.

"I thought you were just going to walk me to my door," she teased, giggling as he spun her around and pulled her close.

He smiled and sighed against her neck. He loosened his hold on her and groaned, stepping away from her. Taking her fingers in his, he drew her toward the stairs. "A date is never over until I kiss a lady at her door," he smiled at her.

They stood outside her door in silence, Lou dancing from foot to foot while clutching a bottle of water in each hand. She had just enough beer in her system to feel loose and uninhibited. Stretching on tiptoe, she placed her lips against his, softly encouraging him to kiss her back. He groaned and clutched her to him, tilting his head and deepening the kiss, his tongue meeting hers.

He broke the kiss yet still held her clutched against him and said, "You're going to make me throw all my good intentions right out the window."

She smiled, slowly kissing his neck. "You had good intentions?" she asked against his skin.

He gasped and ground out, "I started out with some," as her lips found his earlobe and she suckled gently.

"And if I don't want you to have good intentions?" she whispered against his ear.

"Then your wish is my command," he growled, cupping her bottom and lifting her from the floor. He pulled her legs around his waist and felt her lock her ankles behind him. The bottles of water hit the floor with a loud *thunk* as she grabbed tightly to his shoulders. He held her bottom with one hand, turned the doorknob with the other and walked into the room.

He groaned loudly as her teeth nibbled gently at his collarbone. "If you don't stop that, this isn't going to last nearly as long as I want it to."

"Then we'll just have to do it again, won't we?" she mumbled as she unbuttoned his shirt and placed her hands against his skin.

"You bet we will." He continued to hold her bottom in his hands, her legs around his waist as he lowered his mouth to her shirt. He tugged gently against the fabric with his teeth. "Take this off," he murmured.

She grabbed both ends of the top and drew it over her head, exposing her breasts to his gaze in one quick move. He hissed and said, "I watched them move with every step you took tonight, but I couldn't touch them." He lifted her a little higher and teased her nipple to life with his tongue. She threw her head back, clouds of hair falling over her shoulders.

"And here I thought you would have been thinking about the thong all night."

He grunted, " You wore that just for me, didn't you?" She nodded as he slid his hands beneath her skirt and lifted it just a scant few inches to expose her bottom. When it was bunched around her waist, he walked over to the dresser. "I just have to get at least one good look at this thing." He held her in front of the mirror and the look on his face changed from one of desire to pure lust. He watched his own hands in the mirror as they squeezed her bottom, his thumb tweaking the thong like a guitar string. His heartbeat thudded in his ears at the sight of his hands stroking her bottom in the mirror and the length of her naked back.

"God, you are so beautiful," he breathed as he stared at her in the mirror.

"I am not," she started to protest.

"Oh, yes, you are," he said as he set her on her feet and unbuttoned her skirt. He pulled it down her legs and she stepped out of it. She stood before him in nothing but the thong. He grabbed the material at her hips and slowly pulled those down as well. He stood up in front of her and shucked his own clothes quickly. "I'll show you how beautiful you are." He picked her up and set her on the bed on her knees, putting himself behind her. From this angle, she could see herself fully in the dresser mirror. She gasped and turned toward him, looking away from the mirror.

"Oh, no, you don't," he mumbled against her neck, placing his arm around her waist and pulling her back against his chest. His hand cupped her breast and teased her nipple between his thumb and forefinger.

****

Lou closed her eyes, trying to avoid the sight of her own naked body in the mirror.

"Open your eyes," he breathed against her ear. She did so and gasped at the sight of his hand as it crept down her body and tangled in the curls at the juncture of her thighs. She gasped as he found the small nub that was her center and gently coaxed it to life. Her eyes closed again as her body was awash with sensation. She leaned back against him, her head thrown back over his shoulder. He kissed the side of her neck that was exposed to his gaze, nipping gently with his teeth.

With Brody resting on his knees, she sank down on his lap, still facing the mirror. He removed his hand from her curls and pressed it flat against her stomach, drawing her back to him. She gasped as his length slid into her. He filled her completely as she sank down on him, gripping him tightly. He began to move slowly and she rocked above him. She drew in a quick breath as his fingers stole back into her curls and teased her anew. Her heartbeat pounded in her ears as the pressure begin to build. She bit her bottom lip, reaching back to grab at his buttocks to bring him closer and faster to her.

Through the fog of passion, she heard him say, "Open your eyes." She did and inhaled quickly at the sight of her own passion-filled eyes as they met his in the mirror. His gaze did not waver from hers as he took another stroke, then another. Then her world exploded as she found release. She watched his face as he did the same. She leaned back against him and felt him envelop her in his arms before he lowered her to the bed, pulling her close to him, her head upon his shoulder.

He stiffened. "Shit, Lou. I forgot to use protection. I had it in my pocket but I got carried away."

She patted his face gently. "It's okay, we don't need it." *I'm already late*, she wanted to scream.

"You took care of it?" he asked casually, obviously relieved.

"We don't need it," she said again, kissing his cheek.

"I'm glad. Because you feel so good," he said as he squeezed her bottom.

He laughed as she said, "I hope the second date is half as good as the first."

****

Lou woke before dawn to the slow kisses on her neck and a heaviness pressing her into the mattress. Brody spread her thighs and settled himself between them. She stretched slowly and her eyes opened to meet his.

"What a way to wake me up," she breathed at him as he filled her.

"I could wake up like this every day," he said against her skin.

Just until you go home. Aloud, she murmured, "You make one heck of an alarm clock."

She sighed as he began to move. His movements were slow and languorous, drawing out the pleasure until she quaked around him and he stiffened above her.

He rolled, taking her with him, her front pressed to his. "What time is it?" she mumbled, her face pressed against his chest.

He groaned. "Time to get up, unfortunately. I turned the clock off a few minutes ago. I was just watching you sleep." He brushed the hair from her forehead.

"You're not supposed to watch me sleep," she scolded quietly.

"How would you know?" he teased. "You've never slept with anyone before. Never woken up beside someone you care about."

Her heart started to pound. "You care about me?" She tried to sound playful but her heartbeat echoed in her head like a hammer knocking on wood.

He tweaked her nose. "Of course, I do, silly. Why else would I be here?" He smacked her bottom soundly. "Better get up. Bunch of hungry men downstairs."

Lou groaned, trying to catch her head up with her heart. "I almost forgot Sadie is gone." She rose and tiptoed to the bathroom. She turned on the shower and stepped beneath the spray, then felt him slide in behind her. He took the soap from her and washed her back and the rest of her body. Then he shampooed her hair, gently rubbing her scalp. He pushed her back beneath the spray and kissed her soundly.

"Better get out before I muss you up again." He turned her around and pushed her out. He washed himself quickly and tied a towel around his waist. He winked at her as he went out the door to go to his own room to get dressed.

She was getting way too attached. He was only going to stay for a short time, and then he had his life and his work to return to. There was no way she was leaving the only family she had ever known, not that he had even asked. She wasn't a city girl, and he had made it clear he didn't want to be a country boy. He didn't want to be embroiled in a family, even if it was his own.

As soon as he was out of earshot, she rifled through the clothes that had been flung on the floor the night before and pulled out the small jean miniskirt. She reached into the back pocket and retrieved the phone number Wes had slipped to her. Her heart pumped a crazy rhythm in her chest as she dialed the phone.

A sleepy voice answered and said, "Hullo?"

"This is Lou Smith. You wanted me to give you a call?"

She heard him shuffle on the other end.

"I need to meet with you. You're in serious danger and I can help."

"I thought you were the danger," Lou replied, deadpan.

"Not me, Lou, but I know who is. How soon can you meet me?"

"I'll call you when I can get free."

"I'll be waiting."

****

Brody whistled while he dressed. He had never felt as content as he did at this moment. He was home. He was with his family. He was with Lou. He had missed this. He had let his anger and his drive to succeed at all costs keep him from the people he loved the most. He barely made it home before his mother's death but that just made him more determined not to miss one single moment from here on out.

He skipped down the stairs and stopped briefly in the office. He picked up the phone and dialed. He reached the night secretary for his boss, the chief of surgery. "Surgical suite. How can I help you?"

A smile lit his face. "Hi, Beautiful! Do you miss me yet?"

He could hear the smile on her weathered old face. She was sixty-five if she was a day old. "Is that you, Brody?" she chuckled.

"Oh, shucks. How'd you know it was me?"

"Nobody else tries to sweet talk me the way you do. What can I do for you?"

"Is the chief around?" Brody asked.

"Nope. He's in surgery. We just happen to be short one hand around here, you know," she said candidly. "When are you coming home?"

"Well, that's what I want to talk to the chief about. I spoke to him last week about maybe transferring to the local hospital here. Do you know if he looked into it for me?"

"Leaving us, are you? What's her name?" the old woman asked. He could hear her fake fingernails tapping on her desk.

"What makes you think there's a 'her'?" Brody asked.

"Because only a woman could make you want to stay away," she replied.

The chief's secretary was known for spreading rumors so he said, "There's no woman, Rita. Just a lot of obligations that are going to take up my time for a while."

He heard a noise in the doorway and looked up to find Lou staring at him blankly. He turned his back to her and said quietly into the phone, "Can you get with the chief and have him call me about that matter as soon as you see him?"

"Sure thing, Hun. I'll take care of it for you."

"Talk at you later, Rita."

"Bye, Brody."

****

She knew it, knew it, knew it, knew it. There was no "woman back home." At least not one that would make him want to stay. He just had some obligations. She slammed a frying pan on the counter. She guessed he needed to stay long enough to tie up the estate and the farm and was asking for an extended leave. Too bad she hadn't heard the whole conversation.

"There's no woman," Lou mocked under her breath just as Brody walked up behind her.

"What'd you say?" he asked.

"Nothing," she snapped.

"What can I help with?"

"Nothing," she snapped, again.

"You can't do this all by yourself, Lou. Just tell me what to do," he requested.

"If I have to tell you what to do, it's really not a very big help," she replied.

His eyebrows drew together. "Something bothering you?"

"Why would something be bothering me?"

"I don't know. You just seem kind of tense."

John walked into the kitchen at that moment.

Lou sighed loudly and smiled at him. "Thank God you're here. Can you help me get breakfast on the table?"

"At your service, ma'am," he replied as he filled the coffeepot and started setting the buffet.

"Well, hell," Brody said. "I could have done that."

"Never mind. We have it under control." Her smile did not quite reach her eyes.

"If you say so," Brody said as he walked outside and sat down on the steps of the porch.

"You guys okay?" John asked.

"Why wouldn't we be?"

"You seem kind of tense."

"Must be your imagination."

The three of them ushered the hands out and cleaned up after breakfast with Brody pitching in as he saw what needed to be done. Lou wiped the sink dry with a towel and hung it over the edge.

"You feel like running today?" Brody asked.

"No," Lou replied, touching her forehead. "I have a headache. I'm just going to go and lay down for a minute."

"I'll go with you," he said, starting to approach her.

She held up a hand and pressed it to his chest. "I won't be able to rest if you're with me. Just give me an hour."

Brody stepped back and quietly said, "Whatever you say."

She turned and walked upstairs alone.

Chapter Twenty-One

Lou quietly closed the door to her room and reached under the mattress to remove the envelope full of photos Wes had given her. She dumped them onto the bed and thumbed through them. She smiled as she saw the solemn teenager and her worn-out mother, looking so alike yet so different. Her mother had looked tired even after a full night's sleep. She didn't look much older than Lou. She had gotten pregnant at such an early age.

Lou stood up and looked into the mirror, comparing her image in the photo with the one in her hand. She had changed. She had grown. She had become more than she had ever dreamed of being as a child. Her bleak existence had become rosy, filled with love and laughter. Instead of living in squalor, she lived in a fine home with wonderful people whom she could call family. They cared for one another, worked side by side and went to bed looking forward to each new day.

"This, too, shall pass," Lou mumbled as she put the photos back in the envelope and tucked them back under the mattress. These feelings of hopelessness and worry would soon pass. They would be over. Something had to happen to change it all. Now she just had to wait and see what the climax would be.

Lou lay down on the bed and fluffed the pillow beneath her head. She closed her eyes and thought of her daughter and Jeb and Sadie, all of whom were safe. Then she thought of Brody and John, who were downstairs, keeping a watchful eye. She drifted off to sleep with a smile on her face.

Lou woke a short time later to the feel of a hand brushing the hair from her forehead. She felt strong fingers linger over the scar at her temple. She reached without opening her eyes and clasped the fingers in her own hand, squeezing gently.

"Ready to get up, sleeping beauty?" Brody asked.

"Why?" Lou groaned.

"I need to run some errands. I wanted you to go with me." Brody said. "John is going, too."

"So, you don't have anyone to babysit me?" she asked.

"You don't need a babysitter. I just wanted your company."
"Yeah, right," she said, swinging her legs off the side of the bed. Her stomach protested the quick movement and she covered her mouth.

"Are you okay?" he asked, reaching out and touching her forehead.

She nodded, fighting back the nausea. "I'm fine. Must just be the stress." She moved into the bathroom and brushed her teeth. "I feel like someone has sawed off my right arm with Sarah not here. I just don't know what to do with myself."

He wrapped his arms around her and drew her close. "I know what to do with you," he said low in her ear.

She smiled and touched her lips to his. "We had better go if you want to be back before lunch."

He patted her bottom and said, "I need to grab something out of the safe. I'll meet you downstairs."

Lou walked down the steps and met John, who was pacing in the kitchen.

"What's got your tail in a twist?" she asked playfully.

He pointed to his cast. "I get this thing off today. Hallelujah!" he yelled. "I might just have to keep it because it sure does get me some points with the ladies."

"You get any sympathy dates last night?" Lou asked.

"Not yet but I got some sympathy phone numbers." He grinned like a child.

Brody walked into the kitchen.

Lou walked by John and tapped his shoulder. "You're incorrigible," she stated.

"And you, Lou, my friend," he paused for dramatic effect and then pointed at the base of her neck, "have a hickey right there." He laughed uproariously and Brody had to cough to cover his own laughter.

Lou tugged at the neck of her shirt, raising it higher. Her face colored instantly and she huffed out the door, sure the two grinning men were trailing her to the Jeep.

Brody got behind the wheel of the Jeep and started the vehicle. He opened the glove box and placed a large wooden cask inside along with a small velvet box. He closed the glove box, his hand brushing Lou's knee as he did so.

"What's that?" she asked.

Brody smiled at her. "The attorney brought me a list of my mother's assets, jewelry, and things that were in the home at the time of her death. There was one piece of jewelry in the safe that wasn't on the list. I want to take it and have it appraised so it can be accounted for." He shrugged. "That's all."

She pointed to the small box. "And that one?"

"Oh, that's just a ring of my mother's. I want to take it and have it cleaned. Sentimental reasons, I guess."

John chimed in from the back seat. "Can you drop me off at the doctor's office?"

"Yeah," Brody nodded. "Can Lou go with you while I go to the jeweler's?"

"What if I want to go to the jeweler's?" Lou broke in, her eyebrows drawn together.

"I'll need a few minutes at the jeweler's," Brody answered. "John looks like he could use some company."

"But…" Lou started.

"Please?" Brody asked patiently.

"Well, if you don't want me to go with you…" Lou frowned.

"I knew you would understand," he said, clasping her hand in his own and squeezing before he pulled into a parking space at the jeweler's. He leaned over and kissed her soundly. "Stop by when John's done and pick me up."

He left no room for argument as he retrieved the jewelry cases from the glove box and slid out of the Jeep. He slammed the door behind him. Lou sat still and watched him cross the street, until John bumped her arm.

"I'll be glad when I can drive again," he said, bringing her out of her reverie. She slid into the driver's seat and fastened her seatbelt, unable to figure out what bothered her so badly about this one trip to town.

****

Brody walked into the jewelry store and approached the sales clerk.

"Can I see the store manager, please?" he asked casually, clutching the boxes in his hand.

"Is there something I can help you with, sir?" the gentleman smiled at him.

"I need to have a piece appraised that I feel is quite valuable. I need to speak with the manager about it, please," he stated, his voice quiet.

"Certainly, sir. I'll see if he's available," the clerk replied, ducking behind a black curtain into a back room.

A portly, balding gentleman shouldered his way through the back door and approached Brody. "May I help you?" he asked austerely.

Brody turned toward the man and held out the smaller of the two boxes. "Let's start small, shall we?" He opened the lid of the small jewelry piece and held it out.

"This was my mother's engagement ring. I would like to have it cleaned and restored. Can you do that for me? It's an antique."

The man smiled as he took the box from Brody. "Quite a treasure you have there," he said. "Are early congratulations in order?" he asked, his eyebrows arched.

Brody nodded. "Only if she accepts my offer," he answered, smiling.

"With a betrothal ring like this, how could she refuse?" The salesman was obviously a man who appreciated a good piece of jewelry. He passed the small box to the sales associate. "Set this up to be cleaned and restored." He turned back to Brody. "You had another piece?" he asked.

Brody held out the larger wooden cask. "This was part of my mother's estate when she died but I couldn't find paperwork to go with it. All the other jewelry had appraisals or valuations so, I just need to find out the value this piece and get official papers for it."

The balding gentleman cracked the lid of the cask slightly and gasped at the huge diamond that winked back at him. He immediately grabbed a small eyeglass and looked closely at the large gem. Brody saw beads of sweat form on his forehead and the man's breathing increased to the point where Brody thought he was going to pass out.

"Are you okay?" Brody asked, gripping the man's shoulder.

The inspection glass fell from his eye and hit the floor as he opened the eye to regard Brody with fascination. He stuttered, "W…w…would it be ok with you if I take this in back for a m…moment?"

"If you're sure you're okay," Brody answered hesitantly.

The man held up one shaking finger and whispered, "Just one moment."

Brody watched the storeowner go through the curtain and was slightly perplexed when he saw the man pick up the phone. He held the large cask open, talking to the person on the other end, his voice a frantic whisper. He peered over his shoulder and noticed Brody looking at him. He drew the phone closer to his mouth and continued talking. He motioned for an employee to draw the curtain closed.

Brody turned and surveyed the shop. He walked around, admiring the watches and earrings, wondering what type of jewelry Lou would like. Nothing so ostentatious, as he regarded a large piece of jewelry. She was an understated kind of girl. Just the kind he liked.

Brody smiled at the sight of an adolescent girl who was with her parents, choosing her first pair of earrings, obviously her birthday present. Brody glanced at his watch, wondering what was taking so long.

Growing frustrated by the wait, he rang the bell for an associate to come out and just give him a receipt for the jewelry so he could leave them and come back later. From the back of the store, a larger gentleman entered the room. He pushed the curtain aside, yet held the jewel cask in his hand. He approached Brody quietly and looked him in the eye. Brody recognized the gentleman as someone familiar but he couldn't place where he knew him from until he smiled. Crooked teeth and a sneer belied the feigned good cheer. Brody stood up straighter and flexed his own hand, remembering when he had broken those same teeth the night the larger man had tried to steal Sarah.

The man slowly lifted the edge of his jacket and showed Brody he was armed, the feigned smile never leaving his face.

He began quietly, nodding his head toward the young girl and her parents. "Do you see that nice little family over there?"

Brody nodded, every muscle in his body on alert.

"You don't want anything to happen to them, do you?"

Brody shook his head.

"Then I'll tell you what you're going to do." The smile became sinister. "You're going to turn around and walk out that door with me and you're going to do it without making a scene. I can take that whole family out." He showed Brody the gun in the holster again. "Before you can blink. Understand?"

"Understood," Brody replied.

The man walked from behind the counter and to the door of the jewelry store, with Brody following behind. He held the door open and Brody walked through it. Gary motioned him toward a large SUV, the one he remembered from the dance.

He opened the door of the SUV and indicated Brody should get in. Just then, he heard a loud and friendly voice behind him.

"Brody! How's it going, man? It's been years since I saw you last!" The man cuffed Brody on the shoulder. Then he stepped closer to Gary and stretched to his full height. He reached into his own holster and pulled his gun, holding it down by his leg. He said a little more quietly. "I got the same call you did, Gary. Boss said to tell you this one is mine." He reached and took the wooden cask from Gary's outstretched hand. "You want to make a big deal of it?" he asked Gary.

The big brute finally spoke. "Boss told you to come, too?"

The second man reached into his pocket and pulled out his cell phone. He held it out to Gary. "You want to give him a call to verify?" Gary reached for the phone and Wes held it out of his reach saying, "But I give you fair warning. If you want to make him take his attention off that little brunette and the blow job she was giving him, you go right ahead." He chuckled. "Let's just say he was a little busy." The man made an obscene gesture with his own hand.

Then he motioned to Brody, who was still silently watching the exchange.

"Get in the car," he said brusquely as he motioned to his own car which was parked beside them.

Brody weighed his options. He could either go with the big brute that had nearly kicked his ass or take his chances with this guy. He chose the latter. He walked around to the passenger side of the car and got in. Wes slid in beside him and started the car, backing slowly out of the parking space. He drove down a few blocks and parked again, watching his rearview mirror.

"We only have a few minutes, so I have to make this short. You're all in danger. I need to talk to you all together. Can we go to your house and do it?"

"How do I know you're not the danger?" Brody asked.

"If I was, I wouldn't have just saved your life."

Brody nodded, still unsure. He held up both hands in surrender. "Whatever you say."

"Where's Lou?" the man asked.

"At the doctor's office with John. Then they're going to the pharmacy before coming to pick me up."

"Let's see if we can head them off, shall we?" Wes asked of no one in particular as he backed out into the street again.

****

Lou waited patiently while John had his cast removed. He walked out of the doctor's office with full use of both feet, only slightly limping as they walked out the door together and into the pharmacy next door.

"What did you need in here?" John asked.

Lou pretended to blush. "Some girly stuff, if you don't mind," Lou said, batting her eyelashes at him.

"Does that mean you want me to get lost?" John asked.

"Only in the nicest way," Lou replied. "Couple of minutes?"

He pointed his finger at her sternly and said, "I'm going to be one aisle over, so don't go far."

"I promise," Lou replied as she walked back toward the pharmacy counter. She quietly said to the clerk, "May I have a pregnancy test please?"

"Sure thing, Hun," the clerk answered as she slid the test into a brown paper bag. Lou paid for it and walked back toward the front of the store. John joined her at the door, placing his arm companionably around her shoulders.

"Get what you need?" he asked absently, taking in his surroundings.

"Yep," she smiled back at him.

She opened the door of the Jeep and slid her package beneath the front seat. She jumped as a brown sedan pulled up beside them and Brody stepped out. Her hands started to shake as she recognized the man driving.

"Get in the car, Lou," Brody said, picking her up and lifting her into the front seat, then sliding in behind her. John scrambled into the back seat, realizing the seriousness of the situation even though he had no idea what was going on.

"What's going on, Brody?" Lou asked.

"I have a funny feeling we're about to find out," he mumbled as they pulled out into the street. He verified the sedan was following in his rearview mirror.

"Did I miss something, Brody?" Lou asked insistently.

"Do you remember the night of the dance when that man tried to take Sarah?"

"Yeah," she replied, her eyebrows drawn together.

"Well, that same man just showed up at the jewelry store."

"What?" Lou asked. "What would he be doing at the jewelry store?"

"Hell if I know," Brody breathed. "I went to take in that piece of jewelry to be appraised. The owner of the store took it in back, made a phone call and then that goon showed up. He walked out, carrying my diamond and told me I was going with him or he would kill everyone in the store. He was armed, so, I walked out with him and was about to get in his car, then that other man showed up."

"Wes," Lou stated.

"Who?" Brody asked, glancing in her direction as he drove.

"Wes." Lou rubbed her forehead. "He knew my mother."

"You know who this guy is?" Brody asked incredulously.

"No. But he knew my mother. He gave me some photos and said he wanted Sarah."

"I still can't figure out why they want Sarah," Brody said. "Unless it's to use her to get something else."

"I don't know," Lou sighed. "He just kept telling me he wanted what was in the black bag."

"Uh, guys…" John said from the backseat.

"What?" they both snapped.

John replied, "I remember that bag."

"So?" they both asked.

"Sarah wasn't the only thing in the bag," John replied quietly.

Chapter Twenty-Two

They stopped in front of the house and turned off the engine. Lou heard the gravel crunch as Wes pulled in beside them and did the same.

Brody took Lou's hand and pulled her across the seat toward him. He slid out of the car and she followed before he wordlessly pushed her behind him.

Wes hopped out of his own car quickly, looking around, taking in his surroundings. He made a let's go sign with his hands and said, "Let's move this inside where it will be a little more private."

They regarded him wordlessly and walked into the house. He followed them in through the screen door and then closed the hard back door, shooting the lock home when he turned the knob on the deadbolt.

"That's to keep other people out. Not to keep you in," he said quietly.

She regarded him wordlessly, her brown eyes meeting his own. "What do you want?" she asked.

"It's a long story, actually," Wes said, taking a deep breath and raising his cigar to his lips.

Lou glanced at her watch. "I'll make time." She looked at him coldly.

He began, "Nothing has worked out the way it was supposed to, Lou."

"You mean you had hoped to kill me by now? Or to steal my daughter?"

"I hadn't planned to do either. I had hoped you would just give me what I wanted and then we could be finished with this," he sighed. "I don't know why I thought this would be easy," he groaned.

"Why do you want her?" Lou asked.

"Because she's priceless," Wes answered.

"What?" Lou asked, dumbfounded.

Wes motioned to the kitchen chairs and indicated they should all sit. Lou sat slowly and warily, regarding him suspiciously. He sat down beside her, absently kicking at the floor with his heels. "Maybe we should start at the beginning." He turned to face her. "Your mother was in some deep shit, Lou."

"I kind of figured that when she was murdered," Lou said sarcastically.

"She was working for a man named Jerry. Jerry Hayes." Wes said.

"I remember him. He was a friend of a friend from when she was a kid," Lou nodded.

"Jerry is no one's friend, Lou. He's bad news. He's a thief and murderer. He single-handedly pulled off one of the biggest jewelry heists in history a few years ago. He stole some priceless jewelry as it was being moved from a private collector's home to a museum for display."

"What does that have to do with my mother?" Lou asked impatiently.

"Your mother met Jerry, and he hired her to run errands and make some deliveries. A pregnant lady was the perfect cover. She could go almost anywhere and no one would suspect a thing." He smiled at the thought.

"You knew my mother when she was pregnant?" Lou asked.

"Yeah. I knew her. I watched her get deeper and deeper into the shit. I couldn't do anything to stop her." He adjusted the ball cap on his head. Lou flinched as he reached into the inner pocket of his sport coat.

He opened his jacket and showed her the gun that was still in the holster on his side. "Just going in my pocket."

She nodded, her mouth suddenly dry.

Wes pulled a wallet out of his pocket and flicked it open. Lou read the bold letters, FBI, and looked closely at his photo on the paper.

"FBI?" she asked.

He refolded the wallet and put it back in his pocket.

"I've been working this case for a long time, trying to get in good with Jerry and his crew. It's taken me years but I did it." He looked proud, yet defeated. "My first job was to track down the missing jewels from that jewelry heist. I've been able to do that, or almost all of them at least. But once I got involved, I realized Jerry is involved in a lot more than just some thefts. He's responsible for killing a lot of people, but he's really good at covering his tracks. Everyone who works for him is expendable. If they know too much or they become trouble, he just gets rid of them." He drew in a breath. "That's what happened to your mother. She knew too much."

"Knew too much about what?"

"No one is sure." He shrugged. "There at the end, she got a little too cocky. She went too far and she got a little greedy. It was almost like she knew he would kill her and she was going to get everything from him she could before it happened. Your mother took a piece of jewelry from him, one of the most valuable pieces. It was a huge diamond, priceless." He laid the wooden cask on the table before them and opened it. Lou gasped as she saw the huge diamond winking back at them. She reached one finger out to touch it.

"What did she do?"

"She tried to blackmail him. Turns out this piece of jewelry can actually tie him to a whole string of robberies and murders which could put him away for a long time. She knew it had a ton of value to him, even if she couldn't resell it on the open market. He bit. He agreed to give her $50,000 for it, a fraction of its value, but still a lot to someone like your mother. She had no idea what that piece was actually worth. She made arrangements for the money to be left in a black canvas bag and she said she would swap. But the swap never happened. I still don't know how she pulled it off but she got away with the diamond and the money. Then she ran."

"But they found her," Lou stated blandly.

" Jerry hates to lose. So, he killed your mother but before she died, she gave the bag to you. You were seen running away with it. It was a black canvas bag and this was in it." he said dramatically.

"I thought the only thing in the bag was Sarah," Lou hissed as she stood up and began to pace.

"What?" he asked blankly.

"The night my mother died, she threw Sarah into a black canvas bag and I ran with it. I never knew anything else was in the bag." Her eyes reached his, pleading with him. "I swear it." She held up one hand. "I don't even know what happened to the bag."

"It took me seven years to get in with these people, Lou. I know how dangerous they are. They'll kill you and everyone you love to get that diamond."

"All this time, I thought they wanted Sarah," Lou moaned.

"They'll take Sarah. Along with everyone else you love. There's not a damn thing I can do to stop them. Unless you help me."

"How can I do that?"

"They know you have it. Especially now that Lover Boy here took it in to the jewelry store."

Brody shook his head. "It was in my mother's safe. I thought it was hers. I just took it to be appraised." He sighed. "What now?" he addressed Wes.

"Now, we just need to make a date so you can transfer it back. We'll wire you up and be sure you're protected. You will need to get him talking. It's not hard to do. He loves to boast. Get him to talk about the diamond and the people who died at the robbery. Then we'll come in and arrest him once it's in his possession. He'll never see the light of day again. Simple as that."

"Simple as that?" she asked sarcastically.

"Absolutely not!" Brody barked, coming to stand behind Lou.

"Well, what's your plan, big guy?" Wes bit out. "If she doesn't do this, he's not going to go away."

"What do I have to do?" Lou broke in.

"We have a lot of details to work out, but I can take care of that part. Are you in?" he asked, as though he was just asking for a tennis match.

"Will this make it all go away? So I can go back to the way things were?" she asked.

"I think so."

"No." Brody said just that one word.

Lou stood and faced him. "Do you want me to have to hide for the rest of my life? To constantly have to worry about the people I love? That he's going to hurt one of them to get to me? You can't keep me locked up forever."

"You're not under lock and key." He placed his bent finger beneath her chin and forced her to look up. "I don't want anything to happen to you."

She melted immediately, all thoughts of his earlier phone conversation gone with that simple statement. "You don't?" she asked tentatively.

He shook his head, blond locks falling across his forehead. "I don't." He pulled a lock of her hair. "You say that like it surprises you." His eyebrows drew together in question. "Why else would I be here?"

"Your mother's will...settling the estate...familial obligations," Lou replied.

"Let's get one thing straight, Lou. I'm here because of you. Jeb called and asked me to come and I'm here. Because of you. Because I care about you. I might be able to get some things done here while I'm with you. But you are the main reason I'm here. I want to try to keep you safe. But that's hard."

"Is that why you slept in my room?" she whispered to him. "To keep me safe?"

"Hell, no." He grinned. He stepped closer to her and said in a low voice, "That was because I wanted to make love to you."

Her heart started to pound in her chest. Making love and being in love were two different things. *But not to me. I love you*, she wanted to scream. But she didn't. Instead she wrapped her arms around his waist and said, "I'm glad you're here." *I'll take what I can get until it's time for you to go. Even if it's temporary.*

Lou turned to Wes and said, "I'll do whatever it takes."

"Can you promise me she'll be safe?" Brody asked.

"I'll do my best," was Wes's response, as he flipped his phone open and started barking orders into it.

****

When darkness fell, Lou slid her fingers between the slats in the window blinds and spotted the headlights of a vehicle coming down the drive. When it was highlighted by the lights from the barn, she saw it was a pickup with a camper shell.

"Who is that?" she asked, turning to Wes who was still on the phone with his crew.

Wes craned his neck, looking out the window. "Those are my guys." He spoke into the phone. "Yeah. Just pull into the barn." He snapped his phone closed.

Wes turned and unlocked the back door. He pushed Lou in front of him through the doorway, whispering, "Show time."

Brody and John followed them out to the barn. When they walked through the barn door, they saw six men climbing out of the back of the camper, all dressed in jeans and work clothes. Some wore cowboy hats and others baseball caps. All of them looked like they belonged on the farm.

The driver of the truck spoke first. "We don't have much time. We need to get her wired up." He turned to Lou. "Take your shirt off, please."

"What?" Brody barked. "Why does she need to do that?" he said, stepping toward the group.

"It sure ain't so I can see her naked," the man said sarcastically, appraising Lou from head to toe. "Although that might be fun, too." He winked playfully at Lou and held out a black box and a long wire. "We need to wire you up, darlin'." He looked toward Brody. "I have kids older than her," he flung at Brody caustically.

Lou still looked at him hesitantly. Brody stepped forward and took the black box in his own hand. "I'll do it."

"That all right with you, darlin'?" the man asked with one eyebrow raised.

"Yeah." Lou nodded, stepping into a stall and motioning for Brody to follow. Brody closed the door and turned around to find Lou had already drawn her shirt over her head.

"We don't have time for a tickle in there," the man called out.

"We'll hurry," Lou called back.

"Just draw the cord up between the breasts. Make sure the end of the mic isn't smothered in there," the man said as he adjusted his own headset to listen to the static in the line.

"Nice," Lou whistled.

Brody threaded the microphone up between her breasts and taped it in place. "I hope you can get that sticky stuff off later," Lou huffed.

"I heard that," the man called from outside the stall. "Just tape the black box to her stomach and make sure there's no loose cord."

Brody ran the cord across her abdomen and taped it in place. Lou squirmed. "Would you be still?" he asked.

"Sorry," she mumbled.

"You sure you want to do this?" he asked, his breath blowing across her belly.

"I don't think I have a choice," she responded quietly. "Not if I want my life back."

Brody stood up and Lou drew her shirt back over her head. He leaned down and kissed her gently. "I'll be right with you," he said.

"You certainly will," Wes replied as they walked out of the stall.

They had placed two chairs back to back. Wes threw some tape to John. "Tape the two of them up. We need for it to look like I tied them up out here to wait for Jerry."

Brody and Lou sat back to back in the tall chairs. John tied Brody's hands behind his back with the tape, yet made it loose enough to allow for some movement. Then he taped his mouth shut and taped his ankles together. Brody glared at him.

"I always did want to tell you to sit down and shut up," John teased, drawing attention to himself. Brody felt John wrap his hands with duct tape once more and then he felt the give of the tape between his hands as he cut it where no one would notice. He did the same between his legs. When no one was looking, he slipped his pocket-knife in Brody's back pocket. "Just in case you need it," he whispered.

Brody nodded.

John moved to Lou and held the tape out in front of her. "I always had fantasies about you and me and duct tape," he said with a grin. Brody protested with a grunt. John tied her hands in front of her and left her mouth free.

"That's enough for her," Wes said as they heard the crunch of gravel in the driveway. He nodded to John and the other men. "It's business as usual on the farm, fellas. Get to work." They all went out the side door of the barn and found positions near the barn. One man wore a Bluetooth headset that looked like it was probably paired with his smartphone, yet in reality it allowed him to hear any conversation from inside.

"Ready, Lou?" Wes asked. She nodded.

"This is always the worst part," Wes muttered as he raised his hand. Lou didn't realize his intent until after he had already hit her with the back of his hand across the side of her face. Blood dripped from her split lip and tears came to her eyes.

Brody flinched and mumbled against the duct tape covering his mouth. The tape that bound him to the chair held strong.

Wes wiped the blood from the back of his hand on his jeans and held Brody in the chair by pressing down on his shoulder. "If that's the worst that happens to her today, we'll be lucky." Brody took in a deep breath through his nose as he saw Wes ball up his fist. Darkness clouded his vision as he took the blow to his chin. He slumped over in the chair, suddenly unconscious.

"It hurts less if you don't see it coming," Wes said to Lou over her muttered protest.

"Is he okay?" she lisped, her lip already swelling.

"Yeah. He's just unconscious," Wes mumbled as he walked around Lou. His cell phone rang. He flipped open the cover.

"I have them secure. In the barn," he said, then closed the phone and put it away.

Moments later, Gary, the goon from the jewelry store, and Jerry, the boss, walked through the door of the barn.

"Well what do we have here?" Jerry asked casually, as though he was attending a social event.

Wes replied, "Sleeping like a baby is Brody Wester, who is still trying to figure out what the hell is going on." He pointed to Brody and smirked. "And here we have Mary Lou Smith," he said, pointing to Lou.

"So nice to finally meet you," he said quietly as he lit a cigarette, then looking at Lou from head to toe. He reached to caress the side of her face. "Such a shame he had to hit you," he said.

Lou was surprised to see that Jerry was a physically fit gentleman in his early forties.

"You killed my mother," Lou stated blandly, using the back of her taped hands to wipe spit from her dripping lip.

"A necessary part of doing business, I'm afraid," Jerry said as he raised the cigarette to his lips again.

"What do you want?" Lou asked. "The diamond?" Her eyes met his without fear.

"Among other things," he responded.

"What other things?" Lou asked.

"Where is it?" Jerry asked, turning to Wes. Wes reached into his coat pocket and removed the large cask. He held it out to Jerry and flipped it open.

"I had forgotten how big that thing was." He picked it up and held it in his hand, testing its weight. "That was what your mom saw. How big it was. She was desperate."

"She beat you at your own game," Lou sneered.

He grabbed Lou's chin and squeezed hard. "No one beats me."

Lou threw her head to shake her chin out of his hold. "What are you going to do?" she asked.

"The only thing I can do," he said, taking his gun from the holster beneath his jacket.

Lou stiffened as Jerry pulled his gun from the holster. She sat forward slightly, getting ready to move. She looked over her shoulder at Brody, his form still at rest.

"The only thing you can do is kill me." Lou stated. "I never had any hope of coming out of this alive."

Jerry shrugged. "I don't have a choice. You're a liability, just like your mother was."

"You won't walk away from this," Lou said, hoping to antagonize him.

"Oh, sure I will," he boasted. "Just like I walk away from all the others."

"What others?" Lou asked. If she had to die today, she would at least get all the info the FBI needed to put Jerry away for a long time.

He waved the gun and took on an air of self-importance. "All the others who got in my way," he said absently.

"Like who?" Lou asked.

Jerry got a gleeful gleam in his eye. He nodded toward Wes. Then their gazes locked. "You think I don't know who you are?" he asked, raising his gun and pointing it at Wes.

Wes raised both hands as though surrendering. "Whoa, there," he said, the corners of his mouth lifting slowly. "What's going on?" he asked.

Wes reached for his own weapon but it was too late. Jerry pulled the trigger and the bullet slammed into Wes's midsection. He fell to the floor of the barn with a groan, a surprised look upon his face. His eyes closed and he was still.

Brody used the opportunity to flex his hands and legs, unwinding them from the loosened tape. Then he stood quickly and stepped behind Gary, grabbing the shorter man around the throat with his forearm. He touched the knife to the man's neck.

"Step away from Lou or I'll kill him."

Jerry shrugged. He raised his gun and fired. The shot hit Gary in the forehead and Brody felt him slump down toward the floor. He knelt over him, feeling for a pulse. There was none. Brody looked up at Jerry. "There are FBI agents all over the place outside. You'll never walk away from here," he said candidly.

"My guys took out your FBI agents ten minutes ago," Jerry said. "So, now it's just the three of us." He raised his gun again and fired. Brody felt the bullet rip through his shoulder as he fell onto his back. Lou ran to his side.

"Brody! Are you all right?" she screamed, afraid because of all the blood. She touched the wound and brought her hands back, covered in red. Her hands shook violently.

Jerry stood a few feet away, absently cleaning his fingernails with a pocketknife. "Isn't this touching?" he asked sarcastically. He turned his back to them and raised his phone to his ear, sure he had won.

Lou leaned over Brody and they both heard a "Pssst." They looked over and saw John crouched by the door. He pointed over his head to the light switch. In the darkness, Lou and Brody would have an advantage. Brody nodded at him.

Seconds later, the lights flickered off in the barn. Brody whispered to Lou, "Run!"

"What about you?" she whispered back.

"Run!" he said again, and shoved her toward the door, slowly rising, himself. "I'll catch up," he said, trying to reassure her. "Go!" He shoved her again.

Lou silently crept toward the door and out into the night. She clung to the shadows created by the barn until she rounded the corner of the paddock. This particular area did not house horses so Lou crept silently and slowly forward, hoping to make it to the trail behind the barn, where she could run down the path and to safety. Just before she found freedom, she heard a voice behind her.

"Turn around slowly, Mary Lou, and look at me."

Lou turned and raised her hands in the air. "Why don't you just kill me and get it over with?" she asked.

"You're so much like her, you know?" Jerry said quietly, walking toward her. "You could be her twin."

"Is that a compliment or an insult?" she asked.

He shrugged. "You take your pick."

She nodded, biting her bottom lip. She watched him as he raised the gun again. She flinched as he pulled back the hammer. He straightened his arm and played with the trigger.

"You're just too much of a liability," he said. Then he felt it, a loud snort right beside his ear and he jumped, swinging around. He lifted his arms to cover his head as he caught sight of the horse rearing over his head, hooves flying in his face. He screamed as he took a blow to the temple and the shoulder. He dropped the gun as he fell to the ground.

Lou dove for it as she saw it fall and clutched it in her hand. She stepped back and pointed the gun but was unable to distinguish one form from another as hooves pounded the earth. The shrieks were the only thing that let her know he was still alive. Then the screams stopped and Jerry lay still on the ground. The once-wild mare stood above him, heaving in great gasps of air.

Brody and John heard the screams and walked close to Lou. Brody slowly took the gun in his own hand and pried her fingers from it. He passed it to John and said, "Hold this."

John took the gun and aimed it at Jerry's form, which lay on the ground. Brody walked slowly over and felt for a pulse.

"He's still alive but he took one hell of a beating," Brody stated, wincing as pain shot through his own shoulder.

Just then, the grounds came alive with the sound of police cars and ambulances. Wes walked closer toward them.

"How did you…?" Brody started.

Wes patted his chest and said absently, "Bullet-proof vest."

Swarms of uniformed officers walked closer and a gurney was brought for Jerry.

Lou, barely able to stand on her feet, felt Brody's arm slide around her waist, holding her up. She clasped her arms around his neck but he tensed beneath her hands.

"Oh, my God! You were shot!"

"Yeah, but it went all the way through." Brody stated, brushing her hands away as she touched his shoulder.

She laid her head on his other shoulder and took a deep breath. "Is it over?" she asked.

"Looks like it," Brody said quietly before kissing her on the nose. Then he let himself be led away by paramedics.

Chapter Twenty-Three

Lou rode along with Brody in the ambulance to the hospital. It took hours for them to get x-rays, clean the wound and give him some IV fluids and start antibiotics. Wes came and went, updating them on Jerry's health through the night. He suffered from a concussion, several broken ribs, and a broken femur, but he would survive.

"At least he can do his time in prison," Lou sighed. Then she narrowed her eyes and looked at Wes. "He will go to prison, right?"

Wes nodded. "We have him on attempted murder, murder, theft, and a number of other crimes. I can guarantee he'll never live another day outside of prison in this lifetime."

Lou sighed and sat down on the side of Brody's bed. "Thank God it's over," she said, taking his hand in hers. Wes walked out of the room.

Brody rubbed the back of her hand with the pad of his thumb. "Are you okay?" he asked quietly.

"Much better than you, it seems," she responded, smiling at him. "I don't know what I would have done without you."

He puffed out his chest and grinned, "Happy to be of service."

She leaned forward and kissed him quickly on the lips just as John walked into the room.

"Oh, man. Would you two cut that out?" he joked, covering his eyes.

"What are you doing here?" Lou asked, turning toward John.

"I thought you guys could use a ride home," John shrugged. "Besides, I didn't have anything to do after they cleaned up all the mess at home."

"Everyone gone?" Brody asked as he sat up.

"Yep. They all cleared out. I called Jeb and Sadie. They're coming home tomorrow."

Lou smiled. "I can't wait. I just want things to be back to normal."

"What's normal?" Brody asked, joking.

"Who knows," Lou shrugged. "But I want some of it."

The doctor came in a few minutes later and discharged Brody. They went home and, when they walked into the kitchen, John hung his hat on the peg by the door and turned to Lou. He kissed her gently on the forehead.

"When did you get to be so grown up?" Lou asked playfully as she reached up to hug him.

"Same time you did, I reckon," he shrugged and smiled.

"You saved the day today, John," Brody said, clasping his hand.

"Aw, shucks," John replied. "Weren't nothing you wouldn't have done for me."

"You better believe it," Brody said.

John turned to walk down the hallway to his own bedroom. "Night, all," he threw back over his shoulder as he did so.

Lou turned to Brody and took in the sling holding his arm in place and the pained look on his face. "I am so sorry you got caught up in all this," she said.

"I'm not," he replied.

"You're not?" she asked.

"Nope. I wouldn't have missed it for the world," he said, sliding one arm around her waist and drawing her close for a kiss.

"Ready for bed?" he asked.

Lou helped him undress, gently removing his shirt and then replacing the sling for the night. He slid between the sheets naked, and she crawled in with him, fitting her head against his neck. They fell asleep instantly, his breath blowing against her nose and hers tickling the hair on his chest.

****

Brody and Lou slept late the next morning and, after she helped him shower and dress, they shared a box of Lucky Charms in silence. She stood quickly when she heard tires crunch in the driveway and ran out onto the porch. Sarah jumped from the truck and flung herself in her mother's arms, talking animatedly about the trip she had just taken. Lou hugged Jeb and Sadie and then John took Sarah to play so Brody and Lou could fill them in on what happened.

They sat quietly discussing the past few days at the kitchen table when they heard a short, crisp knock on the door. Lou opened the door to find a small, wiry little man wearing thick glasses. He extended his hand to Lou and said, "Nice to meet you. I have an appointment with Dr. Wester today."

She stepped aside and let him walk past her into the room. Brody rose from the table and extended his good hand to shake with the small man. "We have an appointment to read your mother's will today, sir," he gently reminded Brody.

Brody turned and introduced him to the group as "my mother's attorney."

"Let's go to the study where we can have some privacy, shall we?" Brody said, walking toward the hallway.

The small man stuttered, "Actually, Dr. Wester, I need to assemble a group of people. I need to see Jeb, Sadie, John, Sarah, Lou, and you, all together." He walked over to the kitchen table and laid his briefcase down, flipping the locks. He removed a file full of papers and looked expectantly at the group. "Is young John in residence?" he asked hesitantly.

Lou went to the door and called John and Sarah inside. When everyone was assembled at the kitchen table, the attorney started to speak.

"Dr. Wester, your mother left explicit instructions on how her estate is to be divided. It is quite a large estate. Your mother has invested heavily in the past years and those investments have always paid off." He took a deep breath. "To Dr. Wester, she has left the home and the grounds on which the home sits. This includes the contents of the home on the date of her death and the all possessions herein. To each person seated at this table, Margaret Wester has bequeathed an equal sum of $500,000 per person. That includes the child."

Lou took a deep breath and looked over to see tears rolling down Sadie's cheeks. Jeb reached over and took Sadie's hand.

"The business known as Western Skies is now jointly owned by each of you. Jeb and Sadie receive twenty-five percent, which they will share. Brody, Lou, and John each receive twenty-five percent as well. If any one person does not want to be a part of Western Skies, they can sell their share to the other three. They cannot sell outside of this group. Dr. Wester, you living at Western Skies is not mandatory. Your mother made specific instructions as to this fact."

Brody nodded tightly.

"The business is currently valued at ten million dollars. Much of this is tied up in racing stock. But enough is liquid that it can provide generous salaries for all who participate in the running of the business."

The attorney closed the file. "There are other clauses and bequests to various charities and paperwork that need to be completed, but they can be done at a later date. This takes care of the biggest portion of the will. We will be in touch in the coming weeks and finalize all the details." The man slid the file back into his briefcase, flipped the locks and walked out the door as quickly as he had arrived.

Everyone at the table sat quietly for minutes on end. Finally, Lou spoke, though it broke her heart to do so. "At least your mother made no conditions about you having to live here," she said.

He raised his head and looked at her. "I hate to have my choices taken away. If she had done that, I would have walked away from it all." He smiled softly. "She knew me so well." He took a breath. "She also knew each of you and put the business in perfect hands. I look forward to working with you all."

Jeb and Sadie left the table to go and soak up the information while John did the same. Lou turned to Brody and steeled herself. "What's your plan?"

He shrugged. "I have to go home. I have things to do there."

She wilted. He reached over and bumped her chin with his index finger, forcing her to look at him. "But I won't be a stranger. That's for sure." He kissed her swiftly and got up, walking toward the study.

He sat down behind the desk and picked up the phone. He pulled his credit card out of his wallet and laid it on the desk in front of him. As Lou listened at the doorway, he made flight reservations to go home that night. She walked down the hallway, not stopping to listen to the rest of his phone calls. He spent the afternoon packing and left his bags by the back door.

Lou avoided him for the rest of the day, unable to bear the thought of him leaving. *I could tell him about the baby, and maybe he would want to stay. But if I take his choices away, he'll hate me. Better to let him figure it out on his own.*

Lou decided it would be less painful to leave home for a while than to face the fact he was leaving. She whispered to Sadie that she would be home soon, and she and Sarah went to the park. Better to be oblivious than deal with the pain.

****

Brody paced back and forth through the kitchen.

"What's got you so worked up?" John asked.

"I have a flight in a few minutes and Lou's not back yet," he snarled.

"Well, hell, I can take you to the airport."

"I can't exactly kiss you goodbye, can I?" Brody said sarcastically.

"I think that was what she was trying to avoid," John mumbled.

"What do you mean?" Brody asked.

"To be so smart, you sure are stupid," John said around a mouth full of Sadie's pound cake.

"What's that supposed to mean?" he growled.

"She loves you, dumbass," John growled back.

"Well, I love her, too," Brody said, dumbfounded.

John grinned wildly. "You haven't told her that, yet, have you?"

"No. I'm going to surprise her when I come back. I quit my job back home and I'm just flying back to get a U-Haul to bring my furniture and stuff. I got a job at the hospital here." He still looked unhappy. "I took my mother's ring to be cleaned last week so I could ask her to marry me and put it on her finger."

"You picked it up yet?" John asked.

"No. Why?" Brody wanted to know.

John grabbed his hat off the hat rack and slammed it on his head. "You ain't flying nowhere. Your apartment can wait a few days. Hell, I'll pay your rent, if I have to. I'm rich now." He guffawed. "Let's go get that ring. I know where Lou is."

Brody steeled himself by grabbing the back of the chair in front of him. His doubtful eyes met John's. "You think she'll have me?"

"Only one way to find out," Jeb said from the hallway as he and Sadie walked into the kitchen, both smiling.

Brody and John walked out to the car and Brody took the keys. "I'm still not riding with you, even with a bad arm." He slid into the seat but dropped the keys when he went to put them in the switch. He reached down and slid his hand along the carpet. His fingers brushed a bag beneath the seat and he pulled it out. His eyebrows drew together as he opened it, and then his eyes grew wide.

"Hey, that's Lou's girly stuff she bought the other day."

"This is Lou's?" Brody croaked before a huge grin tugged at his lips.

"Yeah," John replied hesitantly. "I never would have thought a box of tampons would make a man so happy," John mumbled.

"You have no idea, John," Brody said, flying out of the driveway.

Chapter Twenty-Four

Lou stood by the pond at the park, watching Sarah as she played. Her mind was so full of problems she couldn't tell which way was up and which was down. She was definitely her mother's daughter. She was pregnant and alone. Brody didn't want her enough to stay or even to ask her to go with him.

Lou squared her shoulders, though, and sat up straight. "I've done it before and I'll do it again," she whispered quietly against the wind.

Then Lou heard a male voice behind her, breaking into her thoughts.

"Lou?" Brody said.

"What are you doing here?" she asked, looking at her watch. "I thought you had a plane to catch?"

"I do. I did." He ran a hand through his hair. "But, when you ran away, I realized I needed to explain a few things to you before I go."

Lou's eyebrows drew together. "What do you need to explain?"

"I wasn't leaving you," he said slowly.

"But you had a plane to catch," Lou said, bewildered.

"I did. It was supposed to be a surprise. But I am afraid I might have waited too long."

"Would you stop talking in riddles?" she said, growing cross.

"I was going to go home, pack up my apartment and rent a U-Haul to bring it all back here. I quit my job. I have a new job at the hospital here in town."

"You do?" she asked quietly.

He sighed. "Do you remember that day we went to the jewelry store and I had the big box and the little box?"

"Yeah," she said cautiously.

He reached into his pocket and pulled out the small box. He flipped it open and held it out for her to see. "I took it to have it cleaned."

"It's beautiful," she said, still not understanding.

He dropped to one knee. A tear rolled down her cheek and she gasped, covering her mouth with her hand.

"I took it to be cleaned so I could give it to you..." he said shyly. "When I ask you to marry me."

"Why do you want to marry me?" she asked, taking the box from his outstretched hand.

He stood up and drew her close to him. He kissed her forehead.

"Because I want you," he said.

Her face fell.

He kissed her nose.

"Because I need you."

She frowned.

He lifted her chin and kissed her lips. He looked into her eyes and said, "Because I love you and can't live without you."

She immediately threw both arms around his neck and pressed herself against him, tears rolling down both cheeks.

He peeled her off of him and said, "Can I take it that this reaction means you feel the same way about me?"

"Oh, Brody! I love you, love you, love you." She rained kisses across his cheeks, chin and nose. Her lips finally met his tenderly. "I always have." She paused. "I feel a little guilty, though," she said as he slipped the engagement ring onto his finger.

"Why?" he asked.

She said quietly against his ear, "I think I may be pregnant."

He clutched her closer.

"You think or you know?" He smiled against her neck.

"I think I know," she said. "I was afraid to tell you because I didn't want to take your choice away. I didn't want you to feel like you had to stay. Or like I trapped you."

"Woman," he said, swatting her bottom. "You had me trapped from the first time I saw you."

"In a good way?" Lou asked.

"In a wonderful way," Brody replied.

Brody felt a small tug on his pants leg. He looked down to see Sarah standing there with John beside her, grinning like a Cheshire cat.

Brody dropped to a crouch and picked Sarah up with his one good arm. "Yes, ma'am?" he asked.

"Are you in love with my mommy?" Sarah asked directly.

"Absolutely," Brody replied.

"Are you in love with Brody, Mommy?" she asked, gazing at Lou.

"All the way," she replied, smiling fondly at her daughter. Then she added. "Brody just asked me to marry him. What do you think of that?"

John took his hat off and flung it in the air, whooping loudly.

Sarah laughed out loud. "Sounds good to me," she said, kissing Brody on the cheek. She whispered in his ear. "Now we'll all be a family?"

"You better believe it." Brody said.

****

The four of them left the park and headed for home. Sarah rode with John while Lou and Brody took the Jeep. Their hands were clutched together on the console, his fingers toying with hers. He flipped the engagement ring around on her finger and said, "You sure you want to marry me?"

"A better question would be, are you sure you want an instant family? There will be Sarah and me, and baby makes three." She fondly placed his hand on her flat stomach.

"I sure hope so," he said, his eyes meeting hers.

"Really?" she asked. He nodded. "There's a pregnancy test under the seat," she informed him shyly.

"You don't say," he replied, suddenly swerving into the parking lot at a gas station. Lou grabbed the dash and shrieked.

"What are you doing?" she gasped.

He reached beneath the seat and pulled out the brown paper bag. "We're going to take a test," he said.

"Here?" she questioned.

"Here," he said, opening her door and ushering her out.

Lou giggled and followed him to the restroom. He pressed the brown bag into her hand and whispered in her ear, "Need some help?"

She blushed and went through the bathroom door.

Inside the stall, Lou's heart raced as though she had run a four-minute mile. She capped the test and slid it back into the bag without looking at the results.

She washed her hands and ran her fingers through her hair in front of the mirror.

Brody knocked insistently on the door. "You had better get your cute little fanny out here," he said.

She blew the hair from her eyes as she walked back out. Her eyes met his, her cheeks rosy and her heart still fluttering.

"Well?" he asked.

"Well, what?" she toyed with him.

"Are we?" he asked.

She held the bag out to him. "I don't know. I'm afraid to look."

He snatched the bag from her hand and opened it. He read the side of the stick. His face fell. "I'm sorry, Lou."

"We're not?" she asked, her hand over her heart.

He grinned wildly. "Oh, no! We are!" He picked her up with his one good arm and swung her around as she clutched his shoulders, tears pouring down her cheeks.

"Then why are you sorry?" she scolded, slapping his shoulder.

He dropped low in front of her and kissed her belly. "'Cause now, you're stuck with me forever." He stood back up and kissed her lips. "You would have been stuck with me anyway. This just makes it better. Let's go home."

Lou and Brody drove up to the house and saw Jeb, Sadie, Sarah and John sitting on the porch. They got out of the truck slowly and walked up the steps to join them. Lou held out her left hand to show it to Sadie.

"I just heard the good news," Sadie said, clutching Lou to her in an embrace.

Jeb held out his hand to Brody. "Congratulations, son."

"Thanks, Jeb," Brody said.

Lou shaded her eyes with her hand as a cloud of dust rumbled up the driveway. "Who could that be?" she asked.

The dark sedan stopped in front of the house and Wes stepped from the car. "I hope you guys can stand one more surprise," he yelled as he walked over and opened the passenger door.

They all held their breath. Lou watched as one beaded shoe hit the ground and then the other. Then she gasped out loud to see a woman stand up and look over the tinted glass of the open door.

Lou stood still for just a moment and then said, "Mom?"

The woman nodded and started to run toward Lou. Lou met her halfway and grabbed her in a tight hug. Everyone on the porch was silent.

Lou stepped back and grabbed her mother's hands in her own. Barely able to talk past the lump in her throat, she asked, "How did you...?"

Wes answered for her. "Witness protection program. We were watching her the whole time. We let Jerry think they had killed her by reporting to the newspapers that a woman's body was found inside after the fire. In fact, I got her out through the back door as the fire started."

Lou felt a tug on her shirt and looked down to find Sarah's brown eyes, so like her own, staring back up at her. "Who is that lady?" she asked in a whisper, one hand cupped around her mouth.

Lou's mother dropped down to kneel before Sarah. "You must be Sarah," she said, taking in the girl's dark hair and eyes. She ran her hands up the child's arm, as though checking to ensure she was real. "I'm..."

"Mom, wait," Lou interrupted, suddenly nervous. Brody's arm slid around her shoulders, offering moral support.

Her mother held up one finger and placed it to her lips, saying, "Shh." She looked at Lou. "It's okay," she added softly.

She looked at Sarah again and said, "I have not seen you since you were a little bitty thing. But," her eyes met Lou's as she ended, "I am your Grandma, your mother's mother."

Sarah took her Grandma's hand in her own and said pleasantly, "My mommy is getting married."

"She is?" Lou's mother said with wonder, tears falling from her eyes. She walked along with Sarah as she pulled her over to the swing set, talking non-stop.

Brody pulled her closer. He kissed her softly.

"Does it get any better than this?" she asked.

"Oh, yeah," he said with a smile. "It only gets better from here," he said as they turned to go inside.

Keep reading for a sneak peek at the next book in the Wester Farms trilogy, A SOFT PLACE TO FALL.

A Soft Place to Fall

Prologue

Olivia Barrett rolled over in the hospital bed and clutched the pillow to her middle, fighting back the tears that threatened to fall. The door to her room opened with a click and she held her breath. She glanced over her shoulder and visibly relaxed when her doctor, dressed in baby blue scrubs, entered the room holding a small plastic cup in his hand.

Dr. Stone passed the cup to her. "This will help with the pain," he said gently. Olivia took the cup and dumped the pills into her mouth, washing them down with water. She slowly looked up at the man beside the bed.

"Anything else I can get you?" he asked quietly. Olivia refused to meet his eyes as he took in the bruises on her face and forearms. He sighed long and loud before he reached for her wrist so he could take her pulse. "I have been your doctor for six years, Olivia. I had my suspicions, but I never expected anything like this to happen. You've lost something precious –," he started.

But she cut him off. "Stop! I don't want to talk about it," she cried. "I will not discuss it right now."

"You do know that he could kill you next time? Right?" Peter asked as he pulled a chair closer to the bedside. He flipped through the chart in front of him and then sat back and crossed his legs, one foot over his knee. "If you're not going to talk to me, you have to talk to someone," he said, blandly.

"What's to talk about?" Olivia asked, rolling over onto her back. "You had better go. He'll be back any minute. He just went for coffee." She glanced anxiously toward the door.

"I'm not afraid of him," the doctor said, shrugging his broad shoulders. "But I'm afraid *for you*," he said, his tone completely different from that of the even-tempered, thirty-something doctor that she'd seen through the years.

"I'll be fine," Olivia grunted, wincing as she adjusted her body in the bed. "It was just an accident."

Peter flipped anxiously through her charts. "There's no reason for a healthy young woman to fall down a staircase three times in four years." He flipped again. "No one is unlucky enough break their forearm on two different occasions, all because of stupid mistakes."

"I'm just very accident prone," Olivia said, avoiding his gaze.

"Why haven't you ever reported him to the police?" the doctor asked solemnly.

"He *is* the police," Olivia groaned helplessly as she rubbed her eyes with her fists.

"I guess you can go home," the doctor sighed. "I don't want to send you back there, but until you're willing to talk to me…"

"I want to go home," she said quietly.

The doctor reached into his pocket and retrieved a business card. "Next time you even get a hint of it – that he's about to get violent – call this number." He hastily scribbled his personal contact information on the card and held it out to her.

"He promises that he won't ever do it again," Olivia said, pushing the card back at him.

"How many times has he told you that before?" he asked.

"He just gets really stressed out at work," she started.

"That's not an excuse," he said, cutting her off.

She startled as her husband entered the room carrying a dozen roses. The cloying scent of his heavy cologne reached Olivia long before he did. She hated the way he smelled. It reminded her of a rest-stop bathroom smell.

"You 'bout ready to go home, babe?" he asked as he bent to kiss Olivia on the cheek. She flinched.

"Yeah, Richard," she tried to recover and smiled slowly back at him. "All ready to go." She sat up slowly in the bed and realized that the doctor could see the faded bruises that shadowed her back through the opening in her gown. She reached back to close it. She couldn't help but notice doctor gritting is teeth as he watched her walk gingerly into the bathroom.

He was gone when she came out of the bathroom, but a discharge nurse had taken his place. She gave Olivia a bottle of pain pills, discharge notes, grief pamphlets and she added Peter's business card to the top of the stack. Olivia took them all and tucked them in her purse.

"The doctor said for you to call him if you need him for anything." Olivia fought the urge to cry as the nurse's eyes met hers. They all knew. They knew about her shame. And what had happened to her. "He said to call him for anything, even small concerns."

"I understand," Olivia said slowly, hissing through her teeth as she slid her swollen foot into her sandals.

****

Olivia spent the next few days in relative comfort. She stayed in bed for two days, per the doctor's orders and then cooked and cleaned and did all the things that she normally did and Richard was calm and comfortable, patronizing even. But those days usually didn't last very long and Olivia knew it.

It lasted for about a week before she started to see the signs again.

They sat at the dinner table, eating their meal when Richard suddenly spat his food across the room.

Olivia jumped up and grabbed a napkin from the table to clean the mess off the floor. She bent to clean the carpet and heard him say, "You can't even get a simple dinner right, can you?" She hung her head and took a deep breath.

Olivia knew better than to respond. She walked into the kitchen and threw the food in the trash and turned to wash her hands in the sink. They trembled as she soaped and rinsed them. It was happening again.

She looked longingly at the wedding photo that hung on the wall in the den. Where had that man gone? Where was the man that she had fallen in love with? Where was the man who loved her back?

Run! Her inner voice screamed.

"Can you get me a beer before you come back?" he bellowed at her.

"Yes, Richard. I'll be right there," she replied. She reached into the fridge and pulled out a beer, opening it and watching the steam rise from the mouth. As she stared into it, she noticed her purse hanging on the back of the informal dining chair in the kitchen. Dr. Stone's phone number was on that card. She unzipped it and reached in, retrieving the card and the bottle of pills that the nurse had given her at the hospital.

Just a few minutes. Just a few minutes was all she needed to get away.

She jumped as she heard him bellow again. "Olivia!" She pinched the skin on the bridge of her nose between her thumb and forefinger and took a deep breath before turning the cap of the medicine bottle with the flat of her hand and shaking the pills into her palm. How many? There were ten in the bottle.

Two would probably make him tired. She took two spoons and put two pills between the fronts and back of the spoon and ground them into powder. She shook the powder into the beer. But two more would make him sleep. She ground two more. Unable to remember how many she'd already added to the beer, she ground two more and dumped them in for good measure. She tucked the bottle into the pocket of her jeans.

She jumped as she heard him step up behind her. "Did you get lost, bitch?" he asked, snatching the beer from her hand.

He lifted the beer to his lips and took a sip. "You just better be glad it's still cold," he said as he sat back in his recliner and put his feet up. He lifted the beer to his lips again and took a long draw. She watched his Adam's apple bob as he swallowed. He drained the bottle dry. Anticipating his needs, she pulled another from the fridge and held it out to him, taking the empty one.

She cleared the table and loaded the dishwasher. There was nothing that Richard hated more than a messy home. She watched from under hooded lashes as he turned on ESPN and settled deeper into his chair, watching him as his lids grew heavier and heavier. She frantically searched her pocket for the business card. Richard didn't like for her to be able to make calls when he was at work, so there was no phone in the home.

She tiptoed quietly over to his side and saw that his cell phone was still in its place on his belt. She slowly reached and touched it. She jumped as he flinched in the chair and stood quietly to see if he would settle back down.

She gingerly tugged the phone and twisted it to remove it from the cradle at his belt. She turned and walked quickly with it down the hallway to the bedroom, closing the door behind her and pressing her back to it. Her breath rushed in and out as she flipped the phone open. She glanced at the slip of paper that was held between her thumb and forefinger and dialled the phone.

Ring.

Ring.

Ring.

"Hello?" a male voice said.

"H-hi. M-my name is Olivia. Can I please speak to Dr. Stone?"

"Hi, Olivia. This is Peter. What's up?"

"Y-you said that I could call you if I ever needed help," she stammered.

There was a pause for a second. "Do you need help?" he asked.

"I think so," Olivia replied.

"Where is he?" Peter asked.

"Sleeping," Olivia whispered, tears escaping from beneath her eyelids as she the clenched them tightly.

"Tell me where you are."

She gave him her address.

"I'll be there in twenty minutes. Pack what you want to take with you. We'll provide the rest."

"Who's we?" she asked quietly.

"Friends," he replied and she could hear the smile in his voice. "I'm on the way. Meet me outside."

Olivia took a sport's bag from the closet and filled it full of her clothes. She turned and swept the jewellery from the top of the dresser into the bag. Then she walked around to her husband's nightstand and bent to open the drawer. It was, of course, locked. She tiptoed into the office and lifted a letter opener from the top of the desk. She had contemplated this scenario in her head hundreds of times but was always afraid to break the lock. She inserted the tip of the letter opener into the flimsy lock and twisted with all her might. Olivia felt the lock break and she slid the drawer open.

She rummaged through the drawer until she found a small, locked rectangular box. She placed it on the bed and turned to open the lock, not entirely sure what she was taking. Then lights shot across the window from the headlights of a car. She threw the metal lock box into the bag and walked back down the hall. Olivia grabbed her purse and threw it over her shoulder.

Richard still sat in the same position in the chair. She looked longingly at the wedding photo. That man no longer existed. And neither did that girl. She pulled her wedding ring from her finger and dropped it on the coffee table, watching it roll until it settled with a clank.

She opened Richard's phone again and called 911. When the operator picked up, she simply said, "I think my husband has tried to commit suicide. He won't wake up." She gave the address and clicked the phone closed. She put the phone on the coffee table beside her wedding ring.

As she opened the front door and slipped outside, she saw the door of the car open as it was pushed from the inside. She bent and looked into the car, meeting the smiling eyes of Dr. Peter Stone.

"Ready?" he asked as she slid into the seat.

"As I'll ever be," she replied as she closed the car door and sat back, drawing in a deep breath. She met his eyes when he turned to look at her.

"Why do you care?" she asked quietly.

"I had a sister, once," he replied.

"Once?" she asked. "What happened to her?"

"She died," he answered, cracking his window and lighting a cigarette. "Do you mind?" he asked as he flicked his Bic.

"No," she shrugged. "Go ahead. Nasty habit, though," she couldn't help adding. "What happened to your sister?" she whispered.

"Same thing that was happening to you," he said, blowing a stream of smoke toward the crack in the window. "He would have finally killed you. Or beaten you down to the point where you wanted to die." He looked at her.

"I would rather die than live like that for one more day," she said with conviction in her voice. "I'm just sorry that it took too long for me to realize it."

"Good. I have good things in store for you."

"What?" she asked.

"First, we're going to get you to a safe place. You can stay with my wife and I for a few days."

"Then what?"

"Then you get a brand new start. You'll be self-sufficient, responsible only to yourself," he said. "What skills do you have?"

"None," Olivia said blandly.

"He's told you that for way too long," Peter replied and tapped her nose playfully. "What's the thing that you enjoyed most as a child?"

Olivia thought long and hard. "Horses," she stated.

"Horses?" he laughed. "Never heard that one before," he said, throwing his cigarette butt out the window. "But horses it is. You afraid to get dirty?"

She laughed. "Why?"

"I think I have the perfect place for you," Peter stated, tapping his forehead. "One of the doctors at the hospital inherited a horse farm. Name is Dr. Broden Wester. Place is in the middle of nowhere. Might be the perfect place to get a new start."

"I'm willing to try anything," Olivia stated.

"You'll like him. He's a nice guy. And his wife is pretty fabulous, too."

"Can't wait to meet them," Olivia replied, her voice full of excitement for the first time in a long time.

Chapter One

John Wester found himself bowing to his partner on the dance floor and lifting his cowboy hat from his head to mop his brow with his forearm. His red hair was plastered to his forehead and he relished the feeling of air moving under his cap. The smoke inside The Pour House was thick and the heat from all the bodies crushed together on the dance floor made it seem doubly so. He made his way from the center of the floor and weaved through tables to the front door, stopping to talk to friends on the way out.

The Pour House had a long, wide porch that ran around three sides of the building with a wooden railing on which patrons could lean. John jovially walked down the length of the porch and entered the shadows, sitting in a rocking chair that he knew was hidden in the darkness. He sat back and lifted his boots onto a wooden wire spool. He raised the hat from his head and balanced it on his crossed feet. He sat back and took a deep breath, enjoying the breeze as it blew across his skin. The music pounded through the walls of the building. He tapped his long fingers on his thigh along with the rhythm of the band.

He smelled the scent of her perfume before he saw her. She smelled like baby powder, simple and clean. John slowly sat forward as he saw her slink into the shadows with him. He reached for his hat and replaced it atop his head, slowly lowering his feet to the floor. The woman stepped further into the shadows.

John heard her stop breathing as a uniformed officer walked by, heading for his car.

"I thought you would never get here," he said quietly in her ear, his arms sliding around her waist from behind in the darkness.

The officer stopped in his tracks and turned, hearing the murmured voice behind him. He pulled out a small flashlight and started searching the darkness.

John felt the woman spin quickly in his arms, her hands moving to clutch the back of his neck as she pressed herself against him. She danced him around until her back was against the wall. She lifted one leg and wrapped it around him, her lips meeting his fiercely.

John tried to pull back, saying, "You're not-."

But heard a whispered, "Please," as she weaved her fingers together behind his neck.

He grabbed her behind her knee and ran his hand under the skirt of her sundress and then up her thigh to her bottom, squeezing gently as he did so. He felt her gasp as she drew in a breath against his lips. His mouth touched hers, gently at first. But she clasped the back of his neck and drew him down to her, her tongue sliding into his mouth. After recovering from the initial shock, he met her tongue, thrust for thrust. He grabbed the back of her head and slanted his mouth against hers, feeling the kiss deepen and his pulse begin to quicken.

John saw the beam of the flashlight as it moved over them in the darkness and lingered. He broke the kiss and lifted his head, calling out, "Do you mind?"

"Sorry," the officer called back as he got into his car and drove away.

John felt the woman in his arms relax but he still held her leg up by his waist, her back pressed to the wall.

"You can let me go, now," the woman said softly. "Please," she added.

"Who are you?" he asked against her ear, his heartbeat still pounding.

"Certainly not who you were waiting for," she replied. "Can you let me go, please?"

John heard the urgency and fear that entered her voice and loosened his hold on her leg. He felt it slide down his side as she released his neck. John stood up to his full height. He was a full head and shoulders taller than she was. He reached out to touch her hair. Her short, choppy red hair stuck out in spikes. Was burgundy a natural color for hair? Her face was devoid of makeup. But lashes heavily coated with dark mascara fluttered against her cheeks. Green eyes danced from one object to another as she looked around, obviously looking for an escape route.

John reached up and resettled his hat upon his head. He stepped back and regarded her quietly.

She moved to walk around him. He grabbed her hand before she could walk away. "You want to tell me what that was all about, ma'am? Maybe I could help," he added.

"You already did," she replied, smiling shyly at him. "Thanks," she threw back as she walked away, her fingers slipping slowly from his grasp.

Olivia remembered their encounter, differently. The uniformed officer had been following her for miles. Her hands shook as she changed gears in the small rental car. She furtively looked into the rear view mirror again and saw that he was still there, despite her efforts to lose him. She checked the speedometer to ensure that she was not driving too fast. Then she spotted the full parking lot of The Pour House. She turned the wheel quickly and slid into a parking space. She looked in her rear view mirror and saw the patrol car stop as well. Her heart clamoured in her chest as she slid out of the car and stayed low, walking toward the front of the building. She walked through the double doors and squinted at the sudden flash from the strobes on the dance floor. She saw a sign pointing to the bathroom and headed in that direction.

She stepped into a stall and closed the door behind her, chewing her fingernails as she walked in a small circle. *What do I do now? He can't be looking for me? But what if he is? It's just a coincidence*, she told herself, taking a deep breath as she walked out of the stall. She primped in front of the mirror, fluffing her hair and wiping the sweat from her brow.

She stepped out of the bathroom and glanced around. Spotting the officer at the bar, talking with the bartender, she quickly skirted the room and went back out the front door. As she was about to step off the porch, she heard someone yell, "Hey!"

Not sure, and not caring, if it was the officer who yelled, she ran into the shadows of the porch and stood very still, watching his dark uniform as he crossed the parking lot. The only sound that she heard was her heart beating in her ears. She did not hear the man as he crept up behind her and slipped his arms around her waist, speaking low in her ear. But she saw the officer as he heard the noise.

In desperation, she turned to the man in the shadows and pulled his head down to hers. She used his large body to shield her smaller one. When he hesitated, she grew desperate and wrapped her leg around him, deepening the kiss. She fought the flutter in her belly that she felt at having a strange man's hands on her and did her best to act like a lover hiding in the shadows with her beau.

When she heard the patrol car finally drive away, she could feel the tears that threatened to fall from beneath her lashes. It was more than she could bear. How long would she jump at shadows? How long before she could feel safe being alone? The man almost broke her down when he asked if there was anything he could do to help.

Rather than let him see her cry, she ran back to her car and got behind the wheel. She asked the navigational system in her rental car to find the nearest motel. She backed out of the parking space and toward the motel, stopping at the dingy registration office. She almost forgot her new name, Olivia Gale, when she signed the registry.

She carried one bag up the stairs to her room and dumped it onto the bed. She pulled the wig slowly from her hair and let her blonde locks fall over her shoulders, using her fingertips to massage her scalp. Then she traded her green contacts for brown ones. When all that was done, she climbed between the sheets and asked God to please give her one day where there was no fear. And to let tomorrow be that day.